Hearts in Danger

COME WHAT MAY

SANDRA CARMEL

ENTWINED PUBLISHING

Come What May
ISBN # 978-1-80250-287-9
©Copyright Sandra Carmel 2025
Cover Art by Kelly Martin ©Copyright November 2025
Interior text design by Entwined Publishing
Published by Entice, an Entwined Publishing imprint

Published in 2025 by Entwined Publishing, United Kingdom.

Entwined Publishing is a division of Totally Entwined Group Limited.

COME WHAT MAY

Dedication

"Wherever my travels may lead, paradise is
where I am."
Voltaire

Chapter One

May Caledon's car clunked and sputtered and came to an abrupt halt, steam streaming from beneath the bonnet.

Noooo! Just what she needed.

Not.

She was almost there.

She huffed and shook her head. "Great. So bloody typical." Of all the times her car could break down, it had to happen on the way to her first serious job interview. The first position that had piqued her interest since she'd left the military.

Only a short couple of kilometers away from the location, according to her GPS. So close, yet still so far. Thank fuck for mobile phones so she could at least let Solve Security know she'd be running late.

And thank fuck she knew the intricate workings of a car. With or without electronic diagnostics. Intimately understood how to fine-tune an engine.

Hazard lights on and with car horns blaring, she threw the gear stick into neutral, jumped out and steered her current labor of love to a safer spot on the side of the busy road.

Extracting a hair tie from her purse, she wound her untamable, rebellious locks into a ponytail then popped open the hood. Once she had the prop rod in place, she hitched up her skirt and leaned over to get a closer look.

The early-morning sun, harsher than she'd expected, beat down on her, adding to the inflamed, unanticipated, infuriating circumstances.

She sighed and swept the wayward strands of hair off her sweaty forehead, the hot, merciless, northerly breeze whipping across her back.

Her classic red and black Holden Torana, affectionately called Ladybird, didn't have any of the electrics so couldn't tell her straight up what was wrong. It absorbed the unprecedented heat to its detriment.

The persistent hissing haze emanating from the radiator suggested a water problem. Most likely a crack or possibly a leak. Fucking great. Just what she needed. Her limited budget hadn't catered for major car issues.

Hopefully the engine hadn't totally overheated. Like her internal thermostat, the pressure had built, teetering close to boiling. It would only take one more inconvenience and she'd blow her last gasket.

The air vibrated with the anxious hum of people desperate to get to work, or wherever they were headed, on time. And halted by traffic. Fumes mixed with a humid mist, creating a fog that rose off the sun-soaked bitumen, and road rage horns blared at semi-frequent intervals.

Instead of playing into responses out of her control, she shifted into mindfulness meditation mode and focused on what she needed to do to ensure a successful interview.

Stop start.

Stop start.

Stop start.

Noxious exhaust gases, musty and smoky and sulfur tinged, permeated the environment, making her nose crinkle and melded with her already high stress.

Frizzy, curling strands of hair stuck to her face. She tried to blow them off, but they flopped back into place, plastering to her hot, perspiring, pollutant-exposed skin.

Unable to do a thing about her ruined hair, she'd have to wait to have a good scrub in the shower after the interview…if she ever made it.

Although tempted to check the radiator, she wouldn't risk removing the cap until the car cooled down. Yes, she wanted to maximize the meeting opportunity, but not at the expense of her safety. Not unless she accepted adding the high possibility of scalding burns to her already compromised condition.

Vehicles continued to crawl on by, the stifling northerly breeze buffeting her body, the tar heating the soles of her shoes like a convection stovetop. She debated whether to walk the rest of the way to Solve Security, then return to Ladybird later.

May refused to call roadside assistance—she was a better mechanic than all of them strung together. She dug her fingers into the back of her neck. What to do? She had to make a decision, and quickly. Did she set off on foot now, or stay put and wait until she could get her car running?

From a risk-first perspective, she didn't want to remain standing on the side of the road, or even sitting in her broken-down car for longer than needed, or else she'd increase her chances of being hit. Injured or possibly killed.

How many times had she heard news stories, how many times had accidental or sometimes purposeful deaths resulted from someone's vehicle breaking down on a busy highway? She refused to be another statistic. Losing Ladybird would be traumatic, but a fuck-ton more preferable than losing her life.

Maybe she should stand on the median strip and wave someone down to help her push Ladybird into an even safer side street.

No.

She shook her head. No.

Not worth it.

Who knew what weirdo might pull over?

Her current irritated, annoyed mood reduced her tolerance to fending off questionable-character advances. With her short fuse shortening by the second, she might lash out on a well-meaning male and be arrested for assault.

In the event of an opposite outcome, she trusted her extensive armed-forces training to enable her to adequately and effectively defend herself, if the need arose. However, in order to best protect herself and others, she should avoid both scenarios.

A car blared its horn and shot up the emergency lane, in an attempt to overtake a slow driver, barely missing the rear of Ladybird, and screeched back into the slow flow of traffic. Heart hammering, she retreated off the road onto the median strip. Not a ploy for male attention. A self-preservation decision.

She didn't need a guy in her life to make it worthwhile, to prove her value, to feel complete. She didn't need him to do anything for her, other than offer his mouth and hands and cock for a good, thorough screw.

May blew out a frustrated breath. It had been too long between men.

A random, no-strings-attached fuck for fun, when she felt like it — which was most days — would do the desired trick. It ticked her sexual-relief boxes.

Nothing serious. Never anything serious. Serious turned into mundane boredom and the death of freedom. May knew from years of personal experience.

She'd tried the boyfriend thing a few times and it hadn't worked. For a countless number of reasons. If anything, it caused her more stress and anxiety. Too much emotional crap, too much pain and baggage to trudge through. She sought a mutual, enjoyable escape.

Instead of easing, the traffic congestion increased, decelerating to a super-slow crawl, the heightened pollution making her cough. She could practically feel the black specks of smog clinging to her face and arms and semi-bare legs. Inhaled it into her lungs.

She'd wait a few more minutes, reluctantly lock Ladybird, then attempt to meander her way to Solve Security and pray she wouldn't feature as a hit-and-run news story.

An army camouflage-print Jeep rolled up in the far lane, a bunch of fresh-faced soldiers sitting in the back. Were they new recruits? Or returning after holidays, to wherever they were deployed, to further defend their country?

The military... She sighed. She'd loved it. Maybe too much. The insular, close, cliquey community had had her back. And she'd had theirs. She'd trusted her team with her life. Even though it had taken a while for her to convince the guys of her mechanical expertise. But it was worth every second of her hard slog.

Bittersweet tears burned like flaring fire behind her eyes. It had taken her months, following a few persisting over-use injuries, to finally pull the I-need-to-go pin.

Losing one of her close team members had finally rammed home the point that no one was ever one-hundred percent safe, didn't matter how well trained. That, plus burn-out, had started singeing the edges of her sanity. Not helpful, not healthy for her or anyone.

If she had any chance of a 'normal' life, a civilian existence with the possibility of children, she had to leave. Before it was too late. Opening up options provided a greater, more satisfying number of choices. Or so she tried to convince herself.

Having worked in the forces since she left secondary school — they'd provided her the education to learn her trade — her team had become her second family. Although unsure of how she'd cope, she'd taken the scary plunge, and much to her surprise, had seamlessly transitioned into her new carefree single life. Contrary to the ex-military PTSD horror stories she'd heard.

Mind you, she hadn't tested herself in a new civilian job. *Yet.* But mounting financial pressure meant she needed to find something soon so she could live the free-and-easy lifestyle she envisaged.

Having a reasonable pension helped, created a comfortable buffer, however she still needed purpose, and an additional income to pay for the accelerating high-cost-of-living expenses in Melbourne.

Going out for dinner at a pub and having a couple of drinks pretty much equaled her grocery shopping bill for the week. Not maintainable. Far from sustainable. The biggest shock since she returned to Australia.

Although still seeking the odd adrenaline rush, overall, she now needed a more supportive, lower-key life. Something with the occasional thrill but more stability. Hence her application for a Solve Security agent position.

If she ever made it to the meeting.

Her car losing its shit—not a good start. Definitely the opposite of making a great first impression. An employee needed to show reliability, efficiency, effectiveness.

May reached into the driver's side door, snatched her cell phone from the center console and searched for the Solve Security number in an email, confirming her interview date, time and venue. She copied and pasted the contact number into her mobile and pressed the call button.

It rang and rang and rang, and went to voicemail. "Hi, you've reached Solve Security. Please leave your name and number and a brief message, and we'll get back to you as soon as possible."

Fuck.

She summoned her calm voice, and waited for the beep. "Hello? It's May Caledon here. I'm scheduled to attend an interview at nine-thirty a.m. but my car has broken down. Just wanted to let you know I'll make it in as soon as I can. Sorry for any inconvenience. My number is…"

She hit the call end button and gritted her teeth. Eight-thirty-seven a.m. She should have been there, would have been there, given herself some quiet, relaxed time to get psychologically prepped for the interview if… No point focusing on that. It wouldn't change the present situation.

The early-morning summer sun had turned scorching. Already. Actually, the temperature had been unbearable most of the night, dropping to a muggy 'low' of twenty-six degrees Celsius, and the weather bureau expected it to rise to forty degrees today.

Great. She fucking hated having a sweaty, unsettled sleep...unless a hot man was involved. She fucking hated summer. She fucking hated turning up to her interview a dripping wet, frizzy-haired, grimy, flustered mess. She really had to get a reverse-cycle unit installed in her bedroom. And maybe a more reliable everyday car.

Normally she'd call a taxi or an Uber, but given Ladybird had decided to die in the peak of peak hour, it'd be quicker for her to walk. Though she really didn't want to leave her pride-and-joy so exposed. What if someone plowed into her baby? Radiator replacement she could handle, but major bodyworks...no. Just no.

May closed her eyes and took a couple of big, deep breaths. She threw her phone onto the driver's seat, and with the steam dissipating, she bent over the engine again, earning her several honks and a couple of wolf whistles.

The short skirt — big mistake.

Was this an omen? Her morning had gone from promising to disastrous. Maybe she wasn't meant to work at Solve Security? Between the congested trudge of traffic, and the whoosh when they took off at the odd interval, her phone started ringing.

Shit.

She raced to retrieve it and answered. "Hi, May here."

Holding the phone tight to one ear, she blocked the other with her hand to filter out the persistent traffic noise, the relentless heat and racket radiating off the road.

"It's Alex from Solve Security. Got your message. Thanks for letting me know what's happening. Get here when you can. Safely. Don't rush." A firm, no-nonsense male voice, yet he exuded empathy. Caring. Gave her a good vibe.

Just the kind of employer she'd enjoy working for…if he continued to demonstrate his positive initial impression with action. Maybe the universe wanted to reinforce she should follow through with the agency.

Give it her best go. Didn't David Bowie say something about needing to step into the deep end, where your feet barely touched the ground to enable growth?

"Thanks, Alex. I'll give you a call when I'm on my way." She yelled over the line after line of chugging car and truck and motorcycle engines, and swiped the sticky sweat from her forehead, the wispy strands of hair from her eyes.

"No worries. Hopefully see you soon."

First-world problem somewhat sorted. Beads of perspiration formed between her breasts and trickled down her stomach. She could only imagine how shit her hair looked. Why had she even attempted to straighten it on such a sultry day? Because she'd assumed she'd make it in air-conditioned comfort to the Solve Security office.

Massive Murphy's Law mistake.

Her clothes stuck to her damp skin, and she fanned her face. Hopefully her mascara hadn't run in dark rivulets down her cheeks. She didn't want to turn up to her interview looking like one of those creepy porcelain clowns popular in the eighties.

Or Alice Cooper. Great for rock and roll, but not so great for a security agent…unless the role called for it. She definitely didn't consider dress-ups a deal breaker.

May checked the time on her mobile — eight forty-five a.m. — then dumped it on the dashboard and went to dislodge the prop rod.

Car tires crunched along the emergency lane.

She swore under her breath, closed her eyes, and froze.

Fuck no.

Please don't be some single, predatory guy.

Yes, okay, she appreciated the concern, the possible help, the attempt to assist, as long as the person didn't show serial killer signs. As long as the 'do-gooder' didn't have some other personal, financial, or pick-up, date-me agenda. As long as they hadn't responded to her practically half-naked body on display as some sort of free-for-all come on.

"May I help?" A man with a refined English accent that contrasted with her born-and-thoroughly-bred Aussie lilt. Nothing too full-on, but still noticeable. The Queen's or in this case, King's English, if she had to guess.

Here we go.

Didn't matter how great he sounded, he could still prove to be a prick.

No matter how sexy his voice, he gave off an old-fashioned, I-must-help-a-lady-in-distress mentality. And she'd experienced that enough in her life, even more in the male-dominated forces.

Already annoyed and frustrated, she couldn't help but sigh. She only just held back from telling the 'selfless' guy to fuck right off. Men always assumed a girl was helpless when it came to cars. Assumed she'd want some big, tough, car-expert to save her.

How could she possibly know a multigrip from her mascara? A makeup bag from a tool kit? As a woman, she'd have no inkling where to start, how to fix anything mechanical. Of course she'd have no idea, and he'd have to swoop in and save the day. Massive ego trip on his part, and most likely some sick attempt at flirting.

Jaded much?

Could her day get any worse? She rolled her eyes and huffed, more than ready to tell the man, in the nicest way possible, to shove off.

May left the prop rod in place and turned.

Whoa.

Her breath caught in her chest. He was fucking stunning. Straight out of her fantasies. Very Tom Ellis, *Lucifer*. Tall, dark hair, built without being overly buff. Dark jeans, a chocolate-colored T-shirt, piercing coffee-colored eyes. And he had an amazing Jaguar F-Type R black car.

Fucking hot. Sexy. Expensive. This guy wasn't some opportunistic, I-desperately-need-a-fuck type. He had wealth. Choices. Going by his outward presentation. Not at all what she'd expected. She'd accused the stranger of assuming and yet she'd done the exact same thing.

But was he dodgy? Appearances could be totally deceiving. For all she knew, he might have hired or stolen the car. Ted Bundy epitomized attractive and charismatic and look what had happened to those who engaged with him.

She stood up super straight, her emotional battle-armor in place, and glared at the apparent good Samaritan. "Can I help *you*?"

Chapter Two

Not technically, no. But...even with grease streaked across her face, the cute, sexy, confident woman, got the blood boiling in Westley's veins. "Have you called roadside assistance?"

She crossed her arms over her chest, and clenched her jaw. "No. I don't need it." She paused and exhaled hard through her nose, as though forcing herself to speak a few more words against her will. "Thanks all the same." Her curt tone suggested the opposite of thankful, more like offended.

"I know a bit about cars. I can have a look."

She rolled her eyes as though she'd dealt with this an innumerable amount of times. "I'm sure you can. Thanks for offering, but I'm already well aware of the problem."

O-kay. She didn't want his help. Fine. She'd made that explicably clear. Was she fobbing him off or did she really know what she was doing? With no way to know for sure, and not wanting to be one of those misogynistic dicks who believed only men knew better when it came to cars, he'd honor her explanation and not-so-subtle request to leave her alone. "I'll be on my way then."

"Thanks for stopping." Her forced smile entirely contradicted her statement.

For her ability to hold off on giving him the third degree, he gave her silent kudos. This woman had belief in herself, assurance, and what did the Aussies say? Balls? And she did. No one with any sense would want to screw with her...in an unfun way. Her actions suggested she wouldn't let a tosser take advantage. She'd vet any man, even if he seemed well-meaning.

Admirable. Sensible. Made him honor the lady's wishes. Though, leaving her behind activated his internal savior complex. Had his stomach clenching and his mind overrun with questions, querying his choice.

Even though they'd only spoken a few words, he didn't doubt her resourcefulness. Didn't doubt she would continue to refuse his assistance. And yet, he hesitated, wanting to ensure her safety. He'd always struggled to rein in his protective instincts. Strong, capable woman or not.

Giving her a shit-ton of time to change her mind, he slowly, under self-imposed duress, got into his car. Indicating back into traffic, he continued to work, watching her as long as possible in his rearview mirror. Within safety limits.

Thankfully the traffic started thinning out, and he wasn't too far from Solve Security headquarters. So he should make his nine a.m. check-in with the boss. Or close to it.

After that, dreaded paperwork. He was a field guy. Through and bloody through. Hated the bureaucratic, red-tape part of the job. Loved the thrill of the chase, the strategy, the excitement of setting up to capture a culprit.

His previous case had dragged on way longer than anticipated. How many times had he been called to different roofs and sat there, gun aimed. No result. Just waiting and more waiting.

Cold, alone, isolated. Focused. But it was worth it. How many times had patience paid off. How many times had the team apprehended the assailant. Too many to count, ever since he'd been employed. Alex and the small team had trust in him, the new guy, and his skills, and he appreciated that. In the end, patience, persistence, perseverance and consistent results were the name of the success game.

In his past, his colleagues had worked together for a while before they trusted each other. Before they felt confident putting their lives on the line for work, a cause, society. With an evolved team, they quickly identified the key required traits of a new recruit.

Reaching the secure agency car park, he scanned his pass. The boom gate opened and he traveled toward his regular spot in the multilevel complex.

While most people had to turn to social media or TV or any other means of escapist entertainment, he loved the challenge of concentration. He loved being a part of bringing in the bad guy. Or girl. Or person, no matter what gender.

Brought up in Britain, he carried his justice mentality with him to Australia. Although people outside of the UK assumed residents had a conservative view, he'd been reared within a diverse environment and applied the knowledge to his work, to his decision to leave his antiquated military regiment and migrate to Australia.

Anyone living in the UK, probably even in broader Western society, would be familiar with their risqué television programs and live theater over the years. They'd pushed social boundaries through comedy for as long as he could remember. Since before he was born. However, with the change in times, questioning people's perspectives ceased to remain funny, accepted.

Not a worry for him. He kept a foot in both politically and non-politically correct camps. Whatever it took to apprehend criminals. He focused on doing his job and getting any relevant reports in on time. Then he'd go into repeat mode for each new assignment.

Westley rolled into his usual spot, grabbed his satchel, and locked the car. He showed his ID pass at the manned checkpoint, then entered the lift and rode it up to the Solve Security office, the sexy little blonde woman impossible to eradicate from his mind. And those large, sea-green eyes…breathtaking.

Yes, okay, it'd been a while since he'd wined and dined and bedded a beautiful lady, but still… *Fuck*. He normally had more control. He *normally* moved on when an opportunity didn't work out. But there was something intangible yet captivating about the woman. Maybe the damsel-in-distress thing?

On his break, he'd detour down there and make sure she hadn't stayed stranded. If he'd stopped, who knew how many predatory men might use the circumstance to their advantage.

Though, he had to admit that some guys might have the best intentions. Like he had. And not just because she was stunning, enchanting, unforgettable.

The elevator dinged and the metal doors slid open. He blew out a big breath, stepped into the cool sunlit floor, said a quick *hi* to Sage on reception, and strode straight to the staff kitchen-lunch room to grab a strong black tea.

Stereotypically English, yes, but required when he'd surpassed his regular stress levels. He needed a kick start out of his woman-focused fog if he planned to get anything of significance achieved.

He rushed into the large bright climate-controlled area, a long table and chairs running down the middle. Thankfully empty. Running late had its benefits at times. As a self-confessed non-morning person, he preferred not to speak too much until he'd had his caffeine fix. Good quality coffee or tea did the required job. But today, he needed a reconnection to his roots, something to center him.

Snagging two tea bags from the huge clear canister on the bench, he popped them in a cup with boiling water from the plumbed tap. The scent of the leaves steeping wafted into his nostrils and had his mouth watering, his mind settling.

Westley glanced at his watch. Eight-fifty-nine. *Shit.* A shorter-than-short-lived high. He added some cold water to the brew, sculled the rest of his tea, hoping it'd give him the required buzz, washed his cup, and strode to his boss's backlit office.

"You're late." Alex gestured to the chair opposite his desk, looking like a god on a throne. And he kind of was, his dark brown hair and intense blue eyes clearly stating *Don't mess with me.* No doubt he'd made it his life to show dominance in order to protect himself and others.

His employer was a stickler for punctuality, and an excellent, experienced boss. Westley took a seat and met Alex's explain-yourself stare. "Sorry. I stopped to help the driver of a broken-down car but they didn't want my assistance."

"A woman?"

"Yes." *Another unfounded male presumption?*

"Did you get her name?"

Weird. Why did it matter? Did the guy have some sort of psychic abilities or cameras on the streets Westley didn't know about in order to ensure his staff told the absolute truth? Was this a test? Was it a CCTV check? "No. Why?"

"I have interviews today and one candidate rang to say she'd possibly be late because of car trouble."

Intriguing. Was it a coincidence, or could the woman he spoke to be the interviewee?

"She didn't specify her circumstances or offer her name." In fact, she refused to give much away, pushed him to go ASAP without relinquishing more than the smallest amount of information. Out of safety, annoyance? Probably both.

"No worries. But next time, call and inform me if you're held up." He peered into Westley's eyes and leaned forward on his forearms, the rolled-up sleeves of his black shirt revealing a myriad of intricately interwoven tattoos. "Thankfully the business is booming but that means I need to keep to scheduled times, or rejig them accordingly, or things get out of hand, and we all get behind."

Made total sense. Westley needed to snap out of his singular mindset and think more broadly. Think with perspective. Think collaborative colleagues. A tricky task when he was used to working alone. Predominantly.

The sniper profession didn't exactly attract extroverted team-player types. And yet, he'd been told time and countless time again he had a natural charisma. Might be his British accent. And yes, he

23

played on it where he could, particularly to gain trust. A requirement of the security profession.

His boss scrolled through his tablet and stopped. "Where are you at with the documentation for the Remington case?"

"Finishing it up today."

"Good. Because I've got another job for you."

Thank goodness. He didn't need the money, but he needed the work. "What are the specs? When do I start?" Not that he cared. He'd do anything Alex asked because he trusted him implicitly. Knew the guy wouldn't assign him to something that didn't suit, that didn't need his expertise. And it helped that Westley had no personal life.

"Still working through the details. All I can tell you is it's offshore and you'll be paired with another agent. Once I've appointed both of you, I'll go through the finer aspects."

"Suits me fine." As long as he had some space. As long as he didn't have to be hauled up with his work partner twenty-four-seven. One night, two nights, all good. Longer than that, he needed his own room to re-energize, to recover.

Time to allow him to think through the day's events and develop a workable strategy going forward. Hard to do if overwhelmed. He needed a clear head with no other extraneous distractions and complications.

"I thought it would. I appreciate your dedication and reliability."

Westley appreciated having an all-consuming job. One where the workplace got him and how to maximize his skills. One that didn't allow him enough time to think about the big black hole in his personal life. "Unless there's something else, I'll get back to finishing the Remington report."

"Nothing else at the moment. I'll be in touch when I have more info on your new assignment."

"Excellent. You know where to find me." Westley stood, circled around to the door and headed to his office, down the sunny corridor—the frequent Melbourne sunshine so unlike the UK—thoughts of that sassy woman reappearing, bouncing back and forth in his brain.

Could she be one of the potential new agents? No. That sort of shit only happened in the movies, right? Though his gut hoped he was wrong. If by some sort of miracle she was the candidate Alex spoke about, what then? If she met all the agency requirements, ticked all the stringent Solve Security boxes, he might have to work with her.

Shit. How could something so simple, so innocent, get so complicated so quickly? If she showed up, and Alex chose her to fill the vacancy, it'd be prudent for Westley not to get personally involved.

Prudent, but not necessarily possible. Not if they both had a mutual attraction. She'd definitely sparked desire in him, but had he triggered the same lustful chemical reaction in her? Even if one-sided, she'd be impossible to ignore.

Hopefully he'd be fully invested in the new case soon, focus all his scattered energy on that and be way too busy to give her a second thought. *Yeah, right.* Who was he trying to fool?

However, he needed a pre-emptive plan. Just in case she made a permanent appearance. Shouldn't be too difficult, given it formed part of his regular processing and strategy when taking on a new assignment. And maybe, just maybe, once he knew her better, he'd lose interest.

Concentrate.

He needed to concentrate on utilizing his fine-tuned skills, his high-end accuracy to get the required job done. Quickly, efficiently, effectively. Without succumbing to any emotional worries. He had to switch off his overactive mind and go into work-compartmentalization mode.

Entering his stifling workspace, he swiped the back of his hand across his forehead and, using the remote, switched on the air con—thank fuck Alex had shown the foresight to install reverse-cycle units in each office and communal area or else he'd have expired.

Westley stood in front of the icy airflow until he stopped sweating, then logged into his computer and waded through the backlog of emails. It always amazed him how many messages piled up in such a short time. Most of them he'd been carbon-copied into, thank goodness. For his reference. Not requiring any action.

After deleting a fair chunk of his inbox, he grabbed a strong black coffee and got stuck into completing his latest report. Once in the flow, time flew and next thing he knew, a familiar female voice penetrated his door, caressing his ears.

A client? The new worker? Either a woman he'd spoken to or someone he'd met or someone he'd fucked. Maybe even someone who sounded like someone he knew. He stopped typing, straining his ears for more seductive snippets but…nothing.

Maybe an interviewee? Or a random? The nature of Alex's business meant that people sometimes walked straight off the street seeking assistance. Either way, the need to know further details about who accompanied that distinctive, libido-inducing voice overwhelmed his mind, caused an almost compulsion.

Could it be the sexy little don't-screw-with-me lady with the broken-down classic Holden Torana? If so, he'd had his luckiest bloody day in years! In terms of seeing her again.

Not that she'd seemed the least bit into him during their mini, stressed-circumstances, side-of-the-road, accidental meeting. But they remained unacquainted. Their short interaction relied on limited first impressions. With more information, familiarity, trust, initial opinions could change. For the positive...or negative.

Except his professional expertise made dating extra hard. He could do his whole English accent charm, which had a history of winning over women from a range of countries but then...what? Honesty and security agent didn't exactly go together.

A romantic date wanted truth, to get to know a potential partner in their entirety in order to consider whether they were aligned enough to pursue the relationship. So if he couldn't be upfront with her, what did it say about him? What did it say about the women he was attracted to? What did it say about his priorities?

He shot up out of his office chair and paced the length of his suddenly stuffy office, the air con no longer able to counteract his inner emotional flare up.

How much did he want a compatible, loving woman in his life? How much was he willing to sacrifice to find her, keep her? How much did fear prevent him from relationship success?

Oh, he'd be honest and frank in terms of his feelings, but he refused to tell the prospective woman what he did job-wise in case it put her – and him, and everyone he was intimately connected with – in additional jeopardy. The more he opened up, the more it elevated the risk.

Aside from that, looking at it with a wider perspective, it added extra awkwardness to the whole scenario. What woman wanted to introduce their boyfriend as a sniper, a shooter, a security agent?

A guy who might, and most likely would, kill people…if he hadn't already. What woman would feel comfortable with his skillset and the accompanying danger?

None that he'd met so far. Then again, he'd dated ladies outside his profession so had consistently lied about his occupation, hadn't tested their true reaction to his career choice. Not the best foundation, pretty much setting a precedent for failure. Anyone external to his work, he didn't let close enough to really know him.

The voices grew louder, nearer.

Alex's distinctive, firm-but-considerate rumble, followed by a sultry, intoxicating woman's laugh. *The* woman.

Westley stopped right in front of his door. His curiosity dared him to make an appearance, determine how she fit within the Solve Security puzzle.

Not yet.

Take a breath. He leaned against the door and raked his hands through his hair. He needed a believable excuse, something that didn't sound pathetic. Something that sounded legit.

Pushing off the door, he started pacing again, darting his eyes about the room, zoning in on his almost empty coffee cup.

Yes, he could take it into the kitchen under the pretense of cleaning the caffeine-stained thing. He needed to act before he missed this rare opportunity.

Westley dropped his face into his hands. For years, he'd lived as a loner. Up until he secured the gig at

Solve Security. Prior to that he'd done his job without concern that someone else might get hurt.

From his experience, enemies knew how to target a person's weak spot. So he'd kept his vulnerabilities, and connections to family and close friends hidden, to retain a strong resolve.

Although he wanted a wife, his own children, he refused to put anyone he loved at risk. Hence his continued single status. His immediate family lived in the UK, and he made sure to keep communication with them to a minimum, for their own protection, and he had no familial connections in Australia.

Just how he liked it...professionally. Made it a shit-ton easier to do his role. If criminals worked out who he loved, they'd use them as pawns, as bargaining chips, making him less effective and reducing his ability to follow agency protocol and stipulations.

It would significantly impact on his job integrity. Because although he enjoyed what he did, he couldn't sacrifice those he cared about. Never. Ever. Protecting those close to him held the highest priority. Always would. As a result, he'd compartmentalized his life into personal and professional, ensuring neither crossed.

Hence why working alone had held added appeal, playing into the whole noble cause thing while increasing his and his family's chances of survival. His family, friends, and partner came first, closely followed by keeping the broader community safe.

More voices joined the mix, ebbing and flowing in volume down the hallway. Normally he had fantastic concentration and attention to task, but not today. Every little sound pulled him out of the moment. Every little noise jolted him into his external surroundings. At the very least, he needed to appease his curiosity.

Westley stretched his arms above his head. Yoga had a way of helping him refocus. He closed his eyes and drew his attention to his breathing, then shifted into the next pose in the sequence. Forcing himself into mental stillness, attuning his mind to create calmness in his body.

Since he moved to Australia, he hadn't returned to an in-person class, but he hadn't forgotten the movements or the positive impact. Once he settled into a more established routine, he'd seek out a session close to home. Assist him to de-stress, refocus.

Achieving balance held the key to success in everything, according to his old yoga instructor, and his life experience. As a natural protector, he strove for safety, equity.

He had a history of putting others ahead of his own needs. But he couldn't if he suffered an emotional breakdown. Westley had to find a way to continually strengthen his psychological battle-armor, his resolve. He had a more interactive job now.

What would it take to successfully reconfigure his brain from years of solo missions, of a skewed perspective? What would it take to ensure he did everything to the best of his ability and eradicate work-biased indoctrination?

Eradicate internal conflict and potentially deadly compromise. His role always entailed a certain amount of danger, however he needed to decipher how much he was willing to accept for himself, for those he cared about, for the broader community.

Snatching his cup off the desk, he drained the dregs of his now-cold coffee. Did he even want to draw more complexity into his already chatty, overloaded mind? Add more considerations into his already close-to-capacity brain?

Create conflict with his current boss? Although Alex and the team had been accepting of him, in Westley's eyes, he still needed to prove himself, his skills, his reliability, his consistency…if he hoped to establish himself in Australia.

Did he have the required maturity, the stamina, the emotional endurance to stick out a security role? Did he have the fortitude to deal with persistent challenges and not get triggered? Only the passage of time would tell. Taking a deep breath, he opened his door and stepped into the corridor.

Chapter Three

Once the gorgeous guy got back into his car and took off, as per her request, May tinkered with the engine for a few more minutes. Long enough for her heartbeat to return to a regular-ish rhythm. And her brain to recalibrate. Why couldn't she have met the man under more normal circumstances. Non-triggering circumstances.

His dark, impeccably styled hair tempted her to run her fingers through it, to rub and tug and tease. And those delicious coffee-colored eyes... *Oh my...* They stimulated the deepest recesses of her soul.

She sighed.

His accent and external appearance piqued her sexual interests. He totally ticked all her physically and aurally attractive criteria.

So ridiculous. She'd known him for how long? Five minutes max. And yet... Renewed images of him flooded her mind and she sighed. Lust. Pure and simple. A base, non-rational, primitive response. Nothing more.

The mysterious good Samaritan had towered over her, but not in an intimidating way. In a way that got her extra hot and moist and interested.

With lean, muscular, broad shoulders and a narrow, tapered waist, he'd more than met the standards on her man-I'd-love-to-ravage checklist. Whether he could consistently string a sentence together...she'd have to assess that later. If she somehow got another chance.

His suave, over-polite manner—an almost old-school, over-the-top chivalry—contrasted with the devilish twinkle in his stare. A total turn on...normally. If she wasn't in such a hurry. If she hadn't had a job interview scheduled shortly, if he hadn't assumed she couldn't possibly know how to fix a car. Asking if she'd called roadside assistance might be practical, but why not check if she knew what to do first?

The guy could look hotter than hot, but overall it didn't mean anything. May required a progressive man, one without 1950s stereotypical thinking. Sure, his chiseled, angular jaw, dark designer stubble, and olive complexion pressed all her arousal buttons, every centimeter of her skin rising into I'd-love-to-do-you goosebumps.

But no. *Fuck no. No way.* His appealing outward appearance didn't deter her from his backward male-centric presumptions. And if he did it in one area, he'd do it across the board. The type that would buy their female partner a vacuum cleaner and call it a present.

Although she appreciated his decision to stop and help, his unexpected eye candy, and his sexy King's English, she didn't condone his damsel-in-distress assumption. Having worked on a huge range of military vehicles for years, she'd almost bet her life she knew more about cars and engines than he did.

Using her forearm, she swiped the sweat off her face, hoping she didn't leave any dark, dirty streaks. Once she dropped back into the driver's seat, she'd check in the rearview mirror.

Standing on tiptoes, she reached over the large expanse of engine, and tentatively touched the radiator cap. *Cool enough to remove. Finally. Thank fuck.* Definitely one positive of the sexy guy stopping. He'd eaten up some time.

She carefully unscrewed the cap and, sure enough, the receptacle had barely a breath of condensation, let alone water. As she'd accurately assessed.

Unable to locate an actual hole, and putting the issue down to a slow-seeping hairline crack, she grabbed an emergency stop leak bottle from her boot, as well as her one-point-five liter, water-filled Thermos from the front passenger seat. First, she poured in the leak solution, then the entire amount of water.

She screwed the radiator cap back on, secured the hood, then jumped in the driver's side. After throwing her Thermos into the back seat, she waited a few agonizing minutes before successfully starting the car.

Yes!

In less than five minutes, she turned into the designated guest car park at Solve Security, found a spot as near as possible to the lift and killed the engine. May flopped back in her seat, eyes closed, and took a much-needed moment to reset and prepare. A much-needed moment to collect herself.

Late. But she'd made it unscathed…physically.

May rang Alex to let him know she'd arrived. Sage answered and confirmed he could see her in fifteen minutes or so. Which worked perfectly because she desperately needed to freshen up first. Then when she finished the interview and got back to her car, she'd check the radiator water level to ensure she had enough to get home.

If not, she'd refill her Thermos and top it up. Once she got Ladybird into her garage, she'd work on her until she sorted the issue and deemed the car safe to drive.

After a security check and sign in at a manned checkpoint, she found the ground-floor ladies' room, and entered the sparkling-clean facility, blessed with large windows welcoming consistent daylight. Following a panicked pee, she washed her hands and grimy, sweaty, grease-smudged face at the immaculate white basin.

Scrubbing at her flushed cheeks, her run-away mascara proved the most difficult to remove, but she did it, then patted her skin dry with a paper towel. Her sexy, British, would-be savior must have noticed her shocking, unkempt appearance and yet he seemed…keen. What did that say about him? What did that say about her?

Didn't matter. He was more than long gone. He'd remain a regrettable, yet safer missed opportunity. The less she got involved with a guy the better, especially one who doubted her abilities. She wanted to avoid any added drama.

Plus, her occupational-hazard type of work already compromised her safety. No matter how tempting, she refused to play into her selfish needs and bring others into her risky world.

Scrutinizing herself in the mirror, she patted shine-reducing powder on her face, reapplied some eyeliner, added a swipe or two of mascara, and finished off with a little light-metallic-pink lipstick.

May stepped back and studied her reflection.

Neat, professional, trendy but approachable.

Good to go.

Or at least she hoped. She packed away her travel cosmetics, threw her bag strap over her shoulder, mustered up some self-confidence, and did one last check of herself in the wall of mirrors.

Her hair desperately needed some further attention. Undoing the elastic tie, she wet the mass of frizz, and tamed the rebellious locks into a sleek, low ponytail.

There. She rolled her lips together. *Ready.*

It always fascinated her how the smallest amount of grooming could increase her self-assurance. Increase her ability to face the corporate world in particular. Her mum had always been a stickler for looking immaculate. *All. The. Time.*

Whether she expected visitors at home or needed to get a couple of things from the local shops, she had to look 'presentable'. Whatever that meant. Such an individual concept. So subjective. It didn't have to be a big occasion for May's mum to doll herself up. And she had drummed that thinking into her three daughters.

Luckily for the other two—or maybe she'd underestimated their ability to make more strategic, smarter decisions—they'd relocated with their partners overseas 'for work'. Singapore and Scotland were far enough away to relegate any parent-related financial and medical decision-making to May…if required.

Not that her parents had been a burden…exactly. Yet. Well, outside of hassling her when she chose to enter the military to complete a mechanics course and, since she returned, frequently asking when she'd have a stable man in her life.

Enough.

She tugged at her strappy top and smoothed out her skirt. Better. Slick, professional. Outside of her poor first impression. But it had been beyond her control.

Her temperamental car deserved all the blame. And if Alex didn't get that, it already raised redder-than-red flags. Ultimately, a job interview was about both sides assessing their suitability to work together.

With a single set of instructions, and great signage, she took the lift to the Solve Security floor.

May closed her eyes and drew in a deep breath, then focused on exhaling any lingering negativity. She'd often attempted meditation and it still hadn't been what she'd consider successful.

Her busy mind wandered way too much. However, the associated Resonance-style breathing she'd learned online helped at least focus her for a minute or two at a time. *Better than nothing*, or so she tried to convince herself.

Leaving the shiny chrome lift, she stepped into the sunny, open-plan area and reported to reception. A stunning woman with long cinnamon hair, amber eyes and a welcoming smile introduced herself as Sage, and informed May she'd let Alexander know she'd arrived.

She gestured for May to sit in the waiting area, and she tried but couldn't stop fidgeting. If she wanted to master her stress, she really needed to practice the breathing techniques more often, and keep more active.

May stood and wandered within the large space, attempting to take slow, calm, controlled steps, stopping periodically to check out the stunning abstract artwork on the walls. Fingers crossed Alex would soon call her into his office, or wherever they were supposed to conduct the meeting.

Knowing the outcome, good or bad, would allow her to relax. To refocus and plan her next career move.

"May Caledon?"

Glancing up, she met the piercing blue gaze of a tall, built, imposing man, his smile offsetting any possible trace of intimidation. Going by his height and presence, she could imagine him successfully scaring most people. And yet, he emanated an unexpected warmth.

"Yes, hi, Alex? I'm so sorry I'm late."

"I appreciate you letting me know. Follow me, and we'll get started."

May hurried to join him, Sage flashing her an encouraging, all-the-best smile. And she appreciated that. It assisted in alleviating some of her nerves, some of her mounting anxiety.

"So, did you get your car sorted out?" His deep raspy voice traveled over his shoulder.

"Oh, yes, it was the radiator. I've done a temporary fix."

"I see you know quite a bit about cars. You've already ticked an additional box I hadn't realized I'd required. Great start."

She breathed out a pent-up breath while trying to keep up with him. Their short conversation had already managed to put her at ease. Somewhat. A very welcome relief. "Thank you. I aim to please." *Within reason.*

"Watch who you say that to." He chuckled, stopped in front of a doorway, and turned to her. "A great sense of humor is always appreciated in addition to your mechanical expertise. Especially with the sort of hardcore, stressful work we do."

For the next fifteen minutes he explained his vision and mission for Solve Security, which fit snugly into her belief system, with where she wanted to head, career-wise.

Then he fired off a round of questions—some job specific, some what-would-you-do case-study scenarios, and some conflict resolution style queries.

Pretty much the standard subjects and sequence she'd prepared for. *Thank fuck.*

Alex's body language gave nothing away, but her internal barometer suggested a successful result. She'd find out soon enough. From the moment she'd had contact with the guy, he'd excelled at rapport building. She just hoped her answers to his multitude of questions met his requirements. The place had the exact sort of vibe she'd searched for.

She stood and reached across his desk to shake his hand.

Alex didn't let go and looked her in the eye. "I like you. I like your honest, straight-up attitude. You have the sort of broad-ranging skills I require. So I'm offering you the position. In fact, I have just the job for you." He let go of her hand and gestured for her to return to her seat.

Oh? Already? She hadn't expected her first interview in a very long time to go so well. She hadn't expected to hear the outcome today. Somehow, she successfully managed to plonk her butt back in the chair. "Great. Thank you." She tried not to squeal with excitement. "With everything we discussed, I feel like I fit in here."

"You do."

His confirmation had her buzzing, and she chomped hard at the bit to know more. "So, if you don't mind me asking, what's this job entail?"

The corners of his mouth kicked up as though impressed with her eagerness. "You'll be paired with another agent. How do you go, working in a partnership?"

Professionally, great. Personally, not so successful. Thankfully he only needed to know about her work proficiency. "More than fine. I'm used to carrying out my role as part of a team."

"Good to hear. I know it can be challenging depending on different personalities, so I try to match people up as best I can."

More than most organizations attempted, citing the usual lack-of-resources argument. "Thank you. That's really reassuring."

He smiled, big and broad and super pleased. "Okay, let's make a time for the three of us to meet and we'll go through the mission in more detail."

"I'm flexible. Let me know when and where, and I'll be there." She couldn't tame the ecstatic, gushy tone of her voice. Hopefully she didn't sound too desperate. "I'm looking forward to it." And she was. It'd been a while since she felt so purposeful.

"As am I. I think you and the other agent I have in mind will work well together." He stood, walked around his desk and opened his office door. "I'll give you a call once I speak to him."

Him? *Shit.*

Why was she surprised? A lot more men than women did this kind of work. "I'll wait to hear from you." On a massive high, tempered with some nervous energy, she exited the room, Alex accompanying her to reception.

Making their way down the corridor, he introduced her to other agents, then made a joke about her orientation, or lack thereof, and, both laughing, they turned the corner.

May slammed into a wall of hard-as-fuck muscle, almost dropping her to the floor. "Excuse me, I..." She glanced up and froze.

The guy. The full-on fuckable man who'd stopped to help her out with her car stared down at her with unblinking intensity.

Alex said something, maybe introduced him, but she couldn't concentrate. Shocked and struck with disbelief, she couldn't stop studying the magnificent man, making sure he was real and not some strange illusion. Her heart hammered at a ridiculous pace, like she'd neared the finish line of a race.

Her eyebrows pulled together, and she stepped back on shaky legs. "You were…what are you doing here?"

His potent, one-hundred-percent-cocoa-colored eyes fixed on hers. "I work here. Did you get your car going?"

That English accent. Good God. It did X-rated things to her erogenous zones. "Enough for her to be drivable, thank you." Her super-controlled tone bordered on snippy, but, more importantly, shut down her gushy, you're-gorgeous response.

Lines of confusion creased his forehead. "And then?"

"I'll fix Ladybird. Once I get her home."

"Ladybird?" He stared at her with wry amusement. As though he couldn't comprehend her car having a name, let alone her resolving the issue herself. Like men were the only ones who could ever understand mechanics. So outdated. So *me man, you woman,* caveman shit.

That shut down any rise in her libido. "Women work with cars these days, you know. Just ask Alex. He understands. In fact, some of us girls even comprehend the workings of an engine." She couldn't help the snark slicing through her tone.

"They do, Westley. You should see her CV."

He shook his head, as though not expecting her answer or Alex's staunch backing. "Sorry, I didn't mean to sound condescending, it's just…"

"I'll leave you to it. Westley can see you out." Alex barely hid a smirk, and disappeared down the hallway.

She refocused on Westley and raised her eyebrows. What the hell excuse could he make, except the typical, uninformed, stereotypical misogynistic one? "Just what?"

"Nothing. My mistake." He extended his hand. "Westley Richards. And you are?"

"Like the gun?" He had to be yanking her short chain.

"Yes." The slightest hint of pink stained his cheeks. Was that surprise? Embarrassment? "My dad was a bit of a firearms aficionado."

She glanced at his hand, and finally grasped it, unexpected tingles shooting up her arm and straight to her core. What the...? Did he feel it too? "May. May Caledon. Looks like we might run into each other now that I'm officially an agent."

The smile that graced his sensual lips spread right to his eyes, cutting elated crinkles at the corners. "Congratulations."

"Thank you." Neither of them had attempted to relinquish the grip on each other's hands. Neither of them seemed to be able to break eye contact. Like some sort of ecstasy-inducing electric shock held them spellbound.

She fucking hoped her cheeks didn't flare a fire-truck red. "Um...I need to, you know, get my car home and make sure it runs before I officially start tomorrow." She reluctantly let go of his hand, the pulsing electricity instantly ceasing, like she'd lost connection to the power grid.

"Right, yes. Of course." Like her, he seemed to snap back into the moment. "See you soon. Tomorrow." He stared at her as if to say, don't let me down.

May tried to keep some composure, walking to the lift with slow, measured, devil-may-care steps, even though her pulse pounded, compelling her to expend some energy, to escape. She needed to get out of there. She needed some solo time to work through why she had an attraction to an old-school, Mr. Polite savior type.

The idea of it might sound romantic, but not the underlying assumption. Yes, okay, at this stage he was only a work colleague and may remain that. Any man with personal potential had to believe in her, not be some guy who thought he knew better or didn't trust in her skills to do, well, anything that was traditionally associated with a man's 'superiority', their supposed 'prowess'.

May signed out at the manned security station, then walked to her car, scanned around it and bent down, checking underneath. No pool or even drip of water. A good sign. She prayed the engine would start.

Slotting the key in the ignition, she clamped her eyes closed and turned...*yes!* The motor purred, much like her core, following her Westley-filled morning.

The man's striking face flashed into her mind's eye. Yes, he was classically handsome. But so fucking what? Appearances only scratched the surface of attraction. And now she might need to work with him. And office romances generally caused no end of trouble. The majority failed, with only a very select few making the distance.

Okay, yes, his accent alone practically set her panties on fire, but so what? History proved fire wasn't sustainable. It may initially burn bright, but even with the required ingredients, it soon petered out, adequate fuel needed to keep it alight.

Miraculously, May made it home without incident. Using the remote control, she opened the garage door and shut it behind her. Although her stomach growled, she prioritized getting her car in order ready for tomorrow.

Tomorrow she'd see Westley again. Her heart and her head conflicted. Emotionally she wanted to create a further connection, but mentally, she couldn't accept a man who didn't respect her and her talents.

Her stomach gurgled insistently but she put it on the back burner, popped the hood and collected her well-loved tools of the trade. She couldn't stop her mind from wandering to all the new job possibilities, the combinations and computations. What if Alex paired her with Westley? Her heart kicked into a sprint.

Could she cope? Maybe she should have ignored security-style positions and gone specifically for a mechanic role?

No.

May couldn't let fear consume her thinking. She wouldn't know for sure if agent work suited her best until she gave it a go. With or without Westley. Anyone could find reasons to rule out options when scared.

Worst-case scenario, she'd realize this Solve Security role didn't meet her new needs, didn't sit well with the new her, the opportunities she strove for, and resign. With her military and mechanical knowledge and expertise, it presumably gave her heaps of possible options.

Currently, she didn't have any outstanding debt, which helped. But it wasn't just about the money. She craved purpose, passion. Something to keep her entertained, something rewarding, something she could enjoy without a romantic partner.

Because she couldn't rely on finding a suitable one. One that met her needs. And his. Wasn't even sure she was cut out for sharing her life with anyone, particularly Mr. Forever. If there was such a thing in her world.

She needed to figure herself out and get aligned with her goals before she could even consider searching for, let alone meet, Mr. Right. Before she could set up a loving, sustainable, couple-driven life.

Not develop core-melting chemistry with someone who didn't show trust and respect. She couldn't allow herself to get sucked into the temptation of Westley and his sexy-as-fuck outward appearance and panty-melting English accent.

Stepping back from the heat radiating from the exposed engine, she shook her head in an attempt to reset her mind. She'd never fit the stereotypical female, overly romantic, overly driven by lust mold and yet...she hadn't felt this horny, this activated in such a long time. Eons.

Yeah, she'd done the one-night-stand thing, expecting it to resolve her loneliness, but it only added to it. Took her further away from sustainable happiness. From the possibility of long-standing love. If it existed. Her internal jury was still out on that one.

Westley had caught her in between relationships. Short term, long term. So no wonder he'd won her lustful favor. It had been too long since she'd had a forget-her-own-name fuck. And although it didn't make practical sense, Westley had screwed with her brain. She'd only met him for a handful of minutes, for fuck's sake. *Crazy.*

Tinkering with the engine, she waited until the radiator had cooled enough, then replaced it and screwed the new one in tight. Almost damaging the thread. *Shit.* She eased up, blew errant stands of hair off her face, and stepped away. Done.

Twisting the key in the ignition, she started the motor, and it hummed in mechanical harmony, everything running smoothly and in sync. Bending down, she peered under the car—no fluid. No concerning leakage.

Thank fuck.

In order for her to get ready for her first day on the job, from a pragmatic standpoint, she closed and locked the car, and entered her home, her safe sanctuary.

Except tonight, it didn't protect her from her uninvited Westley-focused thoughts. Somehow, he'd managed to slip past her usually high security defenses. Suddenly, the likelihood of her getting a decent, sound sleep dropped from six out of ten down to zero.

Chapter Four

Meet me and your co-agent in my office at eight a.m. to discuss the new case.

Alex. His boss.

See you then.

Westley tried to rest, but was too wired to even doze after that enticing five a.m. text message. He'd tossed and turned and finally threw himself onto his back, staring at the ceiling, his arm slung over his forehead.

No, it wasn't just the early-morning work call-in. He'd hardly slept the whole night, thoughts of May invading his mind.

Ridiculous.

He hardly knew her, had engaged with the sexy woman for less than ten minutes, and yet the chemistry between them broke down his existing static state and rearranged all his molecules into a sizzling hot new bond. And all the reconfiguration had happened from the moment they met. It made no rational sense.

The spark lit her up like fresh firewood, her kindling ablaze, stoking his internal flame. Spiritualists might argue that like dried-out hay, their connection had flared to life from the smallest ember of hope.

That the conditions had been set on a universal, cosmic-level way beforehand. And maybe they had. He didn't intend to argue. Just acknowledge the reality. How their interaction played out, and how they could work with the complexity.

Reluctantly, he pried his eyes open and rolled out of his king-sized bed, the black sheets rumpled and tangled in the quilt. He trudged to the shower, hoping the hot water would rejuvenate him enough to make an unforgettable third impression. Because, in all honesty, he'd failed the first two times.

Was May a forgiving type? Someone who factored in the challenges of the environment combined with people's longstanding, deeply embedded baggage? Someone who realized not everything ran smoothly first time around. Or even the second.

Did she reserve judgment until she'd weighed up the outcomes over a series of meetings? That alone should confirm whether she was his type of woman.

My type of woman. Fuck. Talk about shoving the cart before the horse. Someone had gotten way ahead of himself. He shook his head. Shit, he needed to shake her from his system. Go with practicality, not his subjective heart.

He turned on the shower taps and adjusted the water temperature until it bordered on scalding. People spoke about cold showers to reset certain urges, but he needed the heat, the full body and mind cleansing.

Stepping under the hot spray, he soaked his entire body. Probably better if she wasn't open-minded, wasn't into him, because he'd most likely need to work closely with her at some point. And it'd make so much more sense, be so much easier, if they remained distant.

Emotions had a way of stripping rational thought, like peeling off pasted wallpaper from plaster, leaving remnants of uncertainty glued in among overinflated optimism and euphoria.

Under the scorching, high-pressure water flow, he washed away most of the remaining stubborn spots in his tight muscles, then dried himself and got dressed.

In less than forty-five minutes he made it to Solve Security, parked, successfully completed the ID check, and went straight to Alex's office.

Up until now, he'd mostly worked solo. Not that he minded making a change. As long as he was paired with a partner who pulled their weight and had similar safety-first ideals. Being stuck with some gung-ho new recruit could possibly get them both killed.

There'd been a few new staff starting, while Alex built up his business. Some agents had commenced before Westley, all with a range of backgrounds, a range of different skills. Who would Alex match him up with and why?

Not that he could or would question his boss's reasoning, but the guy's decision-making intrigued him. What markers made Alex choose each agent? What influenced his decision to select a particular person for a particular case?

Personality had to factor in. Personality, experience, skills. The job cover story. Whatever colleagues worked on a case had to have no conflict of interest, and get along at least at a civil level. It didn't make sense to have staff arguing and compromising the result. Was that how Alex assessed it?

Westley exited the lift, offering Sage a smile and a quick hello as he powered past reception and down the passageway. He knocked on Alex's door with moments to spare. He hadn't even had any time for a second cup of strong, nerve-settling, energy-evoking black tea.

Alex whipped open his office door and waved Westley inside. Gorgeous May, the stunning new agent, sat on one of the guest chairs closest to him, on the other side of his boss's desk, the window pouring light over every beautiful inch of her clear, fair skin.

Westley had hit the partner jackpot. Or at least he assumed she'd been allocated to work with him. Why else would she be here? Whether she was or wasn't his co-agent on this case, his emotions led him down the same torturous track.

Her magnificent sea-green gaze clamped onto him and, like a magnet, drew him closer. No way could he look anywhere but at her, yet he somehow successfully sat on the seat beside the spellbinding woman without falling onto the floor.

A small smile graced her lips before she turned and refocused on Alex. The boss man sat in his throne, picked up his computer tablet and swiped through page after page, finally settling on one.

"If you haven't already worked it out, this is a briefing. I'd hoped to ease you into your new job, May, have some time to help you orientate, blend in, but...not possible. We need to act now."

Westley fixed his eyes on Alex, an unsettling sensation, like tidal waves accompanied by a strong rip in the ocean, tugging at his already tense stomach. "Why? What's happened?"

"A lot. But for the moment I need you both to attend a party."

"A party?" Westley's brow scrunched up like a Roman blind. If two agents were required, it suggested something pretty damn serious. "To do what?"

"Infiltrate the inner sanctum. Work out exactly what's going on."

"Going on with what?" Everything was so vague and cloak-and-dagger so far. If Alex wanted him and May to work successfully together, they needed a heap more details.

Alex powered down his devices and requested they too switch off their smart phones, and afterward, any appliances connected to them.

They both followed his instructions without question, agreeing to turn off any other associated equipment once they returned home. Anyone who'd worked in the security field long enough knew that smart phones and internet search engines listened, used algorithms to follow people's patterns to more successfully target advertising campaigns to their interests. And more, including extortion, utilizing ransomware demands.

To sell. To create buyers. To encourage people to spend. To blackmail them into buying their way out of trouble. As Alex said all the time, search engines knew people more than they knew themselves.

"It's a hush-hush, high-profile case. You both need to assure me you'll treat any information I give you with total confidence."

Alex looked them each in the eye and they nodded. Neither of them would betray his commands...or at the very least Westley could vouch for himself. If his gut had assessed May accurately, she'd do the same.

Uphold the sanctity of her signed employment contract.

"There's been a string of missing persons, possibly deaths, with no real leads. There are a few people invited to an upcoming kick-starter on a private, isolated island, who have most likely met, and hopefully have more information on, the guests who have disappeared.

"The prime suspect is a wealthy stock investor who has either bought silence out of people or blackmailed them, keeping him generally above scrutiny. But as you know, I don't believe anyone should get away with murder."

"Murder?" May said, and shifted to the edge of her seat, her gaze glued to Alex. She really was a newbie. She really had no idea of the complexity of her role, the nuances. What lengths people would go to.

"Yeah, whoever is behind this has been picking off select, supposedly rich people. Talk to the invited investors, work out if any of them have further intel. If any of them knew those that went missing. If they've heard from them since."

And he'd do that, tackle every possible angle, but if the perp purely sought out money, wouldn't he have robbed the relevant people, in the most subtle way, more along the lines of a Ponzi scheme, and moved on? Why kill? It only drew more unwanted attention.

"You need to find a motive, proof. If the organizer is involved, if he isn't. If anyone else is..." Alex met Westley's gaze. "You know the required drill."

"I do." He did. With absolute subtlety — get in close, find out what's happening and eliminate the threat...or at least report it to headquarters. And wait for further feedback. Further direction.

"And what's that?" May's eyes shot between the two of them.

"Westley will guide you. He's very experienced."

Images of him guiding May in the bedroom bombarded his brain.

Stop it. He subtly shook his head to try to clear the salacious thoughts and refocus on the assignment.

As a sniper, yes, he had loads of expertise. In the field, needing to work closely with others, not so much. But it reassured him that Alex had faith in his decision-making. In his ability to adapt.

He certainly had patience and experience when it came to upholding the required team tactics. Westley also backed himself to come up with an effective, strategic plan, factoring in a broader perspective.

Her eyebrows practically touched her hairline. "So am I. I've been in the military, I get the general gist. But I've only met Westley for less than five minutes and I'm supposed to trust him? A guy I hardly know."

"I realize it's not ideal. If things were, Solve Security wouldn't exist, and you wouldn't have a job."

The stark, no-nonsense reality. Alex's superpower entailed him never mincing words.

She blinked and jolted back into her seat, not uttering another sound.

Westley stared at Alex until he met his curious gaze. The perfectionist in him always needed details. Specifics. "So what's the plan? What additional information can you give us?"

Alex powered on his separate, off-the-grid computer tablet and shifted his gaze between Westley and May. "I want you two to travel to the island and make friends with the organizer and the guests. I want you to collate as much information as possible. Determine what's going on, what the undercurrent is, the deeper issues. Why a prominent businessman would risk being involved in murder."

Westley leaned forward, propping his forearms on his knees. "When do you need us to leave?"

"This afternoon."

"This afternoon? That soon?" May stared at Alex as though not expecting such a short turnaround time. A sign she hadn't yet worked long enough with Solve Security, or in this field. Agents had to be ready to go whenever ordered. Things turned on an unpredictable dime.

Alex focused his piercing blue eyes on her, toning his gaze down to 'concerned, caring' mode. "Is that a problem?"

May averted her eyes to her hands, fidgeting in her lap. "No. If that's what's required—"

"It is. Flexibility is a key trait to work in this area. We don't always have the luxury of devising a thorough plan. We often have to strategize as we go. Part of that is because we usually have limited details, so need to slip in, as covertly as possible, and find them out."

A frustrated frown crinkled her forehead. "Then please provide me with the details you do know, so I can at least somewhat prepare. I understand we can't possibly be aware of everything, but surely the more we utilize the knowledge we have to our advantage the better."

She glanced up and locked her gaze on Alex. "Things like, what's the suspect's name? Where is the island located? What clothes should I pack? How long am I likely to be away? What's our cover story? What time are we leaving and from what airport?"

The start of a smile tugged at the corners of Alex's lips. "You're a smart woman. I knew I needed to hire you."

"Thanks." The hint of a blush tinged her cheeks, reinforcing she wasn't used to compliments. From what he'd garnered so far, she'd spent her life trying to prove herself, her skills and abilities. "I intend to continue to improve myself."

"Another reason you're right for this role."

And another reason Westley had to show her balance. Not all men underestimated women. Not all men felt threatened by a woman's talents. When he'd stopped to check if she needed help with her car, it wasn't because he didn't think she had it under control, it was to ensure she did. He'd do the same for anyone, male or female. He refused to leave anyone stranded.

Alex grabbed a couple of reports off his printer and handed one to May and another to Westley. The security abridged equivalent of *War and Peace*. Westley had a quick scan through the pages. Oh, this Marcus guy had been busy. And amazing at avoiding detection. Which suggested this wasn't his first foray into the criminal world.

He'd most likely used his wealth, and possibly blackmail, as a trade-off for silence and protection. And it had worked an absolute treat...until now.

"I'll let you read this in your own time. And I'll also send a more in-depth electronic version for you to take with you and refer back to."

Thank fuck. In order to have a thorough scan, he and May needed to do it outside of Solve Security, unless Alex expected them to sit in his office for the next couple of hours. Westley could speed read, but even so, given the size of the document, it'd take a while to get through.

Especially considering they needed to practically memorize every aspect. No skimming allowed. As May had touched on, they needed to make the most of the info they had, to give themselves the best chance of success.

Westley lifted the document in front of his face and murmured, "As in the last ridiculously rushed hours we've got left to get everything sorted."

Out of the corner of his eye, May clamped her lips together as though trying not to laugh.

"What was that?"

Uh-oh. Westley lowered the report just enough for his eyes to peek over the top.

Alex's steel-hard stare said, "Don't-take-the-piss, especially in front of new staff." And he got that. Now. Avoiding nuances was easy as an employee, but a shit-ton harder as the business owner. Avoidance got a person nowhere. Especially an entrepreneur.

Westley gave him his best, sheepish, I'm-sorry, I'll-take-more-care-next-time look, with the accompanying twinge of a smile.

His boss glanced down at his computer tablet. "If you flick to the second page, you'll see a summary of the assignment." He waited until they'd found the right spot and continued. "I'll go over the key information with you now, in case you have any pressing questions."

Alex flicked his eyes up to Westley. "I realize your time is restricted. But you have the flight over and then once you're checked in to your accommodation, you have the evening to finish up your reading and speak about how best to proceed. Individually, as a couple.

"You'll be provided with mobile phones and tablets, associated with your cover identities, in place of your existing devices. Which means you need to leave all your personal gear here. I'll make sure IT set up forwarding so any voicemail or text message goes to your new numbers."

He glanced at May, then back to Westley, neither of them objecting. After a few silent seconds, Alex continued.

"However, to deter people in your personal life from leaving non-urgent messages, update the recording on your current cell to let them know you're away and have poor connectivity, so will catch up upon your return."

Not a problem for Westley. He was used to going solo. He was lucky to receive a call or message once a month. He shifted his focus to May. Did she have interfering friends? Family? Boyfriends? People who might stress if she didn't respond within a few hours, a day, several days?

Oh well, not his issue. She had to work that one out, right?

"Once you're on the island, you'll have sketchy internet connectivity. But don't be alarmed." Alex's deep authoritative voice snatched Westley from his musings. Thank fuck his boss's attention had shifted to May.

"We've organized the most receptive electronic equipment for each of you, but the transmission still isn't great. So keep that in mind. Some areas have better reception than others. You'll need to test that out when you arrive."

Westley waited until Alex's eyes fixed on his. "Any idea where the peak points are?"

"No, unfortunately. It'll be a bit of careful trial and quiet error. If you get my less-than-subtle drift."

As in suss out spots without drawing too much attention. His forte. Stealthy was his middle name. "I do."

"So do I," May said straight after him. "Have you got more details on this guy? A rundown of him and his firm's exploits. Partners, close friends. Business dealings gone wrong. Even a vague hypothesis of why he might be behind the supposed mortalities?"

All great questions. All the same ones he'd had but she'd beat him to the proverbial punch.

"Marcus' wife suspects murder, but technically the cases are currently listed as missing persons. Hence why I need you two to obtain evidence to prove what exactly is going on. The clearer we are, the easier it is to strategize."

Alex flicked his gaze back to his tablet screen and started reading. "Marcus King is a stereotypical reformed-playboy media mogul and stock investor, now married to Penelope King.

"Both families come from a long history of wealth. He inherited the financial advisor business from his father, but in recent times, his recommendations have had a significant decrease in share price. Profits have been at an all-time, record low.

"His dad is retired but has apparently threatened to fire and disinherit Marcus if he doesn't get the figures back on the required track. Penelope reported increasing stress and emotional distance from her husband that started around the time she noticed a pattern of missing persons who'd attended his business 'retreats'."

He scrolled further down the page. "She ignored it at first, thought she'd read too much into the situation until she saw a persistent, recurrent theme. With only speculation, no actual evidence, she took her concerns to her friend, my wife, Sage, rather than the police. And asked her to red flag the issue with me.

"She did, and following some preliminary investigations, I recognized some anomalies, backing Penelope's concerns, hence your recruitment to the case."

May went to speak, and Alex held up his hand in a stop-right-there gesture. "Don't stress. All the details will be included in the electronic file."

"Thank you." She relaxed into her seat.

"Any other questions?" Alex darted his gaze between the two of them.

Westley sat forward and pinned his boss with a curious stare. "So, our cover story is...?" Because the sooner they knew, the sooner they could get into their required roles.

Alex folded his hands on top of his tablet. "Most of the select, invited group of investors, have tended to be rich and partnered, so you've been accepted onto the list as a wealthy newly married couple, searching for avant-garde, lucrative investment opportunities."

"Married?" May sent Westley a horrified, imploring gawp. As in, what-the-fuck-does-this-mean? She'd signed up to be an agent, protect citizens, do her job, but hadn't realized the extent the case could take. Hadn't realized she may have to enter into a fake relationship. Play act attraction and passion. Even so, was he that repulsive?

Real confidence booster. Shot his self-assurance down a huge number of notches. If that was her plan, she'd succeeded brilliantly.

Alex didn't seem to notice his distress, instead focusing on getting May fully up to speed with the situation. "That's right. So in order to obtain the intel, you need to not only play nice, but also show everyone you're totally enamored with each other. You've supposedly just tied the knot, so onlookers will expect you to struggle to keep your hands off one another. Understand?"

May shook her head and buried it between her hands, her voice a soft, stressed murmur. "I wasn't expecting *this*. I didn't think—" Pretty much confirming everything Westley had picked up on. Would she pull out now that she knew the working mechanics of her new position? He had everything crossed she'd stick it out. He couldn't imagine convincingly playing husband to anyone else.

Alex's concerned eyes studied her. "This work is challenging, and not just because it can be physically dangerous. If it's not for you, I understand." Because, yes, they all needed to know. If she couldn't fulfill the requirements, they'd have to rethink their approach.

She jolted up, chin thrust out, and stared back at their boss. "I didn't say that. I'm not a quitter. I have a history of rising to any challenge that comes my way. I wouldn't be here otherwise."

A pleased smile stretched across Alex's lips. His goading could have gone either way. And maybe that had been part of his plan. It gave him an opportunity to test her, review the sincerity of her reply. "Happy to hear it. I'm glad you're willing to continue to push yourself. Solve Security needs a diverse range of staff with a broad variety of skills and an open mind."

His boss swung his gaze to Westley. "Any objections? Concerns?"

Not now. "With our mutual understanding and aligned thinking regarding the assignment, plus our broad skill base, I trust May and I can get the job done." And he did. She might have reservations toward him, but she radiated the required drive and determination for this style of work.

Going by her responses to date, she'd experienced doubters in her past, particularly of the male persuasion. And overcome their ignorance and lack of faith.

May glimpsed at him, her forehead creased, a hint of surprise in her eyes. Like she couldn't believe he'd backed her after her negative reaction, and particularly when they still hardly knew one another. But he got a gut feel for people, an indescribable instinct. And it had saved his life. Time after time after time.

Plus, she couldn't have survived the army otherwise. Although they were more supportive of women in the ranks these days, the establishment still had a lingering old-school, restrictive, boys' club mentality. And that never made it easy. Made it twice as hard for females.

"Great." Alex's no-nonsense voice snatched Westley back from his ballooning thoughts. "It's a tropical island, with the average daily temperature between twenty-five and thirty degrees Celsius at the moment, so pack accordingly, then head to the Solve Security airstrip. Once on board the plane, a staff member will provide you with your identity kit, including your new cell phone and laptop, and answer any other queries about the destination."

His boss's intense blue eyes pierced into him, then May. "Any other questions, contact me. And make sure you send a text when you've arrived and checked in. Keep me up to date with anything and everything. I want to know even if nothing of significance happens."

Of course. Between them, Westley would ensure they gave Alex regular feedback, and abided by agency protocol.

Although not exactly the island paradise trip Westley had dreamed of, he'd somewhat gotten his wish. Yes, it was for work, but who could complain about an all-expenses-paid journey with a captivating woman?

Celebratory circumstances rather than job-related would be wonderful and yet, even though the situation had no romantic or relaxation overtones, the thrill of the tricky task ahead got his heart hammering with anticipation.

Chapter Five

May stood in the shadows beside the private plane, but it did nothing to protect her from the wild, whooshing winds. The airstrip worked like a large tunnel, funneling the squall over and around her, consistently whipping blonde wisps of her hair across her face.

With her forearm plastered to her brow, she blocked out the glare as best she could, but still squinted.

A man walked toward her.

Westley. She could tell by his stride, his posture, his unique, masculine presence, even from over two hundred meters away.

She stifled a gasp.

Looking as hot and cool and relaxed as can be, he strolled along the tarmac of the private-airfield, reflective sunglasses in place, dressed in beige linen pants and a white shirt. Total tropical island attire. In keeping with their instructions.

She did a double take, forcing herself not to fan her face. Part of her had expected him to turn up totally in black. Still fitting with the paradise destination brief while looking stealthy, calm, commanding. Like Alex.

From what she'd witnessed so far, black was the unspoken Solve Security uniform. Plus, Westley had a controlled, loner vibe about him. How had that come about? What sort of work had he done in the past? Did she really want to know? What if he was a semi-reformed hitman?

His answer might be confronting, but the more she knew about the man she'd spend up-close-and-personal hours with, the better she could prepare. And while they had this forced time together, she'd make it her side mission to suss out his story. Though, would Alex have hired a loose cannon, someone untrustworthy, someone who oscillated on the line between sin and morality?

A sly smile slid onto his lips, and he raked his gaze over her long, flowy red linen dress. If he thought his eyes were hidden behind the dark lenses, he was mistaken.

"Hello, May. All ready?" He raised his eyebrows in question, waited for her nod, then snagged the carry-on bag from her hand and gestured for her to step up into the plane ahead of him.

How helpful, how convenient. Some might see his actions as gentlemanly, but she knew his suave type. He had the perfect excuse to enjoy a view of her ass. And she'd make the most of it.

She traversed the stairs, ensuring she swung her hips to full advantage. Not too overt, but definitely not subtle. Served him right. She hoped he had a hard-on for the duration of the flight, and beyond.

Stepping into the spacious, sumptuous, first-class interior, she jolted back with surprise. She hadn't expected such luxury.

The handful of large charcoal seats looked as though they'd extend into a bed, with swing-away desks, and TV monitors. She'd assumed something a lot more basic. Maybe a slight improvement on economy.

But apparently Solve Security spared no expense when it came to agent comfort and support. At least, from what she'd experienced so far.

The business had to have more funds, more consistent cash flow than she'd anticipated, especially for a new enterprise. Before applying for the job, she'd researched the agency and its owner, and its likelihood of surviving its first year.

And all the parameters met the positive indicators. Alex had apparently left the army with no debt and a great lifetime pension. More successful than what she'd achieved. Not that she had any complaints.

The military had embraced her mechanical skills, her drive, and remunerated her for it. However, he'd been a longer standing member, having served several more years than her, and had the connections to obtain everyday as well as government contracts. It all helped. The broader a person cast their net, the bigger the haul.

May selected a seat, and got comfy. She quickly located the remote, tucked away in a side compartment of the chair. So many buttons! It'd probably take her the whole trip to work it out.

A whoosh and accompanying squeak of leather had her glancing up.

Instead of sitting in one of the many other seats, Westley shoved her carry-on bag in the overhead compartment, alongside his own, and settled in beside her. Her thighs clamped together, automatically reacting to his close contact. Trying to prevent any accidental touches.

Could the man give her some space? She subtly shook her head and clenched her teeth to stop herself from blurting out a few choice swear words, annoyed at her response to his magnetizing presence.

Her heart hammered and her face heated, as though her body rebelled against her mind, as though her libido tried to convince her that his close proximity wasn't all that bad. The opposite of bad. Pulse-pounding. Seductive. Tempting.

No. She refused to visit planet Westley no matter how enticing, no matter how much she wanted to explore.

Although his attentiveness was over the top, overly chivalrous, she couldn't deny he made fantastic eye candy. Oozed an indescribable yet palpable dark sensuality.

And that only made her more determined to keep him at a distance. She didn't need a cloying, claustrophobic man, no matter how much her core lit up in his company, no matter how aesthetically pleasing.

Westley could be as alluring and delectable as an expensive, high-end wine and cheese platter, but she had to resist. They had to work together. That was all. The last thing she needed was emotional complications.

He placed a tan, leather-looking satchel at his feet, grabbed a document, and snapped his seatbelt into place. His espresso eyes met hers with the potency of a concentrated, super-strong, short-black coffee, making her heart accelerate. "Have you read this?"

Their identity dossiers? Yes, they'd only had a few hours to get everything done but she'd prioritized memorizing them. "We keep our first names to make it easier to slot into our roles but adopt a new married surname. I believe it's listed as Borgne."

His eyes widened and his provocative lips parted on a shocked breath. "It is. I'm impressed." And everything about his body language—turning more toward her, bright eyes, broad smile—backed his words. "But how about *us*? We need a consistent story. How did we meet, how long have we been a couple? What do we like to do together? How long have we been married?"

Oh. Shit. Yeah. He had a point. She'd memorized the scant relationship details on the page but if they hoped to be successful, the depth of information, their knowledge of each other needed to be congruous. Their responses needed to match. "Um…we met when you stopped to help me with my broken-down car?"

A sexy smirk lifted the corners of his lips. "Nice."

And semi-accurate. Easy to remember. She focused all her energy on ignoring the annoyingly attractive man, and preventing a blush from staining her cheeks. Again. "We exchanged numbers, and you called to check on me. We agreed to meet up for a coffee and quickly realized our interests intersected. That we had a heap of life goals in common."

A flow of thoughts filled her mind and, with a hair's breadth of a pause, she continued. "Only a few dates in, we got serious. Our friends considered it a whirlwind romance but we knew we were meant to be. We've been married for five months and love traveling together, particularly to places far away from typical tourist destinations. To secluded resorts with all the swanky facilities."

He jotted down some notes on his phone and glanced up to meet her gaze. "Wow. You're good at this."

"Thank you." His praise had a smile stretching across her lips. "Hopefully we can both look as convincing."

He crossed his legs toward her and stroked the scruff on his chin. "Yes. Agreed."

What else? They needed to think in layers of coupledom existence. "Do we have pets? Where have we traveled? What do we do for work? How do we entertain ourselves?"

"We love traveling and have extensively toured through Australia and Europe. We don't need to work but we enjoy feeling purposeful and productive. I've been an executive in a corporate weapons company for several years, and you're a blogger with a focus on females with a love of classic cars.

"When we're not working, we prioritize time together visiting local places, especially art galleries and museums. We don't currently have any pets, but now that we're settled back home, we're looking at getting a couple of kittens."

He was a cat guy? She loved cats! "A couple?"

"Two, at least. It's important they don't just have human company."

Her thoughts exactly. "Not puppies?"

"No. Cute, but too dependent. Wouldn't suit our lifestyle." Was he talking their imaginary lifestyle or if they were actually together?

"Okay, so...what are their names?"

"Smoky and Shadow."

She balked. "Really? Let me guess, one is gray and fluffy and the other is black." She huffed out an exasperated breath. "So cheesy. So cliché."

"That's the point. We need to look like a pretentious wealthy couple who fit into the scene."

Like those rich women with spoiled, handbag-size pooches.

The guy had an inarguable point. He'd definitely done this before. A bolt of unexpected jealousy struck her heart. Had he been as flirty with his previous partners?

Didn't matter. They were paired to do a job. And if they had to act as a newlywed couple, she could uphold the façade for a short time…in public. Couldn't she?

In private, they'd do their own thing within their own space. Give each of them a window of recovery from the exhausting fake relationship and challenges of the day, then discuss any observations, and investigate any leads. Keep the whole thing entirely work focused.

"Fine. Our favorite travel destination?"

"The Whitsundays."

All right to suggest a spot, but he needed to know it with some level of intimacy. "Have you even been there?"

"I have."

With who? A woman? When? "Good. Because we need to describe it like we've visited the place. Be able to name what we loved most."

"We hardly saw outside of our accommodation, too busy fucking like horny little rabbits." He stared at her with the most sinful smile, and she tried to hold off a full body flush. Was he flirting, or had she read more into his reply, tapped into a not-so-subconscious desire?

He shrugged. "So, as you can see, no problem for me. Is it a problem for you?" Westley raised an inquisitive eyebrow, his devilish grin widening.

She sat up straight in her seat, almost defensive, adamant to do whatever it took to shut-off the erotic images flooding her brain and tamp down her accompanying aroused response. "No. I've been several times."

"Sounds like the perfect option then. If in doubt, we talk about being caught up in each other, and no one will question it. Everyone will understand that we might not remember too many island-specific details…if we hardly left our room."

Could the guy stop staring? Stop planting more salacious images in her head? The intensity had her struggling not to switch the overhead fan to full blast.

"How about this to ensure general consistency? We stayed at a prestigious resort—we'll google a name—and when we weren't island hopping, walking along the pristine white sands, swimming in the azure water, and wandering in and around the rocky outcrops, we enjoyed exploring each other. Thoroughly. Intimately." His high-potency dark brown eyes hardly even blinked.

May swallowed and glanced out of the window, breaking the mesmerizing eye lock, bordering on eye fuck, trying to erase the fresh influx of fantasies he'd conjured up in her depraved mind.

How could just a few short sentences get her so hot?

Because it wasn't just a few short sentences. It was everything together—his words, his accent, his tone, his innuendo, his intense stare, his fit physique, his sexy scent. He drove her crazy.

She gathered herself, and turned back to him. "So it was our honeymoon then?"

He shook his head, his gaze zeroing in on her eyes. "Oh no. Our honeymoon was in Hawaii. Not the typical Oahu or Maui. We stayed in a guest house on the island of Hawaii, close to the Volcanoes National Park. We spent every spare minute making love so I can't even remember the view from the window."

She squirmed in her seat as subtly as possible. If his verbose, white-knight personality didn't annoy the ever-loving crap out of her, she'd straddle his lap right now and fuck him senseless. "Right. Noted." Her voice came out all husky, and softer than a whisper.

"How about birthdays? Favorite food? Favorite color?"

Safer topics, thank fuck. She let out a relieved breath. "31st May 1993, cheese, red."

"Nice. 31st August 1991, fry-up, green."

Green? Surprising. She thought for sure he'd choose black. A safe, non-committal answer. An I'm-a-cool-guy reply. Interesting. Maybe he had more depth than she'd assumed.

May typed his responses into her phone. She'd make it her mission to reread everything over and over until she knew the info as well as the familiar back of her hand. "So, sounds like we're pretty sorted now, unless you can think of something else?"

"Do you want children?"

What did that have to do with anything? "Excuse me?"

"Does my wife, *May*, want to have my babies?" He leaned his elbow on the armrest between them, one dark eyebrow raised.

Why did her insides flutter? Yeah, he was good looking but really? She wasn't fourteen with a crush on the hot new boy at school.

And kids? She'd considered it, but never thought seriously about having any. She'd focused on finding the right partner first. If that were even possible. Then if that worked out and they both wanted them, sure. "Does my husband, *Westley*, want a family?"

"He does. Three children, minimum."

She snorted out a surprised laugh. "Minimum? Good luck with that. Maybe if *you* carry the babies and go through labor."

His signature smirk slid onto his lips. "Happy to oblige…if I could. But I can't, so I recommend you focus on how much fun we'd have fucking."

Her traitorous body had her pussy tingling without permission. "How convenient, and conceited."

"Not conceited. Confident in my abilities and willingness to please my partner. Happy wife, fucking elated life."

Oh. Oh God. Thoughts of him going down on her crashed into her mind. And with him, right there, physically less than a foot from her pussy, it intensified the fantasy. "You're right — if you please your wife, you can't really go wrong."

His unwavering gaze penetrated deep, not allowing her any room to deflect. Warning her that if she did, he'd redirect her straight back to the topic. He'd persevere and persevere until they'd discussed anything and everything of consequence. In explicit detail. No leeway allowed.

She returned his stare and leaned in, their mouths irresistibly close. "And how about raising *our* children.

It's fine to want them but I refuse to be stuck at home while my *husband* is out gallivanting."

His dark chocolate gaze melted away her belligerence. "Be assured, I would share the duties. If I choose to marry and have children, then my partner and progeny become my top priority. Happy family and all that."

Good call. Great call. The perfect answer... hypothetically. But was it bullshit? When it came to practicality, would he pull his proposed weight? Because if she got lumped with all the child rearing, the last thing she'd want was sex. "Thanks for clarifying." She forced a smile, trying to disregard his libido-enhancing impact on her body.

She pressed the remote to transition her chair into recline. "Well, if that's it, I'm going to try and get some sleep." Because God knew, with him in the same suite, she'd struggle to get any decent rest.

"You do that." He leaned back into his chair and started flicking through his phone.

Did this guy ever go offline, chill? Not her problem. He knew what he needed to do. They both had to manage themselves in the best way possible to achieve the required result. She had to trust his judgment, and he had to trust hers if they had any chance of success with this assignment.

A blanket of wispy clouds filled the sky outside her window and her eyes fluttered closed. She drifted into a dozy dreamscape of surreal Salvidor Dali-style images, featuring her and Westley running in and around drooping clocks. Time ticking.

A sudden jolt had her eyes springing open and her face buried in Westley's neck, his fresh, clean, musky man scent arousing her senses.

What had happened to their shared armrest? Had he flipped it up? Why? When? If the plane had an ejector chute, she'd press the button and disappear into the far-reaching distance.

She squeezed her eyes shut, hoping it had all been a horribly bad dream. The next subconscious chapter of her vivid, scarily real nightmare. Not that she didn't enjoy their intimately entwined position, but she couldn't afford for him to discover her inexplicable attraction. Couldn't stand the teasing, the embarrassment.

When she opened her eyes again, reality hit home, like an arousing slap. Her nose nestled against Westley's jaw, her hand nudging the impossible-to-miss bulge in his pants, her face pressed against his delicious smelling stubble.

Oh God.

After too long a pause, she scrambled back onto her seat, adjusted the backrest, and met his stare, his eyes dancing with mischief. "Thanks for reminding me — I love my wife plastered against me. Preferably naked."

Heat suffused her chest and cheeks, her body temperature soaring to full-on flaming. She didn't even have to see her reflection to know her skin had turned a deep tomato red.

No matter how much she tried to wish the redness away, it couldn't happen quickly enough. No way could her coloring return to normal before Westley clocked her reaction.

He tipped her chin up and slowly scanned her face, his gaze resettling on her eyes. "I couldn't resist, sorry." And, surprisingly, he looked sincere.

Instead of ribbing her, he'd gone the considerate route? So unexpected. Yes, he'd had some fun with her, but he knew when to stop. And she appreciated it, appreciated a man with awareness. It bumped him up several appealing notches.

A nervous, yet relieved laugh spilled out of her lips. Now she needed to take the focus off them and their overly familiar physical contact, and further lighten the moment. So they could move on without lingering awkwardness. "It's not your fault. Blame the plane. And possibly the pilot."

They both laughed. Good, they could shift to another subject. Forget what just happened. Relegate the faux pas to a funny, shared moment. Nothing of consequence.

He stroked his stubble, as though deep in thought. "Blame circumstances out of our control. I like it. I love the absolution. But even so, I can't say I regret having a beautiful woman pressed against me. Quite the contrary."

Oh. So her tactic hadn't quite had the desired result. Or had it? Did he really think she was beautiful? More heat flared from her breasts right up to her hairline. "Such a guy thing to say." She rolled her eyes, hoping he'd laugh and let it go. This time.

He pinned her with a sexy-as-fuck stare. "I don't think so. You seemed right at home, all snuggled into my side."

Her pulse rate kicked up to caffeine-overdose level. Was he trying to keep her permanently embarrassed, question her sexual interest, or get into marriage-cover mode?

Chapter Six

So far, he'd excelled at all three. "I fell asleep! You can't hold me accountable to what I did when I was unconscious."

He searched her eyes. "You're right. Luckily for you, your *husband* is incredibly understanding."

She stared back, swallowed, and clamped her teeth together. Attempting and struggling to keep herself in check. He hadn't said anything provocative, titillating, yet her core throbbed at how that might play out sexually. Her hormones had been well and truly struck by the lust bug.

Could he live up to her presumption of his expertise? He'd hinted at a few things now that suggested he knew how to physically please a partner. But she wouldn't go there. Shouldn't even consider it, given this was a job. Nothing more.

And she couldn't forget that his character drove her absolutely insane. "So is your *wife*." Experience showed she knew how to please a man. Over and over and over.

She could spar with the best of them. Couldn't explain how much of a buzz it gave her to put him back in his place. To have the last winning word.

He adjusted his position, out of frustration, or maybe to ease the pressure on his cock? She hoped it was the latter. Then at least she wasn't the only one plagued by ridiculous, unfulfillable fantasies.

A crackle came over the loudspeaker. "Good afternoon. It's your pilot here, letting you know we're due to arrive on schedule and it should be a reasonably smooth ride. But even so, when seated, please keep your seatbelts on for safety. Weather conditions can change very quickly at this altitude. Hope you enjoy the rest of the flight."

After the announcement, they sat in silence. She returned into a reclined posture and popped in her noise-canceling headphones to block out the roar of the engines mixed with the buffeting winds, both she and Westley soon absorbed by their phones.

May revised her notes about their *marriage* and *interests*. In public, she expected them to hold hands, have their arms around each other, hug, use pet names, speak sweetly and lovingly, but would they have to be more demonstrative? Would they have to kiss?

She gulped the large lump of anxiety clogging her throat. Part of her prayed for a forced lip lock situation, to give her a legit reason to check out his purported prowess. And part of her hoped circumstances prevented it happening. If he kissed as well as she thought he might, she'd be in big trouble. Huge trouble.

This assignment was her first job since she left the military, so she couldn't afford an emotional distraction, couldn't afford to screw up her career options going forward by some desire-driven lapse in judgment. And yet, the temptation to taste Westley—just once—had her practically salivating.

No.

These days she had too much internal strength to fall victim to her temporary, short-lived longings.

In the past, she'd succumbed to her baser needs, gotten sucked in by guys who knew how to seduce but couldn't offer anything more substantial. And she'd learned from that. Not that she desperately sought someone long term. So no matter how appealing an affair with Westley seemed…no, just no.

A wave of turbulence rocked the plane. Nothing stressful, more lulling, and yet Westley gripped the armrests, his knuckles turning a washed-out white. He normally behaved like it'd take a cyclone or volcanic eruption to rattle his cool, calm demeanor. But obviously not. Had he had a traumatic flying experience?

It didn't matter.

No caring.

No investing in him.

No delving into his history—unless it was something that could impact on her—and potentially create a more tenuous, possibly deadly bond.

No getting sidetracked by someone whose personality didn't rate on the deeper, I-want-you scale. No getting sidetracked by a workmate.

She needed to remain disciplined, no matter how difficult. No matter how much lust, and her love of vulnerabilities, pushed her to have a small sample of the wonders of Westley.

Yeah, as if she could stop at a small sample. She'd want to thoroughly feast and indulge, make the absolute most of any opportunity. One night, two, three, no strings. She wouldn't care. As long as they both knew what they had subscribed to.

No.

Too difficult when emotions had their own idea of reality. Too hard when they both had a difficult job to do. Hence why she had to ensure nothing happened, outside of them putting on an act in public.

Although terribly tempting, she had to ignore her curiosity about his personal history, and whether he could live up to his allure. They needed to focus on finding evidence about Marcus, not doing each other and adding unnecessary angst.

The pilot announced their descent, and Westley clung tighter to the armrests, eyes closed, jaw clinched together so tight she thought he might crack his teeth.

Fascinating.

She adjusted her backrest into an upright seated position, wanting to watch him, but yanked her gaze to the window, enjoying the play of whiskey-colored clouds billowing against the wings, the sun slowly descending in the distance.

Spectacular.

An unrelenting compulsion to check on Westley had her glancing his way. He still held on for dear-as-fuck life, eyes squeezed shut. What a shame he would miss the stunning pinks and oranges and purples streaking across the sky.

May's ears rumbled, crackled, air pressure building like blowing into a balloon, and finally popped. Her usual flying experience. Nothing too troubling, nothing too out of the ordinary. But she wasn't sure what to expect from being an agent, from pretending to be Westley's partner. That went way into new-normal, unchartered territory.

Dealing with some slight ear discomfort while descending had nothing on needing to act like a wife for several days.

The tires hit the tarmac and they landed with hardly a bump. The plane roared to a stop and, only a few minutes later, the flight attendant gave them the go-ahead to unclip their seatbelts, then opened the door.

Westley pried his hands off the armrests, collected both of their bags and stood, encouraging May to go ahead of him, which both frustrated and impressed her. She could carry her own stuff, but she couldn't deny that she appreciated his ability to push past his stress and offer her assistance.

She'd half expected him to escape their confined cabin as soon as the moment presented, yet he'd somehow overcome adversity and stayed, apparently wanting to help.

In all her thirty-one years, she'd never gone out with a guy who had such impeccable, seemingly selfless manners. But was it all for show? To satisfy some inner need? The way he coaxed women into his bed?

Did. Not. Matter.

Alex had sent them to do a job. That's all. Pure and indisputably simple. Their burgeoning attraction, from what she felt, anyway, was just a bonus. Or was it?

Personally, probably not. Professionally, their palpable sexual tension should hopefully reinforce the legitimacy of their newlywed status. Whether or not they acted on their lust in reality.

Westley followed her down the steps and, at the bottom, handed over her carry-on luggage. She smiled, clicked the handle into place and walked toward the waiting car, the wheels of her case clunking over the asphalt.

A small airport building stood ahead, with a view of the sea to the right, the scent of sweet lilies bombarding her nostrils. So different from the concrete-jungle, fuel-infused city smell of home.

The driver opened the back door of the black town car and, after leaving her carry-on bag by the boot, she climbed inside. Westley approached, looking all relieved and recovered, and just as fresh and riveting as when they'd left several hours earlier, rolling their two suitcases — with his hand luggage secured to the top of his — behind him.

While the chauffeur loaded their bags in the rear, Westley got on his phone, then slid in beside her, showing May confirmation that Alex had arranged the car and driver to transport them to their accommodation.

His hypnotizing cologne permeated the confined compartment, overpowering the tropical-flower scent. Had he applied more when she hadn't noticed, or could she sense it better in the small, enclosed back-seat space?

Westley provided their destination details to the driver, then shoved his phone into his pocket and pressed a button to close the privacy partition, separating them in a compact little cone of silence. "Ready?"

Not entirely. How could anyone be completely ready for anything, especially when others were involved. But she'd do her best. "As much as our preplanning allows."

"As long as we play our parts convincingly, we'll be on track to achieve the required result."

Sounded great in theory but it wasn't as simple as them behaving like a believable couple. That alone didn't necessarily ensure the outcome they sought. Yeah, it helped paint the trust picture, provided them with more leeway, more access to other guests, to Marcus, to information, but it didn't guarantee they'd find what they needed.

She stared out of the window, the sun casting soft rays of light across the rocky coast. The aqua-midnight-blue sea crashed against the cliff-faces, creating geyser-like spurts in the surrounding rock pools, the sand a fine, pristine white.

Paradise.

Or was it?

Going by Penelope's take on her husband, it didn't come anywhere close to the definition. Quite the opposite. But hopefully they would get close enough to infiltrate Marcus' current scheme. Hopefully they'd use their expertise to determine what had happened — without drawing unwanted attention — and prevent future disappearances and homicides.

The rest of the drive she kept her gaze glued to the aesthetically beautiful landscape. A real lovers' retreat. If only they were there for different reasons. Legitimate, committed-loving-couple reasons.

Except most people couldn't afford the exorbitant prices to experience such 'natural' beauty, if a resort set among nature with sketchy Wi-Fi and no TV defined natural.

Going by the brochure, their accommodation was the opposite of roughing it. Camping in a supposedly untouched area, she'd understand. But they had access to complete comfort. Unless guests were TV or social media addicts. She was neither.

May did love reading, though, as long as she could get into her Kindle she'd be fine. Because she wanted to restrict her private time in Westley's annoyingly alluring company.

How long would the island remain free from additional development, and travelers? Once a place got traction, it lost its mystique. It lost its appeal.

The only way to push back demand yet make the money, relied on resorts hiking up prices, promising visitors they'd have an exclusive experience. Or having wealthy guests buy the island or pay a premium to book it out for themselves and any others. Pretty much reflecting their current situation.

The driver parked in front of a cabin, more like a luxurious beach house, made up of large windows and, given the exceptional position, she could only imagine that it offered a stunning three-hundred-and-sixty-degree panoramic view of the sea, sand, rocky outcrops, pristine parkland, and surrounding accommodation including the spectacular mansion perched on the hilltop.

Each self-contained cottage, dotted along the beachfront, appeared to share the exquisite aspect overlooking the ocean. Plus they had enough space between each other to enable extreme privacy. A positive and a negative, depending on the circumstances.

The chauffeur retrieved their cases, and Westley paid the taxi fare using what she imagined was a pre-paid company credit card. She secured her carry-on bag to the top of her suitcase then rolled her luggage toward the entrance. Using a keycard, presumably provided by the driver, Westley opened the front door, flicked the light switch, and she rushed ahead.

Warm downlights lit up the open-plan space, which featured a kitchenette, comfy couches positioned in front of a large window, and an accompanying courtyard overlooking the beach. She dropped her bags and explored the rest of the interior.

The master bedroom had a king-sized bed. *Nice. Luxurious.*

She raced through the remaining doors.

No second bedroom.

No other bed.

Shit.

Just a romantic, sumptuous en suite bathroom and toilet.

Two toilets but not two beds.

Yes, it was a honeymoon suite but...

Fuck.

Hyperventilation had her almost passing out. She covered her face with her hands and tried to slow her breathing.

The set up was great for *actual* couples. But in this instance... Trying to contain her distress, and come up with an avoidance plan, she slowly wandered back into the main living area. A small table with a couple of chairs sat near the sliding door leading into the private courtyard. None of the couches looked convertible.

Westley stood on the back patio, hand above his eyes, staring out across the ocean, his linen pants hugging his grope-able butt. Looking totally delectable...and off limits. For so many reasons.

The waves crashing into the shore broke her from her lust spell. She needed to step away before he saw her and assumed the truth. That physically she wanted him.

Yes, they had to play the marriage card in front of others, but getting together in private could fuck up everything. She'd expected Alex to have ensured they had more space to do their own thing. Apparently not the case. A huge reminder not to rely on assumptions.

Whether he'd requested a larger cabin or not, the accommodation met all the newlywed criteria, so if she or Westley argued for a two-bedroom option instead it would arouse suspicion. The place radiated romance to the max.

Her own rebellious inner demons rose, demanding attention. The layout ensured she and Westley had hardly a minute away from one another. A carnal positive, a concentration and clear-thinking negative.

Returning to the huge, beautiful bedroom, decked out in whites and blues, she stopped at the foot of the big bed, and ran her hands over her face. How was she going to survive this?

Westley's soft yet distinct footsteps announced his presence. No, not just that. His aftershave, his aura. His distant yet palpable heat. Had he seen her hovering?

"There's only one bed," she blurted, without turning around, still not quite believing their super-forced-proximity situation. Still hoping he'd have an answer to adequately address this dilemma.

"Shhh…"

She spun around to find his dark eyes wary and his index finger to his lips.

"Wait here," he mouthed, then slowly, methodically, inspected the room, and left her alone.

She kept silent and still.

Finally he returned, leaned into her ear and whispered, "Checked for bugs. Looks clear…for the moment."

As in, they needed to be alert, aware, watchful in case something got planted in their place at another point during their stay.

"Oh." She hadn't even thought of that. She still had so much to be mindful of, so much to learn.

He stood upright, a cheeky twinkle in his eyes. "And I'm not surprised regarding the bed situation. I mean, we're meant to be a married couple." His sensual voice penetrated her thoughts, the sun's golden ambience highlighting the darker streaks in his lustrous cocoa hair.

True. Part of her had hoped he'd prove her wrong and confirm that the couch did actually double as a fold-out bed. Or that maybe he'd offer to take one for their team of two, and sleep on it no matter what. Not that it would adequately accommodate him, or her.

Dammit. From what she'd witnessed, no other suitable option existed.

They required a mutually agreed-upon arrangement to ensure they remained refreshed, to enable them to think as clearly as possible. To be able to problem solve and consider the next steps without putting themselves in unnecessary danger.

May breathed out a resigned breath. "I'll construct a pillow wall between us." Not the most effective option but it provided some barrier.

"Don't worry—I can sleep on the couch."

Oh. So he really did consider her needs, her concerns, apparently above his own. A sudden warmth rose up and saturated her heart. "I can too, but it'll impact on the quality of our rest and recuperation. And we need to be functioning on full cylinders, we need to be more than switched on."

Not that she'd end up particularly well rested, knowing he slept mere inches away from her. But a bed was a bed, much more supportive than a couch, even if she did have a somewhat disturbed sleep.

"So we'll sleep together?" The hint of a smirk twitched at the corners of his lips.

"In the same bed but separated. By a barrier, a pillow wall, weren't you listening? So no swiping it aside, no climbing over, no funny business, okay?"

"Cross my heart." And he physically did, like a good, born-and-bred Christian boy. Another interesting anomaly. Didn't quite align with his agent career choice.

Most likely he'd been brought up in a somewhat religious household, and had detoured down a different path. Or he loved mafia movies. "I wouldn't dare make a move on a woman unless I wanted her, and she made it explicitly clear she wanted me too."

Did he mean he did or didn't desire her? And what did it matter? Sounded like she'd have to state her intentions outright, if she craved his touch beyond pretend.

Or could he read her mind? Could he feel the unexplainable chemistry bubbling between them? Not necessarily on a rational level, but the heated mocha swirls in his eyes suggested he'd tuned in to the same lustful frequency.

"Good to know." And she left it at that. Didn't want to reinforce something neither of them had quite figured out. May took control of her cases and organized a designated spot for them. On her chosen side of the bedroom, keeping a decent distance away from him.

Ultimately, she needed space to satiate any buildup of sexual tension. She needed a physical outlet to stop her making a rash, regrettable, morally gray decision. Her only safe solo space, somewhere she could think without distraction, take sensual matters into her own skillful hands without detection — the shower.

Other than a few relief-filled minutes alone per day, May needed to focus on their mission. First and absolutely foremost. "Are there any social engagements tonight?" Although far from religious, she prayed they had some sort of welcome, let's-get-to-know-each-other function to attend. It provided them both a bit of required breathing room.

"There's a cocktail party at the main house."

Thank the universe. "Then we need to go."

Chapter Seven

Westley wished he'd had more than twenty minutes to himself, enough to allow some much-needed self-satisfaction. Without interruption. Except he couldn't guarantee that, couldn't risk her walking in on him, so instead he focused on his agent duties and informed Alex that they'd arrived safely.

May volunteered to shower first, and soon returned to the bedroom in one of the long, white guest robes, her hair dried and makeup done, looking like a sensuous present he'd love to unwrap.

Trying not to stare, not to fantasize about releasing that loose tie at her narrow waist, he'd hurried into the en suite with his clothes and had a hot shower, staying under the muscle-soothing spray until his cock got the memo to back down.

Dressing for the cocktail party in his favorite body-hugging black suit and white French-cuff shirt, silver-black cufflinks in place, he'd had to shove his still semi-erect dick into his boxers and pants. Quite the feat. But he'd gotten there...eventually.

He finished applying product in his hair, washed and dried his hands, and reassessed himself in the mirror, fingering the Saint Christopher pendant around his neck, given to him by his parents when he joined the army. A constant reminder to be careful. A constant tangible charm to give him confidence with flying.

He couldn't wait to see how May had scrubbed up. Not that he didn't find her striking no matter what she wore.

Would she go formal or stick to something more casual, floral and feminine? He ran his fingers along the edge of his lapels, straightening them out, pressing them down and allowed himself one last look before knocking, and re-entering their shared bedroom.

Empty.

"May?" He'd expected to find her still primping and preening, but no.

"In the kitchen," she called out.

Phew. For a split second, he'd worried their ruse had somehow been discovered, and she'd been kidnapped. Possibly follow the Marcus-guest disappearing pattern. He tugged at the bottom of his jacket, slipped on his shoes, then strolled out of the room and froze.

She stood with her back to him in a long, white, figure-enhancing, halter-neck number, her hair whipped up into a loose bun, mixing a tropical-looking cocktail.

"I hope you like mojitos," she said, without turning around, her husky tone teasing. Like she knew the draw-dropping effect of her backless dress. Had confidence it would get a rise out of him. And, oh boy, did it ever.

He adjusted himself, attempting to ease the growing pressure on his crotch. "I do. Thank you."

Finally, his brain got the message through to his feet and he moved forward, joining her at the bench.

She turned, a drink in each hand, and offered him one.

Wow.

She looked…scrumptious. Breathtaking. Sexy as all get out. He had to work extra hard to stop his gaze from roving too slowly over every inch of her exquisite body.

Thankfully, even his express visual assessment gave him plenty of information to digest. Not too slim, not too rounded. Curvaceous and womanly in exactly the way that got him going.

He raised his drink to hers and ensured his eyes remained fixed on May's beautiful face. "To a successful evening."

"Yes. Cheers." She clinked her glass to his, and they both took a sip. "Any particular plan for tonight?"

To let her hair down, strip her out of that dress and thoroughly pleasure the stunning woman. But that's not what she meant. "No set strategy. Let's just focus on acting like newlyweds and make our way around the party to introduce ourselves to as many of the attendees as possible. Whether we get to speak to them all tonight or not, we can still observe their behavior, still suss them out.

"Once we confirm the attending guests' names, we can do some further investigation. Get an understanding of who's been invited and what they have to offer. And determine if anyone has past dealings with the host or threatened him in any way."

May sipped her cocktail and studied him. "I like it. It's subtle, doable and practical."

"Agreed."

She licked a few stray drops of mojito off her lips, and he clamped his hand tighter around his glass to stop him reaching for her. "Let's finish our drinks and make our way over. No need to be too eager, given we've just arrived, and we're newlyweds." If only he could fully enjoy the pleasure of her company.

The bright red blush staining her cheeks showed she got his we-were-busy-fucking insinuation. If only it were true.

She sculled the rest of her cocktail and plonked the empty glass in the sink. He followed suit, his hand brushing hers, sending an overwhelming thrill rushing right up his arm and spiking somewhere much, much lower.

"We're close by. It should only take us a few minutes to reach the venue." His voice came out all low and deep and raspy.

"Yes." She glanced up at him with a fleeting smile and rushed away. "I need to um…grab my bag and shawl."

"You do what you need to do. I'll wait right here." He propped his butt against the bench, and just stopped his hand before it raked through his styled hair. *Fuck.* His heart rate hadn't even come close to returning anywhere near normal. The persistent, unrelenting thump pounded in his ears so loud, he was surprised she hadn't heard, and called him on it. Or called an ambulance.

In minutes she returned, black sparkly shawl draped over her shoulders, matching black clutch bag in her hand, looking a billion dollars. "Ready?"

She blew out a breath. "I don't know."

"Relax. You'll be fine. We'll be fine. I'll be right by your side." He tucked her hand through his arm. And it felt indescribably good, having her so close. If only they were newly married and he could have her naked body plastered to his in real life, rather than just in his mind.

He swallowed, and attempted to redirect his thoughts. "I've got the key."

"I've got the secret." She paused, an anxious laugh spilling from her bright red lips. "It's an old song reference. Forget it. I've got the spare key in my bag."

He laughed, instantly recognizing the retro song. *Thanks for the earworm.* "Good. Pays to have a solid back-up plan." Just in case they had to separate for some reason, she could still get inside their beachfront cabin without him. And call for help.

As he'd predicted, it took them less than five minutes to make their way up the torch-lit path to the main venue—a white, two-story, old-style home. Utterly charming, reminiscent of his English heritage.

They approached the entrance, and her arm locked harder through his. She was nervous, and she should be. It'd worry him more if she had a totally complacent, blasé attitude. Over confidence bred disaster. But so did an overdose of anxiety. They needed to trust each other.

He stopped in front of the big, wooden, glass-panel double doors, leaned down and whispered in her ear. "If we mostly stick together, we'll be safe, believable. If you're unsure at any point, follow my lead. Or ask to step outside for some fresh air and we'll talk. Allay any fears. Regroup."

The tension in her body fell away on her next breath and she squared her shoulders in preparation for what the night might bring. "Okay. Let's do this."

He opened one of the heavy doors and ushered her into the foyer, pulling her tighter against his side. Except, instead of going along with their ploy, she flinched and pulled away. Slightly, but still perceptible for anyone watching.

He got that she hardly knew him, struggled with the forced-proximity circumstances, that he still had to prove she could trust him implicitly, but an undercover agent needed to play their part. No matter what.

If she had any issues, she needed to speak to Alex. But in the interim, she had agreed to follow the discussed plan. The one they'd signed to when accepting this job.

Part of it required them to create a convincing charade in order to increase their chances of solving the case and preventing further deaths. They had to temporarily put aside whatever feelings they had, positive or negative, or risk abject failure. Risk possible demise.

"Take it easy," he whispered into her ear with his best, sinful smile. Anyone else would think he was saying something sexy. He wished he was.

She momentarily stiffened, then shifted closer to him. He could virtually feel her trying to mentally relax her muscles and appear enamored. She needed work to look legitimately loving. "You take the lead."

And he would. Although he excelled at sniper-based roles, he'd worked enough cases to know what it took to successfully come across as convincing. This was her first foray, and she was still learning. He had to remember that. Remember that she wanted this *job*, not *him*.

They entered the dim, red, lush cocktail lounge, hand in hand, and a waiter approached with a tray of tropical drinks.

May pointed to a creamy concoction with a piece of pineapple and green leaves fixed to the side of the glass. "Is that a piña colada?"

"It is."

She grabbed the glass and turned to him. "What are you having, honey?"

Nice. Much better. The tight muscles in his upper back released. He hadn't even realized how much tension he'd been holding. "What are the other options?"

"Pimm's, Hugo Elderflower and Prosecco Spritz, Tequila Sunrise, sangria, and Sex on the Beach."

"I'll go Sex on the Beach, thanks." The drink and with his woman, if he could.

His woman... In his dreams.

The waiter smiled, bordering on a smirk, and handed over his chosen cocktail.

Westley touched his glass to May's. "Cheers."

They each had a sip through their straws, and scanned the rest of the room.

A few other couples milled around on the timber floor, chatting. Most likely they were other invited investors. He assumed Marcus had prevented any uninvolved, holidaying gatecrashers for the week. The fewer witnesses, the fewer complications, the better. Keep it all close and quiet and select.

Westley leaned into her ear, inhaling a waft of her sexy, cock-stirring perfume. "Let's break into the elite circle."

She didn't resist, instead sucking some more on her straw, and giving him a subtle nod.

With his hand still wrapped securely around hers, he led her to the closest couple. Dressed to the absolute nines. "Hi, I'm Westley, and this is my wife, May."

"Sterling." The silver-fox, middle-aged man gestured to his equally attractive partner. "And this is my wife, Felicity."

"Lovely to meet you." Westley raised his glass in a silent toast, and they all had a swig of their drinks.

The ladies got talking and while May sussed out Felicity, Westley shifted closer to Sterling. "I'm assuming you're here at Marcus' invitation?"

"I am indeed. It's apparently a great investment opportunity." The guy's scathing laugh stabbed the air. "As long as there's a return this time."

Oh. So Sterling had been there, probably more than done that, before. And yet he kept coming back. *Interesting.* Did the guy's negative attitude, and openness, with accompanying verbal, maybe even written bad press make him and his wife high on Marcus' next-victims list? "What do you mean?"

Sterling had another swill of his red wine and looked around, keeping his voice low. "We've been sucked in before. The ideas sound great, but I'm yet to see a profit."

"Really?" Westley placed his drink on a high table and moved nearer. "So what made you give this investment option a go?"

"It shows a lot of potential. More than the previous projects. But if it doesn't work out this time, we won't give his ventures another chance. Ever. No matter how great the opportunity sounds, we won't fall for it going forward. And if anyone asks me about my experience, I'll warn them away."

"Is Marcus aware of your feelings?"

"Absolutely. I told him straight up. He needs to know that people won't keep pouring cash into his proposals if they don't pan out, if they constantly lose money."

Knowing Sterling's thoughts, had Marcus asked him to the island for financial backing or to shut him up? Hard to determine until he and May had a chance to chat to the other invited guests. And even then, certainty eluded them. Without a clear motive, they had no understanding of who he'd target next.

"Thanks for your honesty. It's good to know what we're possibly getting into. I didn't realize he'd previously struggled to achieve positive results. He sold this project incredibly effectively."

"Oh, he's great at that, propaganda, promotion. Marketing. A natural salesman. He could sell a cape to the all-mighty Superman. But when it comes down to cultivating profits, he hasn't shared any with me and always gives excuses as to why things haven't panned out as expected."

Sterling surveyed the room and refocused his piercing light blue eyes on Westley. "The outcomes have started to make me question whether these 'projects' are a Ponzi scheme. While we're without earnings, interest, he's taking our money and personally benefiting." Sterling's voice sounded as bitter as an under-ripe lemon.

"Thanks for your candor. I might have to readjust my original proposed pledge."

The disgruntled man stared him in the eye with categorical conviction. "I highly suggest you do. The fact that you're here means Marcus believes you have a lot of money to spend. But if I were you, if you decide to go ahead, I'd limit the amount to a very small percentage of your investment wealth. One percent maximum."

What amount had the guy guaranteed from his financial portfolio in the past? Must have been a hell of a lot, going by his cynicism. "Thanks for your advice. As a first timer, it's great hearing from people with a history of working with Marcus' business proposals. Do you know if any of the others have had a similar experience to you? Or are the rest of the attendees all new?"

Another waiter approached with a range of finger food and high-end hors d'oeuvres, including black and red caviar on toasted crackers, breaking the flow of conversation. Westley's stomach rumbled and he stared at the selection of canapés and hot savory treats. He needed to eat or he'd get hangry.

Westley grabbed a napkin and loaded up a small plate with some caviar crackers, a couple of gourmet party pies, and pork-belly sliders. Out of the corner of his eye, May made a similar selection. Good, they were somewhat in sync. Following a somewhat aligned process.

The first bite into his black-caviar-laden cracker and he almost groaned. So delectable. He could count the amount of fancy food he'd had on one overused hand. But he needed to focus. Couldn't allow even the slightest indulgence when he had such a prime opportunity to garner information.

Sterling selected his preferred appetizer options and scanned the rest of the guests, mingling, eating and drinking. He subtly nodded toward the far right of the bar. "That guy with the midnight blue Armani suit and perfectly styled hair, studying everyone, is Rei Emilio. Marcus' best friend and business colleague. He's been involved every time. Given his expensive tastes, I imagine he hasn't lost out."

Or the guy liked to appear a certain way but had huge debt. Westley would definitely ensure he spoke to Rei and looked into his background in more detail. With him and Marcus aside, and assuming no one else arrived, other than Westley and May, that only left eight possible investors. How did they fit into the convoluted picture?

Sterling crunched into his red caviar cracker. "See that guy with the brown hair and chiseled jaw, that's Franc and the fashionable woman with the titian hair is his wife, Odette. They're speaking to Edgar and his partner, Billie. I know their names but not much else. They're in my wider social circle."

He tilted his head to a young man with stylish stubble and a fresh-faced woman with long golden hair, trying to make conversation. "And those two, looking all socially awkward, are Benjamin and Phoenix. They're on their own, staying in separate villas. From what I understand, both have recently gained access to their trust funds."

Westley would make sure to check all that info, and whether the group were connected in any way other than wealth. Did some of them socialize outside of Marcus' soirees? And if they did, what else did they have in common? What other crucial details did they know?

Did anything create tension? Were they competitive? Jealous? Envious? Were any of them closer to Marcus and his dealings? Were any of them more supportive of his causes? Did anyone harbor ill feelings toward him? All things that required thorough consideration.

He and May needed to assess all the evidence and Marcus' involvement. Determine if Rei was a consistent business partner or whether Marcus had several business associates, as well as consider if someone might have possibly set him up. Unlikely but possible.

"Have you kept in touch with any of the previous potential investors? Do you know if they've fared any better?"

"I'm not sure how they've done. I tried to contact two of the other couples from prior promo trips to arrange a catch up to discuss results in more detail but haven't been able to get onto them yet.."

Interesting. Chances were he'd struggle to get onto them at all. "Bugger. Do you remember their names? I'd love to try and have a chat with them too. Maybe we could organize a meeting together." Westley swallowed the last mouthful of his hors d'oeuvre selection.

"Let me think..." Within ten seconds, Sterling mentioned the guests who'd disappeared. Westley knew those names as well as the back of his tanned hands. Had heard them, read them in preparation for the assignment. The people Penelope suspected had been murdered.

Bloody hell. He tried to school his reaction so he looked interested rather than horrified. He couldn't let anyone see that he suspected anything sinister. He couldn't have anyone wondering why he cared. Otherwise he'd jeopardize his cover story with May, putting them both at significantly increased risk.

Act normal. Now he needed to wind up this conversation, urge May to do the same, and have them start on the rest of the small party. See if there were any similarities, any crossover.

"Thank you. It's really helpful to have an understanding of everyone here, as well as past participants, plus previous and current investment opportunities. If you hear from any of those who attended other retreats, let me know. As I said, I'd love to tee-up a get-together."

"Not a problem. Good to meet you both. Look forward to catching up more throughout the weekend." Had he tried to shut Westley down before he delved deeper or did he want to reconnect with his wife?

"Indeed." Westley grabbed his cocktail, smiled at Sterling and bored his eyes into May, praying for her acknowledgment and attention. Except her and Felicity kept chatting, pretty much ignoring anything and anyone around them. Hopefully she had gathered some useful intel.

He walked over to his 'wife', weaved his arm around her waist and finished his Sex on the Beach. "May, darling?"

She shuddered, her muscles tensing and stiffening under his hand, her unease hopefully imperceptible, and twisted her head toward him. If looks could kill, he'd be struck down dead.

Out of surprise or fear or abhorrence, or an inability to acknowledge their attraction, he didn't know. And he shouldn't care. But he did. Whether they felt it or not, they needed to promote an into-each-other vibe.

Their brief stated they had to portray a loved-up, can't-keep-their-hands-off-each-other couple. No problem whatsoever on his side. He found her absolutely captivating. But over and above that, he would make it his mission to uphold his promise to Solve Security. Switch off any contrary emotions. Focus on doing his job. And he'd encourage her to do the same, lead by practical example.

Westley hadn't wanted to disturb her, but they had a duty to make their way around the room, and use the prime circumstances to show their supposed love. Extract even a snippet of info from people, do some further behind-the-scenes investigation and continue to develop rapport and hopefully dig out more details.

Essentially, they needed to look interested and enamored. He had no issues doing either, given his spellbinding attraction to her and high job integrity. Did she? Her actions would soon show her beliefs. Show her ability to factor in the bigger, broader picture. Show whether she could be selfless.

"Ladies and gentlemen, please make your way into the dining room for dinner," Marcus announced, appearing from nowhere, decked out in a highly expensive, designer suit. Going by his theatrics, he enjoyed surprising people. Had most likely used it to his advantage.

Chapter Eight

All the guests meandered into the designated area. Candles dotted the center of the pristine white tablecloth, covering the length of the table, with seats accommodating the small potential-investor party. But the setup limited speaking to those seated nearby. Was that purposeful, strategic, or coincidental?

Couples had place cards beside one another, in the grand, old-money, massive room, while the newcomer singles were positioned up with Marcus and Rei at the far end of the table.

Did Marcus have a strategy to move the guests through, like musical chairs, until he had a chance to speak to them individually and determine their commitment and support of his kick-starter? Or did he aim to organize separate dedicated times with party members to privately discuss how each investor planned to proceed?

Outside the window, the lingering remnants of the gold and burnt-orange sky petered out, the sun disappearing below the horizon. The overhead chandelier sparkled from the persistent candlelight, casting multiple rainbows across the ornate ceiling.

Westley scoped out the dining room as discreetly as possible. Aside from the wall of large windows overlooking the sea, a spotless, unlit fireplace took up a fair chunk on the opposite end of the enclosed area. He doubted it'd be used often, if ever, given the mostly mild, usually tropical, weather conditions. But it certainly added a formal yet warm, inviting touch.

Everyone moved to their assigned spots, while Westley observed and listened, preparing to ask questions. He intended to take note of body language and eavesdrop on conversations, as well as chat to those within his vicinity — to develop an updated hypothesis, a workable, practical plan.

His forte entailed snagging as much data as possible prior to acting. Yes, he had a sniper background but his insistence on absorbing details had earned him the nickname 'Sponge'.

The guests took their seats, and his natural, gentlemanly tendencies, combined with what he assessed as good husband material, had him absentmindedly pulling out May's chair. She shot him a glare, a frown furrowing her forehead and a forced, delayed smile lifting the corners of her rebellious lips.

"Thank you," she ground out between clenched teeth, sat, and shoved in close to the table's edge. Leaving no room for the eager waiter to fold the cloth napkin on her lap.

"Madam?" He held the white serviette out to her, and she placed it beside her plate.

May really didn't like men doing anything for her, as though she had to constantly prove her capability. In her eyes, if no one else's. Except, pulling out her chair had nothing to do with him believing she couldn't do it, or that he could do it better. From his perspective, it showed signs of caring, manners, appreciating his 'wife'. It showed a level of courtesy that society had almost forgotten.

He didn't have an un-politically correct agenda, didn't want to upset anyone, but couldn't understand why such a simple action was considered offensive. Whatever happened to gratefulness, and the recipient just saying *thanks*? Just valuing someone wanting to do something for them, to help out, to make things easier.

The only explanation was it indicated a massive trigger point for his partner. Something he'd need to try to help her work through ASAP.

In the interim, he'd salvage the situation as best he could and keep an eye on her responses. Because whether she had issues with his behavior or not, in public, she had to suck it up. They had to look in love. It formed a key part of the undercover requirements for their mission.

In order to quash any repeated signs of resistance, he'd have to have a serious word with her. They couldn't afford anyone questioning the legitimacy of their relationship. Not a single person. Any doubt could create additional scrutiny, and undermine their chances of success.

He slipped into the chair beside his 'wife', and hoped she wasn't the type to hold a grudge. She'd shown she had a fairness, equal-rights, sassy streak, but could she move on from her pricked ego and play the required part? He bloody well hoped so, or they wouldn't last another day in paradise.

Felicity and Sterling sat opposite them, with Billie and Edgar next to May, and Franc and Odette across from them. Benjamin and Phoenix faced each other, on either side of Marcus and Rei.

During the decadent three-course dinner, with accompanying expensive champagne, more cocktails, red wine and spirits, they exchanged pleasantries and general chitchat, but he wasn't able to garner any additional stand-out information. The constricted, compact table configuration didn't help. The layout restricted confidential conversation.

Over the next couple of days, Westley intended to subtly segregate each of the remaining guests and have a more in-depth, straight-up chat. Check if they, too, had any doubts about the project, noticed anyone missing, as well as any past negative experiences. And whether they'd been vocal about their concerns, difficulties, reservations. Whether they'd exposed Marcus to potential bad press.

The night ended and the second May pushed her chair back, he grabbed her hand, waved a general goodbye to the guests and led her out of the building into the cool, fresh night air.

"What are you doing?" She yanked her hand from his. "Stop treating me like a possession."

Bringing his mouth right to her ear, he restated their situation with a scalding whisper, "Listen, May, you're meant to be my wife. And whether you like it or not, we need to enact the façade. And that means holding hands, putting my arm around you, pulling out your chair, keeping you physically close. Or else we'll put ourselves and the operation at risk."

Ultimately, she needed a reality check, to de-energize the ball-and-chain beliefs in her current mindset, and positively redirect any reactive negativity. She needed to fully acknowledge their agency's aim, and tap into her acting abilities.

May huffed out a frustrated breath. "I know. It's just... I need to get used to it."

Up until this point, May hadn't disclosed what had held her back. It could be one reason, or several that came together, that influenced the development of her pattern of thinking and behavior. Maybe she hadn't yet worked out the underlying root cause of her decision-making?

Had men let her down? Believed they were stronger, better, more capable? Did she have trust issues? Had people close to her not had faith in her abilities and judgment, increasing her desire to prove herself? Could be any or all of those. Plus many more. The possibilities could extend almost indefinitely.

Westley studied her eyes. "What can I do to make this easier for you?"

"Nothing. I'll sort it out."

Shutdown. She'd stonewalled him from providing any assistance. And he had to respect her decision. For now. But if he saw a repeat of her back-off response, he'd have to intervene. As the more experienced agent, he had a responsibility to take charge where required.

In less than two minutes, they made it back to their accommodation and he poured them a nightcap while she got changed. A neat Scotch for him, a Baileys on ice for her. Maybe he should have checked her preference first rather than assume. But worst-case scenario, it wouldn't go to waste. Unless she threw it over him.

She returned to the living area in a red satin dressing gown, conforming to her sexy figure, and sat on the couch. He brought over their drinks and handed her the Baileys.

She stared up at him with surprise. "How did you know?"

"I had a feeling. But if I was wrong, I'd have had it and poured you something else."

She laughed, and bloody hell, the sweet sound went straight to his dick.

He sat on the couch opposite and they each had a sip. "Find out anything interesting?"

She cradled the bulbous glass in her hand and glanced at him. "I did. Billie and Felicity both explained they'd had underwhelming dealings with Marcus before, but FOMO had encouraged their partners to give him one more shot.

"However, this was the last figurative straw. Both ladies had put their proverbial foot down. They confirmed they'd invested in previous projects at a loss and had begged their husbands to refrain from going there again. But their men convinced them this was the last time...unless they saw a profit."

"Did they mention any heated discussions, any arguments with Marcus, any threats? Any other investors missing?"

"No. Nothing. But I didn't ask them directly. Did the guys say anything?" She stared at Westley, leaned forward and had another swig of her Baileys.

"Sterling mentioned he'd made his displeasure known to Marcus about the lack of gains so far. And he admitted he'd tried to connect with previous investors from Marcus' 'parties' but hadn't heard anything. Yet."

"Oh. It'll be interesting to see if anyone else mentions investment-related issues, as well as people missing, and whether they've confronted Marcus with any of it." May bit the corner of her bottom lip as though in thought, and swirled the Baileys over and around the melting ice cubes in her glass.

"It will." Westley drank the remainder of his Scotch, the delicious heat rolling down his throat.

May polished off her liqueur and swiped her tongue over her plump lips. "What's on for tomorrow?"

He struggled to tear his gaze from her mouth. "We chat to the guests at the set events, and keep an eye on their general movements. The moment they're roaming the island, hidden from the main house, away from possible spyware, we intercept to inquire if there is any bad blood, if there are any other significant details, then make a mental note of the reasons why they might be targeted. Or involved."

May placed her empty glass on the coffee table and propped her forearms on her knees, providing a distracting view of her boosted-up cleavage. "And then?"

He tore his gaze away from the best view he'd seen in a long time, and locked his focus on her inquisitive eyes. "Call it in. Let Alex know the situation. Get his opinion on how to proceed."

"Oh." She shook her head, as if to say, I-can't-believe-I-didn't-figure-that-out. "Of course."

"There's a lot to absorb. And it's been a long, drawn-out day." He hoped that somewhat reassured her. Yes, she'd worked in the military, but her role had focused on mechanic duties.

Solve Security had thrown her in the specialized, undercover-ops deep end. And she'd either sink into stress or swim at the challenge. Whatever happened, he hoped to keep her afloat.

"I suppose we should go to bed…I mean…get some sleep." Her cheeks flared with the brightest, most beautiful pink.

Westley could tease her, wanted to, badly, but decided against it. Their partnership was in its infancy, in the testing and trying and developing-rapport phase. Ruining that could cost them the case, cost them their lives.

Plus, he'd hate for her to think he'd use their shared accommodation situation to take advantage, to sexually harass her, to use the close proximity to force her into a compromising position.

Westley wouldn't. Ever. It went against everything that he believed in. If anything shifted from professional to personal, she'd have to instigate it. He'd love nothing more than to interact beyond pretending but he'd never cross that lustful line without consent.

And he doubted she'd give him an undeniable go-for-it sign. Probably for the better. Romantic entanglements only complicated things. The case, and people's lives, remained their number one priority. "I agree. Go and get yourself settled, and I'll be there in fifteen minutes." That should give her enough time to do any last-minute woman things, shouldn't it?

He washed and dried the dishes, and got himself sorted in the bathroom, which included brushing his teeth, undressing down to his boxers, and giving himself a good, firm talking to. His mind had to stop diverting to the sexy, untouchable woman who'd be lying beside him for the duration of the assignment.

It didn't matter how irresistible she looked, how much her presence had his heart beating off the charts. This was the most restraint he'd had to show in years. And he prided himself on upholding propriety.

Westley acknowledged the allure, the pulsing, unmistakable electricity between them and suppressed it. Tapped into his discipline to quell his desire. If anything ever happened between them, she had to make her intentions without-a-doubt clear.

He entered the bedroom and her eyes widened, redness rushing to the top of her hairline, the covers pulled right up to her neck. "I...is that what you're wearing?" she stammered.

He glanced down at himself and back up at her. "Too many clothes?" He hooked his fingers in the waistband of his snug-fit undies, his gaze penetrating her eyes. "Should I get rid of these?" He couldn't help but tease her. Her reaction embodied enchanting.

She held up her hand in a stop-right-there motion and looked away. "No!"

A deep chuckle fell from his lips, partly in response to her shock, partly to release some pent-up energy. "Count yourself lucky. I usually sleep naked."

She huffed as though frustrated and annoyed, but her body language suggested she enjoyed his semi-nude state, that she protested too damn much. It wasn't his place to question her, though, and definitely not presume. It wasn't his place to do anything but literally sleep beside her, no matter how much chemistry pulsed between them.

She'd accused him of being too polite and gentlemanly, and yes, he generally was. And he prided himself on that thinking. He didn't believe in forcing anyone to like him. Equal enthusiasm and consent was sexy.

May flipped over, her back to him, and he slipped in beside her, a pillow wall separating their bodies. *Good luck with that.* From his experience, they didn't make the best barrier, they never held up. But good try to at least attempt to erect...something. Once they fell asleep, pillows alone couldn't keep them apart.

The climate control retained just the right temperature in the room to comfortably send him off to sleep. And he drifted into a delicious dream. Spooning a supple, sexy woman, his hand cupping her full breast, her nipple beading beautifully in response to his touch.

He groaned and kissed her exposed neck, his cock nudging her gorgeous ass. She undulated into him, as though wanting more, and he couldn't wait to give it to her. Good and proper.

Thwack!

His eyes snapped open to find May jolting out of his arms and turning to glare at him, the pillow wall totally tossed aside.

Bloody hell. He'd felt her up in his sleep.

His gaze dipped involuntarily to her hard-to-miss perky nipples, evident beneath her red satin slip, and straight back up to her squinty what-the-hell-do-you-think-you're-doing eyes.

"Sorry. I didn't mean to, ah... I was asleep, dreaming. I swear."

He must have looked and sounded believable because she shook her head, the hint of a smile on her lips. "I should have known that wouldn't work." She eyed the dislodged pillows, one strewn down the end of the bed and the rest kicked onto the floor.

"I really am sorry." But his asshole, horny, still-sleepy self wasn't one bit. She'd felt amazing. Soft, lush, curvaceous. Right up his attraction alley.

"I know. We can't control ourselves to the same level when we're unconscious." Thank goodness she understood the compromised conditions.

"As evidenced by my touchy-feely good morning."
She laughed. "Yes, exactly."

He grabbed his mobile off the bedside table and checked the time. Just after six a.m. "Ready for breakfast? Or do you want more of a snooze?"

"What do you want?"

A bloody loaded question. *Her.* His cock agreed. But he couldn't go there, no matter how much he craved the chance to explore her exquisite body. He cleared his throat. "To watch the sun rise, then eat."

They had been provided a refrigerated basket with a range of goodies for the duration of their stay, which was apparently topped up each day, and he looked forward to trying out the various options.

Westley wouldn't rate himself as a great cook, nowhere near the vicinity of a celebrity chef, but he could do a fantastic fry-up. He was English after all, and they excelled at cooked breakfasts.

"That actually sounds nice. Really nice, tempting. But I do love my sleep, so let me know when breakfast is ready." She smirked, turned over, and lifted the covers up to her chin.

Right. A wave of unexpected disappointment rolled through him. Why did he care? He gave her the option and she chose one that best suited her, just as he'd chosen what best suited him. Well, sort of. His ideal morning consisted of a lot more hands-on, mouth-on, cock-in May time.

Westley forced a smile onto his lips so he sounded appreciative rather than rejected. "I'll leave you to it then, and call you when I'm done."

"Thanks." Her voice came out all pillow-muffled.

He slipped out of bed, grabbed some clothes, showered, dressed, and stood on the back deck to watch the spectacular gold, pink and rustic-orange sunrise. He sighed and closed his eyes, the warm sunlight seeping into his exposed skin. How he'd love to share the stunning view with her, while sinking deep into her slick heat.

Enough.

Although early morning, the temperature had already reached what felt like twenty-three degrees Celsius. Warm. Temperate. He didn't feel even close to cold in his shorts and T-shirt. He had to give props to Marcus' venue choice. The place was pure paradise. Best assignment Westley had ever had. *Thank you, Alex.*

Half an hour later, he retreated inside, with still no sign of May. Hopefully she had gotten back to sleep because they had a big few days ahead of them. Being on a case was taxing enough, but having to fake a romantic relationship added to that stress. Not that faking the attraction caused him any concern. But obviously it did for her.

Westley couldn't deny he liked his work colleague a bit too much, appreciated her spunk. Found her heart-hammering, knee-weakening hot. Beautiful. However, her snippiness showed her body and mind didn't align when it came to her overall opinion of him.

The conflict had to wear out every last ounce of her energy. And he planned to ameliorate that as best he could. Ultimately, he needed to keep his physical distance in private, and ensure they both ate enough nutritious food to remain energized in public to achieve the best outcomes.

He examined the contents of the complimentary food basket and decided on short-cut bacon, fried eggs, continental sausages, hash browns, mushrooms, spinach and tomato with multigrain toast. They could do pancakes another day. No need to get greedy and end up with a severe carb coma. They needed to be active, responsive, switched on.

Westley plugged in his wireless earphones, synched them with his smartphone and selected his favorite playlist—a mix of industrial metal, electronica and Brit-pop. He washed his hands and got to work on feeding them ASAP. His stomach had gone from growling to roaring.

Music always soothed his mind, especially listening to tracks that took him back to a positive place and time in his life. Even some edgy, hardcore, dark stuff still reminded him of wonderful, shared experiences with friends and colleagues...mostly before he almost got killed.

Songs had gotten him through his long, in-patient hospital admission, his rehab, and his move to Australia. They'd gotten him through break-ups, and frustration and sadness. And now he hoped they'd help him stay centered and not get too infatuated with his pretty, ball-breaker partner.

Once the veggies were cooked and the hash browns crisp and golden, he put them in a tray and placed them in the oven on low to keep them warm while he fried the bacon and eggs. Right in the midst of grinding his hips to *Closer* by Nine Inch Nails, he went to flip the eggs onto a plate and almost jumped out of his usually tough skin.

May stood beside him, hair loose and wavy and wet, wearing a yellow singlet top and colorful floral skirt, a smirk on her lips. "Enjoying yourself?"

She certainly seemed like she was. At his expense. How long had she observed him? He stopped the song and yanked the headphones off, placing them further along the countertop. "I am. Did you have a good rest?"

"Until the smell of bacon roused my ravenous body, yes."

Bacon had a way of doing that. "You've arrived just in time. Everything is almost done."

"Anything I can do to help?"

"Not today. Though, you can make the pancakes tomorrow."

"Sounds fair." Instead of sitting down, she took initiative, setting out a couple of placemats on the breakfast bench, along with some napkins, cutlery and glasses. Tasks he hadn't yet gotten around to but hadn't expected her to do.

He appreciated her team-player approach. If she showed the ability to work with others in a personal area, it would most likely transfer to the professional.

She opened the fridge and turned to him. "Juice or water?"

Truth be told, he could do with a Bloody Mary. "Apple and blackcurrant juice would be great, thanks."

She filled their glasses, carried them to the bench and sat on one of the stools, waiting.

He dished out a decent serving of food onto their plates, and put one on each placemat.

Her eyes practically bugged right out of her head like a shocked cartoon character. "This is heaps!"

"Eat what you want, and we'll save the rest for a snack later." Or tomorrow. Assuming they weren't too full from the rest of the exclusive resort meals. He didn't like to waste food, so he'd just have to make sure he didn't over fill himself elsewhere. "When we're done, let's go for a walk on the beach and see if we run into anyone or notice anything suspicious."

Chapter Nine

Less than thirty minutes after the most delicious start to the day she'd ever experienced—yummy food, and eating with an even more annoyingly mouth-watering man—they exited their deluxe, beachfront cabin and started down the small, sandy gravel path leading to the ocean.

Not even ten seconds into the walk, he grasped her hand and attempted to thread his fingers through hers. She gasped and jerked away as though she'd touched a scorching-hot stove, her heart hammering. Why did he affect her so much?

He leaned into her ear. "We don't know who's watching. We need to act like we're in love." His warning tone said, *don't forget.*

Although reprimanding, his deep whispered voice, and sexy-as-fuck English accent, had her aching with want against her will. Not that he had to know. If she had it her way, she'd never disclose her honest reaction to him. She could barely admit it to herself.

But he was right. She couldn't argue. They both had to do what the job required. And she still needed to prove her ability as an agent to her Solve Security boss, Alex. This was her one and possibly only opportunity with the company.

Alex wouldn't have appointed her to this position if he hadn't believed she had the skills, so she had to demonstrate to him that he'd made the right decision. A decision he wouldn't regret. And even more importantly, she had to make a positive impression with the agents. They had to feel confident working with her.

May stopped at the edge of the sandy beachfront, and he stood right beside her. She had to get past her resistance and do what needed to be done. She faced him, reached out and grabbed his hands.

Glancing up into his eyes, she hoped her unblinking gaze and resolute smile said everything she couldn't. *I'm sorry. I swear I'm trustworthy, reliable. I swear I'm along for the bumpy ride.*

Westley grinned, as though deciphering her non-verbal message, squeezed her hands and pulled her in for a hug, pressing the front of her body up close and incredibly personal to his. Did it remind him of the way they'd woken up this morning? It certainly flooded her brain with delightful, core-clenching memories.

Except his front had been well and truly plastered to her back, his lips grazing her neck, his hand caressing her breast, tweaking her nipple. She'd wanted to lean into him so badly but had played the outraged, get-off-me card instead.

Much to her dismay, her body had loved every second of his hands-on attention, but her brain wouldn't allow her to submit to his sleepy advances.

She tried to rationalize her conflicted response by admitting the keepings-off outcome was the best for both of them...in the broader scheme of things.

With his arms enveloped around her, he once again brought his lips to her ear. "Thank you. I know you find it difficult, challenging, I do too, but just keep reminding yourself that we need to look believable as a couple. Okay?"

He pulled back a little, held her face between his hands, and planted the softest of kisses on her forehead. Just the sort of loving, almost dreamy feeling she'd craved as a teenager, still craved now...with the right man.

But what did he mean by he found it difficult too? Challenging? Was he not attracted to her? Everything about his words and tone and body language suggested he was. However, had she read into his behavior through a lens of, dare she admit it, hope?

She sighed. Whether he found her hot or not, whether she did or didn't have an attraction to him, didn't matter, right? Probably better that they didn't desire each other.

As long as they looked in love, enough for others to subscribe to their newlywed story, while they worked out how to get the required job info.

"I'm going to hold your hand again, all right?" He said it so quietly that only she could hear his whispered words.

She shoved her inner conflict aside, smiled and nodded. Part of her quite looked forward to the renewed skin-on-skin contact.

As he'd warned, he interlocked their fingers, the heat of his hand, the friction, sending a kickstarting, five-hundred-volt jolt of joy to her heart. Every cell in her body thrummed with the thrill of his touch. And that had only been hand holding. Imagine if his naked body pressed and rubbed against hers.

No.

No imagining.

If she even entertained the idea, she couldn't pay the required attention, had no hope of concentrating. And she needed to. They both needed to. They had to put temptation aside. No distractions allowed. None.

They continued to the seaside, him talking incessantly about England, his school and military days, regaling her with his sniper stories — instead of freaking her out, his elite expertise kind of turned her on, not that she'd admit that to him — and his decision to move to Australia.

"And there was this one time I had to shoot from a plane." He stopped and closed his eyes, as though having to work through a possible panic attack.

He glanced at her, taking a few breaths and kept walking. "We were all set up, everything was going to plan and then an engine failed, and the aircraft jolted, dropped. In seconds, the plane dove toward the nearby mountain range."

"Shit."

"Indeed. The whole situation was out of our control. None of the rest of us knew what to do, knew how to help."

She couldn't tear her gaze away from his eyes. "So what happened?"

"The pilot was able to land on a precarious mountain ledge, and a rescue crew came and extracted us. Transported us to hospital. Ever since I..." He swallowed, and didn't finish his sentence. But she understood.

"I'd be the same." Worried, traumatized, reluctant to fly. And she meant it. Got it. She glanced at the pendant around his neck. "Maybe Saint Christopher assisted?"

Westley fingered the charm, a surprised crease crumpling his brow. "Yes."

Had he chosen to disclose some personal details as a way to make her feel more comfortable with him? To further develop rapport, trust? Enhance their intimacy?

No matter the reason, she found it fascinating—because she used words much more economically—and alluring, because she loved the sound of his voice and he'd shown vulnerability, something she found extra sexy.

Yet the more he spoke, moving from one story to the next, with barely a breath, irritation started running through her like a meth user in withdrawal.

How about her? How about her stories? Her life? Did he have any curiosity in others, any selfless thoughts and concerns outside of himself?

Did he always chat so much or was it a nervous trait? She needed him to show some legit, non-sexual interest in her too, who she was as a person, as well as her requiring some silent time to balance out their interactions, allow reflection.

A stroll in nature to appreciate the surroundings and provide her some non-acting space, a few quiet moments to process the best way forward personally and professionally.

She took off her sandals and tried to focus on the feel of the warm, wet sand squelching between her toes, reconnecting with the elements, his voice drifting by her like a distant breeze.

"Westley?"

A man's voice.

The cool water splashed over her feet and she stumbled. Westley grabbed her before she hit the beach, like a true gentleman, like an attentive husband, his eyes warning her before she freaked out and pushed him away.

Automatic, ingrained fear and frustration had built up over years of dealing with men who thought they knew better. Men who thought she needed them to take care of her. How could a petite woman possibly look after herself without a man's support?

"Everything okay?" The same guy. Was he alone?

Westley wrapped her in his arms and planted a kiss on her unsuspecting lips. She gasped but he persisted, his warm, insistent mouth moving against hers. And much to her annoyance, she liked it, *really* liked it, her pliant, aroused body, accepting his unexpected onslaught.

His tongue traced the seam of her lips, seeking entry. Maybe out of shock, or her subconscious acknowledgement that they needed to play the married part, or, dare she acknowledge it, her inexplicable attraction to him, she didn't refuse.

He licked into her mouth, delving gently at first, then going harder, driving deeper. And God it felt good, real. Like he meant it. The man couldn't just talk, he could kiss. With passion. If it was an act to uphold their couple story, he was the best actor she'd ever met.

"Oh, excuse me. I didn't mean to interrupt."

Westley abruptly ended the kiss, leaving her dazed and unsteady. He kept one arm cinched tight around her waist, as though he'd expected her wobbly response, and turned toward the man.

Marcus.

Shit.

"You're not." Though Westley's PC smile and extra-squishy hug suggested otherwise. "What can we do for you?"

Marcus continued speaking, either not noticing the move-along-buddy signs or too tuned into his extremely narcissistic self. "We didn't have a chance to talk much last night, so I'd love for you both to meet me for dinner in the main dining room this evening."

Westley stared into her eyes, and caressed the length of her hair. "What do you think, darling?"

That she wanted his hands and mouth to stroke every inch of her bare skin. But getting involved would be a massive mistake, right? They had to focus on what they'd been employed to do. "Sounds great."

She swung her gaze to meet Marcus' eyes. "We don't have any other plans tonight, and we're eager to hear more about your enticing investment opportunity."

"I'm keen to get your feedback and ascertain your interest." Marcus held out his hand and Westley shook it.

The smarmy guy locked his eyes onto hers. "You sure you're okay?"

What the fuck? Had he seen her resistance to Westley's advances? *Shit.* In public, she had to be so much more careful. As Westley had warned her consistently. People saw things, whether they noticed or not.

She rubbed Westley's lean, muscular chest and rested her head against his shoulder. "Absolutely." Although she struggled to accept it, it felt fucking amazing being cocooned in Westley's embrace. Safe. Arousing.

Marcus wouldn't relinquish his stronghold stare. "And do the facilities and location meet your expectations?"

She hesitated, still trying to get her brain into gear after Westley's mind-melting kiss, the heat and warmth of his hug. "Everything is lovely, thank you."

"Marcus, you've got an urgent call." Rei approached, holding out the guy's smartphone. He handed it over, and redirected his attention to her and Westley. "Hi, folks. Sorry to break up the conversation. Hope you're enjoying your stay so far."

"We are, thank you," Westley answered before she could put another meaningful sentence together.

Marcus walked away, phone pressed to his ear, his voice too low to catch his conversation over the crashing waves.

Rei glanced over his shoulder at his mate. "See you later." He waved and hurried to meet up with Marcus.

Westley swept her hair away, nuzzled in and whispered, "That was close."

Was that all he could say after... She sighed. What had she expected? That the kiss had actually meant more to him? It was all a game, and she represented nothing other than an expendable pawn. But how did a man kiss like that and not feel something?

Men.

Hence why she avoided them these days, unless she wanted a quick, no-commitment fuck. Too much trouble otherwise.

With a bruised ego and activated emotions, she stomped away and, realizing it may look suspect, shifted into a jog. "Meet you back at the cabin, honey," she called out in the sweetest voice she could muster.

May needed some recovery time, some space from him and his allure. She needed some solo time to reconnect with her job role. Focus on that, and that alone.

In a few minutes, May reached their accommodation, used the keycard to enter, and slammed the door shut. Not that Westley would hear, but it helped dissipate some of her pent-up frustration. *Fu-u-uck!* The guy was gorgeously infuriating.

Expecting him at any moment, May kept an eye on the window and marched across the living area, up and back, up and back, up and back, ready to blast him. But he didn't show up. For fucking ages!

By the time he arrived, she'd almost outpaced all her anger. Almost. Obviously, he'd needed some time to himself too. However, her unextinguished emotional embers reignited, and she reared up, ready to confront him.

He couldn't just feel her up and crush his lips to hers any time he thought he had an excuse. Yes, they had to play a newlywed part but they could keep it simple. Less…intimate. Hand-holding, hugging, a brush to the lips. Not something so…erotic, panty-melting.

Westley shut the door behind him and her annoyance sparked to the surface. "You fucking kissed me!" Had he really needed to thrust his tongue between her lips and tease hers so convincingly?

The question had circled in her head since she'd taken off. Surely, he could have cuddled her close, held and possibly even kissed her hand? Skimmed her lips. Kept things the absolute least invasive and still looked loving.

He stared at her with a combination of exasperation and disbelief. Exactly what she felt. "I did. Because otherwise you could have given our whole cover away. I needed you to relax and appear as though you were fully into me, and that I was fully into you. Not show you were uncomfortable with your *husband* touching you."

Westley shoved both hands through his hair and fixed his eyes on hers. "Look, I'm sorry I sprang it on you, but I don't want to give Marcus any reason to be suspicious." He shook his head.

"And your skin is so soft, and you looked so bloody sexy. Your lips parted, your face upturned. What was I supposed to do? Ignore my *wife*? A man can only resist temptation for so long. I took a chance, and it worked. But I'll be more mindful next time, give you more warning."

His piercing stare penetrated her eyes. "I tell you what—I'll run you a bath. By way of an apology."

And she imagined it'd give him a stash of images for self-pleasure. "Stop trying to suck up. Stop all the charming, flirty bullshit."

A grin slid onto his lips. "You think I'm charming."

"Fuck!" She spun on her heel and stormed into the bedroom, trying not to laugh. Trying not to show she actually did appreciate him and his humor.

Of course he followed. "If you insist."

May wiped off her burgeoning smile and glared at him, stepping into his personal space and jabbing her finger into his breastbone. "I'd tread carefully, if I were you."

"Why? Scared if I continue, you'll give in?" He raised his dark, questioning eyebrows, as if he could read her like a smut-filled book.

"Give in? As in have sex? With you?" She scoffed, her heart racing ahead with hope of that exact eventuation.

He wouldn't stop staring. Wouldn't stop evaluating her every response. "Come on, you can't deny there's something here." He waved his hand between them.

Although she wouldn't confess her full feelings, she wouldn't lie. "Oh, there's something, all right." Her tone dripped with sarcasm.

He stayed unperturbed, with that smirky, I-recognize-what's-going-on smile. "You know what I'm talking about. You can practically slice the air, the sexual tension is so thick."

He might be right, but she wouldn't concede. Not to him. Not to any man. Not to anyone who thought they had it over her. Anything she did, she'd do on her terms. "I'll admit you have an attractive outer shell, but personality-wise, you're fucking infuriating."

"So you'd fuck me."

"At this point I'd do almost anything to shut you up!" She pressed her palm to his chest, backed him against the bed and pushed.

He dropped into sitting and went to say something but she stepped between his long, muscular legs and stopped him with a kiss. One that went on and on and on.

Much, much deeper and more mind and body-altering than the one he'd surprised her with earlier. And that had made her toes curl and her core clench...against her will. She'd only meant for this one to shock him into silence.

But fuck. Their chemistry stirred a level of passion she'd never experienced. She couldn't ignore it, and instead focused on savoring the sensation while she had this fleeting chance.

Westley broke away and stared at her, his pupils blown-out black with desire, a confused crease splitting his brow. "What was tha — "

Instead of answering, she pressed her hand to his mouth, pushed his back to the mattress, then threw off her clothes and climbed over him, until she straddled his face, his eyes as dark as an unclouded, moonless night. "This is the only way I can think of to keep you quiet."

He sucked in a breath ready to speak, but May crushed her pussy to his lips, muffling his attempted reply. *Finally, some peace and desperately sought-after silence.*

He groaned, gripped her hips and trailed his tongue slowly over her clit.

She shot up, but he gently, tenderly guided her back to his mouth.

"Mmm...so nice and wet for me." His hot breath singed her skin.

"For *me*. I'm wet because I want to be. I let this happen to satisfy *my* needs."

"Whatever you say."

She could feel his arrogant smirk against her labia. And yet, she wanted to stay in position, see if his tongue proved as talented with tantalizing her lower lips as with talking.

He licked between her legs again, taking his sweet-ass time and driving her crazy with the achy need to come. But she refused to beg. And he'd met her wishes and stayed silent now so... She ground her sex against his mouth, riding his face to move things along, to speed up the process.

However, he refused to take the hint, licking her right to the edge, then easing off. Back to the edge, then easing up. Back to the edge and…she gasped, moaned, came close to climax. Oh yes, he had a very pleasure-giving mouth, a teasing, provocative tongue.

He coated his thumb with her juices, then stroked it between her ass cheeks and…bingo! Straight in her rear hole and rubbed right against the partition, while he sucked her clit into his super-skilled mouth, setting off a mind-blowing orgasm.

She arched into him and cried out, planting one palm on the mattress and gripping his head with the other, holding him to her.

The second she came down from her brilliant high he said, "I told you I always hit the required spot."

The bull's eye, in her case. She didn't know whether to smack him or request round two. "Always so modest," she answered, still breathing hard.

"What can I say? I'm skilled that way."

She didn't have to see his mouth, still buried between her thighs, to register his proud grin.

"Get the fix you needed?"

"Not even close." Yeah he'd satisfied her, but now that he'd proved his oral expertise, she wanted more. More physical pleasure, less conversing.

He went to shift her and sit up but her thighs clamped down, keeping him prisoner. "I'm not finished with you yet."

"Oh?" He relaxed back against the bed and nuzzled his nose along her folds.

The delicious sensation drove her extra crazy with want, excited to have his dick buried deep inside her. But first, she could do with more of his talented tongue.

"Make me come again, and then I need your cock."

He didn't hesitate, lapping at her clit like a man on a desire-filled mission, then sucked her little swollen nub into his mouth and she came once more with a super loud string of moans.

The second she regained her breath, and, desperate to feel his dick filling her up, she swiftly and elegantly lifted off him. "Stay there."

May rummaged through her suitcase and found the packet of condoms she'd packed. Each time she went away, she always brought a fresh lot...just in case she got lucky. And she usually did. She ripped open a foil square, threw the rest of the pack on the bedside table, and freed his cock from his shorts. She gave it a pump, and he closed his eyes and let out a long groan.

She kept going, gripping his dick just right and getting into a stimulating rhythm. Fuck, she loved having an attractive man at her mercy. Such a turn on. A rush of moisture pooled at her opening, and she ground her clit against his knee.

His desire-filled eyes met hers. "You're so bloody hot."

"Take off your T-shirt."

He did and *oh yes*! She ran her gaze over his gorgeous body. Just the right sprinkling of dark chest hair that narrowed into a happy trail, bisecting his sculpted abs. May could admire him all day but if she didn't get a move on, neither of them would make it to the joint pinnacle.

She shifted into a reverse cowgirl position, rolled on the condom and sank onto his magnificent, manscaped cock. He filled her right up and she sighed with satisfaction.

He brushed his thumb over her clit, and she attempted to press into his hand for more friction. But he held her back.

"Come on!" How was the guy not succumbing? She wanted an orgasm hat-trick, and he still hadn't come.

He didn't reply, just continued to torture her with leisurely deep thrusts and gentle rubbing, building unreleased pleasure.

"Please, Westley. Please!" Fuck, she'd promised she wouldn't plead. But he'd made her into a shameless, wanton woman.

As though she'd flicked a speed switch, he started pounding into her, squeezing her nipple hard with one hand, and with the other, pressing her clit.

She detonated, riding out the most earth-shattering climax of her life. Exactly how he'd promised. The bastard. She'd made herself beholden to him. But in this moment, her endorphins didn't care, shutting down her trouble-making mind.

With her hands braced on his legs, she moved faster, harder, taking him deeper. And he kept thrusting into her, perfectly matching her pace and rhythm and hitting every single earth-shattering spot. In terms of everyday decisions, they weren't always in sync, but when it came to sex... *Wow.*

She threw her head back with a cry of pleasure and he grabbed her hips, angling them slightly forward. In seconds she went off again like a winning slot machine. Loud and bright and impossible to ignore.

A grunt, followed by a booming shout and he lost his load inside her. A few moments later, Westley sat up and nipped her neck, then her earlobe. "I told you I never miss my target."

Fucking show off! She wanted to get annoyed and give him an earful, explain that his arrogance was the opposite of a turn on, but that would be a bald-faced, straight-up lie. She'd be prematurely cutting off her nose to spite her ecstatic face.

He snaked his arm around her waist, his other hand hovering further south. "May I please touch your clit again?"

With his big warm hand so close to her pussy, she could hardly string two thoughts together. "You may. But only if you promise me a mind-blowing orgasm in less than a minute."

"Such, a demanding, greedy girl." His hot breath scorched her shoulder.

"Well can you or can't you?" Her voice came out all breathy, needy, frantic.

"If it means I can do this, oh yes." He slid his fingers over her slick, super-swollen clit. "If this is my punishment, you can count on me being a very naughty boy more often." He slowly licked along the ridge of her ear, making her shiver.

His magic fingers stroked her moist clit and *oh God* it felt good, had her core clenching over his still hard cock. Even though he'd come. My goodness. This guy was super-stud stallion material.

Though, his work-life discipline probably helped to develop his admirable, arousing skillset. Speaking of which… "You need to get rid of that condom."

"I do." But instead of moving, he caressed her breast with one hand and with the other, rubbed her clit in maddening circles. "Once I make you come again, as promised."

Oh. Oh! She'd given him an out but he'd prioritized her request. A more than pleasant surprise. She'd totally assessed him as a selfish type. That whole loner, self-absorbed, sniper stereotype. But maybe she'd misread him. She'd presumed without adequate evidence. Maybe his experience had encouraged and trained him to have extra attention to detail. And now, if he came through, she'd question every bit of her judgment.

In an instant, he broke into some nipple-tweaking, clit-stimulating combo—nothing she'd experienced before, not considered, not even fantasized about—and before she could say another word, respond with some smart-ass comeback, he'd taken her over the edge.

He waited for her to settle, nipping and kissing her nape. "Let me sort this out." He gripped her hips and shifted her gently off him, then removed his shorts, and the condom. Westley wrapped the rubber in a tissue and turned back to her. "Where were we?"

May palmed his irresistible, semi-erect dick.

He looked her straight in the eye. "Straddle me." He stilled her hand and held it behind her back.

No stalled on her lips. She needed to do a deep dive into what made her want to do the opposite of what he said, asked. But not now. Now she wanted more of him, to reconnect to their joint satisfaction. She kneeled astride his narrow hips, snatched a fresh condom off the bedside table and rolled it over his eager cock.

May sank down onto it, closed her eyes and sighed. His groan harmonized with hers and they began to move. Totally aligned, totally synchronized, totally in rhythm. And oh, *oh God*. She'd had big dicks before but none of them had filled her up while pressing all her internal erogenous zones. Not like he'd managed to do. Twice, in a row.

She rocked her hips, wanting more, wanting him to thrust harder, faster, deeper. And he did, as though reading her horny, determined mind. He pinched her nipple with one hand and her clit with the other, and she threw her head back and cried out, coming all over his incredible cock.

He kept pumping, fucking, and with rough hands brought her face to his, closing his lips over hers and kissing her with an intense, desperate passion.

Seconds later he grunted into her mouth and came, and she kissed him through it, undulating her hips and rhythmically contracting her core muscles until they both hit a base, aligned, unhinged level.

His breathing started to slow. "See, I told you we have undisputable chemistry, that I could make you scream in ecstasy."

Of course he had to ruin the moment with his maddening, smart-ass, I-told-you-so mentality. She scrambled off him, and yanked on her satin dressing gown, tying it tight at her waist, staring at him and his big smug smile. Refusing to back down, to show any sign of weakness, of submission. "You are so…so…infuriating."

He propped up on his elbows. "You weren't saying that the last hour or so."

"Because I successfully managed to shut you up. Mostly. For once. See the theme?"

"Take off your robe and come and give me a hug."

He had to be joking. Had he heard a single word she'd said? Seen her beyond-exasperated body language? "Excuse me?"

He patted the mattress. "Come and join me."

"I just did." *You arrogant, self-centered…*

"And only you are stopping it happening again."

Ugh. She hesitated. Okay, yes, the sex had been brilliant, and she'd love to have another good go. But should she? She was on a job. A new job. Should she really risk screwing that up? Had she already? Should she risk the high possibility of significantly negative ramifications.

Sure, it worked in the interim, if they kept ninety percent of their relationship focused on work and fucking, but otherwise... No matter how tempting, she had to ignore her stupid, oxytocin-riddled, hormone-afflicted body.

Their already strained relationship didn't need sex to further complicate it. They didn't need extra emotionally taxing distractions to impact on their ability to successfully resolve the case.

He chuckled with that superior, King's English, posh tone of his. "Stop playing the prude. Stop overthinking. Come and do me again. You've far from used up all your tickets on this ride."

She thrust her hands on her hips and tapped her foot. "Well, you've used up yours," she said, not meaning a single word, and stomped toward the bedroom door, intent on keeping her distance from him until they had to go to dinner.

When they returned, she'd make sure she slept on the sofa. Far, far away from him and his arrogant, self-serving attitude. Served him right. He needed to know that the sex could shoot the lights out, but it wouldn't guarantee her continuing to do him going forward.

Yeah, it wasn't the most comfortable option being on the couch, but she refused to give Westley the satisfaction of returning to sharing the bed, especially given the ineffectiveness of the pillow wall. And his fucking egotistical attitude. He may excel at sex, but whatever. It made up the smallest percentage of a person's overall happiness.

She couldn't let his unexpected, amazing ability to press all her arousal buttons, cloud her judgment. She couldn't afford to succumb to his physical charisma. Thank fuck his personality prevented that from happening.

May slammed the door behind her, his low, deep laughter chasing her down the corridor.

Chapter Ten

Bloody best sex of his entire life. So passionate, so fucking hot. The woman oozed sexiness. Westley folded his hands behind his head and relived the past amazing hour. With so many erotic images, he'd fill his spank bank for eternity.

Her smart mouth and snarky comments had surprisingly ramped up his desire. And could she move or what? He could never erase the vision of her beautiful naked body riding him, her hips undulating, his dick disappearing between her legs, her head thrown back in ecstasy.

Behind his eyes, stars had exploded into a confetti of white light when he came. The ferocity of his climax had him bordering on passing out or bursting a hole clear through the condom. But thank the bloody universe the prophylactic had remained intact. Both times.

Whether he wanted to accept it or not, he was officially hooked. Addicted to all things May. They had to have sex again. How could they possibly go back to sleeping beside one another with no touching?

Or maybe that was his skewed take. Maybe she could compartmentalize better. Keep things separate. In his case, once he fell for a woman, he was all in, feelings-wise. However, he'd one-hundred-percent respect her view. If she saw their interlude as a one-off affair, he'd step aside. Never make another fucking move.

Given her string of very vocal, body-shuddering, core-clenching orgasms, he assumed she equally enjoyed herself, but that didn't mean she'd want to keep sexually interacting. If she chose not to, it'd be a massive shame, but he'd totally honor her decision and back right off, even if it hurt like a dagger to his heart.

Whatever he proposed, she'd challenge him initially, because that's what she did. He expected it. That was their unique dynamic. She'd shown through words and actions that she required certainty to retain the amount of control she desired.

Westley closed his eyes, scrubbed his hands over his face, then rubbed his temples using a circular motion with the pads of his fingers. Muscle tension immediately drained from his head, neck and shoulders.

While he had these few calm, quiet moments, he needed to determine the most effective strategy to ensure fear and pride didn't prevent them moving forward positively. In whichever incarnation that took. Because he couldn't take over her thinking or conduct, only take charge of his own.

Two possible options existed—more sex, if they were both onboard, or if they weren't, no more sex.

And he needed to prepare himself to accept each possible eventuality.

He'd back them two hundred percent to pursue this new, exciting, intimate path, but would she admit to craving another session? Everything about her response suggested she'd enjoy going at it again, if not mentally, emotionally, definitely physically. However, she needed to give him the clear-as-day green light.

A subsequent roll in the proverbial hay remained off limits unless she not only agreed but also instigated further contact. For him, non-consensual sex wasn't ever a consideration. It'd provide zero enjoyment. Enthusiasm played an essential part in ensuring an exceptional fun-filled outcome.

Both parties needed to want to fuck or it wouldn't happen. His partner had to show equal interest in order to share the experience, or else he always had his hands to get himself off.

Westley stared at the pristine white ceiling, the fan spinning overhead, right along with his thoughts. What could he say to get her over the already obliterated line without being manipulative?

Nothing. Most likely it wouldn't make a difference what words Westley used unless she had already considered doing the deed with him again.

But he had to say something. Try something. Attempt to win her over with clear, concise reasoning rather than charm. No doubt she'd make her stance known. If she decided on more fucking, fantastic, otherwise they'd revert to pretending in public, to no contact outside of their newlywed act.

Westley shifted his leg position, his dick tenting the sheet. Impatient. Although hard, he had to wait. Impulsivity could kill any chance of success. He had to give May the first opportunity to raise the possibility of hooking up again soon, but if she didn't... Plan B.

Maybe he could suggest they have another go to test if the brilliance of their sexual connection was a one-off fluke? Or even better, if he framed it as a dare?

Yes. From what he'd observed, she'd jump on that, hopefully on him, and they could have a multiple repeat performance. An absolutely blissful next few days away. Ease the mounting job stress. The best sort of selfcare.

Her footfalls thudded heavily through the kitchen and living area. What was she doing? Expelling some energy? Having a drink, something to eat? Thinking through how to best proceed, factoring in their case requirements? *Thinking about me?*

Fingers crossed he wouldn't have to argue with her, and she'd still accompany him to the dinner they'd agreed to with Marcus. But he might. If either of them showed up alone, it wouldn't look good. They had to uphold a no-trouble-in-paradise charade, no matter the difficulties in their interconnected personal life.

Disharmony between them would potentially lead to additional, unwelcome scrutiny. He had to be ready for that, get Alex onside if required. Have a back-up plan.

Westley didn't want things to progress to that point but if they did, he may require stronger, more external support. An unbiased view on how to salvage the mission, causing the least amount of physical and emotional carnage.

How long should he give May to process things on her own? How much should he give himself? His stomach tensed, his heart beating wildly, like a bird trapped in a chamber, desperate to escape.

Westley shoved his hand over his face, wishing he had more time to let her cool down, but they didn't have that luxury. Pressing conditions meant he needed to speak to her shortly to ensure they had an aligned, cohesive approach before meeting Marcus.

He flung himself out of bed, re-dressed and met her in the living area. She sat on the couch, coffee in hand, staring out the window. Didn't even turn to face him, didn't even acknowledge his presence.

And fair enough. His response hadn't helped. He strode to the coffee machine and focused on making the perfect espresso. Something to take the edge off his stress.

Caffeine had him firing on all possible cylinders, helped him concentrate, honed his thinking, ensured he effectively and efficiently completed any and all required tasks. Dosed up on coffee, he'd been known to successfully accomplish a myriad of duties.

She stayed silent, and just the thought of making eye contact had him on absolute tenterhooks. Pressure to discuss things further between them, and their assignment, bubbled up inside him, but how would she react? What would she say? Had their brief time apart enhanced a broader, positive perspective or narrowed it right down?

Had she focused on appeasing her anger and frustration or had overthinking kept her temper simmering, ready to boil over at the slightest provocation? Would she have the presence of mind to consider what they needed to do together personally and in their Solve Security roles? Had she contemplated what it would take to make the most of their working relationship, at a minimum?

He placed a cup under the coffee machine nozzle, the stream of delicious black goodness filling it up, the irresistible scent wafting into his nostrils. Although stimulating, it equally eased his mind. Already had him thinking clearer.

Westley grabbed the mug and psyched himself up to speak to his skittish, bucking mare. Although he blew on the hot brew, the first sip bordered on burning his tongue. A sign not to be impulsive? A reminder to think through every word before he spoke.

He sat beside May, making sure not to crowd into her personal space. "Are you okay?"

She rubbed her eyes with the back of her hand, then pulled her robe tighter around herself, her empty coffee cup on a coaster on the small table in front of them. "Does it matter?"

"Yes, it does. We need to continue to connect with one another, be on the same somewhat challenging page, and do the job we've agreed to do. We need to work out how that looks."

She twisted her head, her gaze fixing on his eyes, confusion splitting her forehead. "I just... I realize we have a façade to uphold."

Is that all it was to her? Or was that a protective mechanism to prevent her heart from getting hurt? "We do. And so much more."

"What do you mean?" The lines in her forehead deepened.

He exhaled, measured, controlled. "We need to be convincing. However we present in public needs to support our happily married status. But we also need to be honest with one another."

She clenched her jaw and shook her head, as though she found the thought alone overwhelming. When they'd come together, they'd seemed so physically in tune. Had she not experienced the same level of elation? "Why?"

"Because partners need to know the full truth, work in tandem. Trust is essential as a foundational base, so it transfers across other areas. If we can't be honest with each other, look believable, how can anyone else have faith in what we say and do? How can we successfully work in a partnership?"

Hands clasped tightly in her lap, she stared into the depths of her empty cup. "What you're saying about working well as a team makes total sense." Except that little twitching crease in her forehead suggested she wasn't thoroughly convinced. She knew how to say the right words, but could she abide by them?

"And how about what transpired between *us*?" Maybe he should have held off, but he needed to know. Had their extracurricular activities had a positive or negative impact? Had crossing their professional boundary placed any potential roadblocks in their path, in their ability to function as a cohesive unit?

Sex changed things. For the better or worse. However, he hoped in their instance the increased intimacy would reflect positively in the way they touched and communicated.

She shrugged her shoulders. "It happened." As in *Move on. I have.*

Her non-committal response had his thoughts rocketing off in a clouded shit-storm of different directions. He needed a definitive answer from her to know what to expect and what to do to strengthen their Solve Security duo dynamic.

His ego clawed at his mind, fixated on finding out whether she'd enjoyed their coupling as much as he had, or if he'd imagined it, presumed based on his own skewed perception.

Although he'd planned to dare her to give sex another go, a warning resistance in his gut had him easing in, starting with a softer, more engaging and considerate approach. "Any regrets?"

She looked him directly in the eye without a second's hesitation. "None. You?"

Absolutely not. He'd do her again in a heartbeat. "No. So what now?"

"We go to dinner with Marcus."

"Then?"

"We see."

"See what?"

"What happens?"

And what did that entail? What signs would she look for to agree to another naked, no-holds-barred session between the sheets? Did she have some subconscious checklist?

Would it come down to how they interacted over dinner? Whether he met her conversational considerations? Touched her appropriately and adoringly enough? Whether he treated her like the doting, spellbound husband she expected? Did she want him to lead, suggest, dominate? Or would she prefer to take their fake-relationship reins while he sat back and provided whatever support she required?

He fixed his eyes on hers. "I don't want to leave it to chance. I want to test whether we can recreate the same sublime circumstances or better. So tell me, what do you need to make that happen?" Yes, he'd put the pressure on her, but knowledge created immense power. The power to ensure they factored in each other's desires.

"I...I don't know." She dropped her gaze and stared at her hands.

"What will it take for you to know? Because the last thing I want to do is cause you added stress and anxiety. The last thing I want to do is have you feel forced into pursuing something you're not entirely comfortable with."

Her forehead pleated, her focus still locked on her lap. "I'm not sure. Can't we just go with the whole consent discussion? As long as we check with each other prior to making a move, and honor the other person's response, it should be fine."

It should, except he couldn't accept *fine*. Westley hoped to hear her screaming his name with total abandon. "Then there's nothing stopping us giving things another go...if we're both up for it."

May swung her gaze to meet his, a restrained smile tugging at the corners of her lips. "I can't predict the future so...we need to reassess from moment to moment."

"And if we both assess the situation as conducive? If I tell you I can't wait to taste you again, can't wait to make you writhe against my mouth, come on my tongue, then on my cock?"

She gasped, her cheeks turning a glorious, aroused pink.

Ah...so she liked dirty talk. Good to know.

May squirmed slightly in her seat. "If you guarantee to make me come multiple times, how can I say *no*?"

How indeed? He had no problem whatsoever making her climax repeatedly. In fact, getting her off got him bloody horny as hell. But essentially, from what she said, she'd agreed to a purely pleasure-based union. She wanted to keep things casual. Not his ideal outcome, but he would follow her terms of engagement.

She shot up, out of his reach, then smoothed over her robe and sashayed to her handbag on the dining table. The slide of the zip caught his attention, conjuring images in his brain of her slowly undoing his fly. He barely held back a groan.

Unfortunately, her intentions and his imagination didn't quite sync. Instead, she reached into her cavernous purse, pulled out a soft pink lip gloss and applied the sexy gooey goodness to her full lips.

He stifled another groan, picturing her glossy mouth surrounding his cock. Taking him deep. Bloody hell. If he didn't give himself some relief again soon, his dick threatened to punch a hole through his pants.

No time. Dammit.

In the interim, he'd just have to redirect his thinking to the precarious nature of their job and how easily they could end up on Marcus' hit list if they buggered up their cover. If they didn't stay aware of their surroundings and take note of details emerging from everyone's conversations.

Impossible to totally switch off his appreciation of May's spellbinding beauty, which wasn't all bad considering it played into their ruse. The extra benefit of fawning all over her meant he'd hopefully keep her on side, establishing some semblance of peace between them and the wider party.

Fingers crossed she could push past any anger and annoyance that might arise, and uphold the loving-partner façade. Or they'd be fucked. And not in a fun way.

If it were up to him, he'd be open and willing to try for a reciprocal, longer-lasting relationship. Something that had substance. Something that survived beyond the situational work environment.

It would be the first time he didn't have to hide what he did for a living. The first time he could be one-hundred percent himself with a woman he desired. And if she agreed, great. Celebrations all round.

If she didn't, the harsh reality meant that the end of their case would signal the end of their hook up. Like with his work, he'd find a way to move on. Find the next fulfilling opportunity. Reality dictated he'd have to, whether he agreed with the circumstances or not.

She spun around to him, the satin dressing gown parting, offering a tempting glimpse of her breasts, stomach and legs. "So?"

Oh, yeah, he still hadn't responded. Had gone on quite the tumultuous emotional journey in his head. "It would be an honor and a privilege, and an absolute pleasure to make you come. Over and over and over." He dropped his gaze to her tempting lips, right on the border of sweeping her into his arms and taking her back to bed.

His leg bounced, and it took all his self-control to stay seated. Because she hadn't asked him to do her now.

She glanced between his hungry eyes and his jumpy thigh. All signs he'd have her again right this moment if she only gave him permission. "I guess I should get dressed."

Oh yes, she really should before he did her up against the kitchen counter. Then on the couch, up against the courtyard window, then on the bed. They'd never make it to dinner.

But they *had* to make an appearance.

His dick wholeheartedly disagreed.

She must have seen the blatant desire in his eyes before she disappeared into their joint bedroom and shut the door.

Chapter Eleven

Dressed in a swishy floral dress and high-heeled sandals, May returned to the living area and searched the enclosed back patio to find it empty. Disappointment rolled through her like the persistent ripple of waves on the nearby beach.

No sign of Westley.

Where had he gone? Had he chosen to run off some frustration? Was he okay? Had she been too...stand-offish? Bitchy? Vague? Probably, but shit. She didn't know what to think or do.

Yes, they'd had exceptional sex but she didn't want to fuck up her future career. Especially now that she'd started to re-establish some stability in her life.

May checked the time on her mobile, her pulse pounding, her hand shaking. No new messages or texts. She'd gotten ready with plenty of time to spare, considering his needs as well as her own.

She'd needed some space. He most likely had too, given his disappearing act. If she'd stayed near him much longer, she'd have jumped the guy. Had he sensed that? Or did he believe she was indifferent?

A cursory glance over the kitchen bench and dining table confirmed he hadn't left a note. Where the hell was he and would he be back and ready on time? If he didn't show up soon, she'd need to go on her own. Not ideal. Far from ideal. The opposite of what he'd reinforced.

Her breathing escalated to borderline hyperventilation. Just the thought of facing Marcus alone, and concern about Westley's wellbeing had her insides churning with worry.

She grabbed her bag and ensured it contained the minimal requirements—money, keycard, mobile, lipstick—and slipped on her shoes.

Still no sign of him.

She checked the wall clock and her smartphone. They had to leave in less than twenty minutes.

May scrolled to her partner's number and called him. His phone rang and rang and rang, and just as she was about to hang up, it connected. "Westley?"

"Yes." His breath pounded into her ear, images of when he'd come bombarding her brain. "You okay?"

"Are you?" Her voice sounded post-sex breathy.

"See you in a minute." He hung up, and she stared at the disconnected phone. What the hell? What was he doing? If he'd aimed to unsettle her, to freak her out, he'd done an amazing job.

Anger, frustration and anxiety came together to create a potent, interactive, volatile mix and she had to refrain from snapping at him the second he entered the cabin. Instead, she clinched her lips together and glared.

He shut the door behind him, bent forward and braced his hands on his knees, perspiration dripping off him onto the floor like a leaky faucet. What the fuck? He knew they had to go out soon. "Where were you?"

He stood up straight and swiped his damp hair off his sweaty face. "Going for a little incognito suss out of the grounds."

"And you didn't ask me? Maybe I wanted to come."

"Maybe I wanted you to as well."

His bold, unexpected, insinuating response had her cheeks flaring with a shocked blaze of throbbing heat. "And yet you didn't ask. Thanks." She folded her arms across her chest and huffed.

He chuckled. "Do you realize how endearing you look when you get all put out?"

She clamped her teeth together and tried not to growl. This man…fuck, he did her head in, yet got her all revved up at the same time. How was that even possible? "Just get ready. On the way to dinner, we'll talk about anything of interest you found."

"As you wish, milady." A sly smile crept onto his lips, his dark eyes shining with a roguish glint.

He slunk past her, the scent of his potent pheromones activating all her pleasure receptors, and she retreated into the kitchenette, waiting for him to close the door and go shower. Waiting for him to stop setting her libido alight like a Guy Fawkes Day fireworks display.

The moment he left her alone, she raced to open the back patio sliding door and inhaled lungfuls of Westley-free air. Not that she didn't like his natural aroma, crave it on a primitive level, but it wouldn't help her brain stay clear, alert…to anything aside from him.

Whether she wanted to admit it or not, his presence had overwhelmed her senses, her objectivity and perspective. Awareness helped her ameliorate that but still, hormones and emotions had a way of hijacking any form of sensible assessment.

She'd always considered herself immune to a man's influence, but in a short time, much to her dismay and distress, Westley had proven that certain characteristics increased her susceptibility.

As long as he remained the only outlier, she should stay safe...ish. Emotionally, at least. She sucked in as much salty sea air as possible, hoping to cleanse right down to the depths of her soul, then returned inside, the sound of the shower water beating down on her. And all her arousal zones.

Unbidden images overtook her mind. Yes, she'd seen Westley gloriously naked but, as delightful as that was, she didn't need any reminders. She couldn't possibly work effectively with that sort of core-deep distraction playing on repeat in her head.

She needed no further sparks to ignite the Westley kindling in her already primed mind. And what worried her more was them doing the dirty again, adding erotic memories to her already extensive back catalogue of arousing images. To relive over and over and over. At that rate, she'd never want to return to reality.

May poured herself a glass of bubbles and sat on the couch, flipping through social media, and checking if Alex or the team had sent through any further info. As though her boss had read her mind, her phone pinged with a text message from him.

Don't forget to include me in any updates.

Of course they'd keep him informed, but she understood his need to reinforce the stipulations, the requirements of their role. With her new to the position, he probably wanted to spell things out, not leave her decisions to chance, not assume she'd comprehended the unspoken nuances.

None of them could afford to be too complacent in case things changed. And things could change quickly. She knew that from her army days. He obviously did too.

May replied to Alex, letting him know she and Westley were due to meet up with Marcus for dinner. He sent back a thumbs-up emoji. Afterward, one of them would let Alex know the outcome, significant or not.

Outwardly, it might mean nothing but inwardly, assessing it from a removed point of view, a removed standpoint, and with access to greater intel, it might mean something. Something neither she nor Westley were privy to.

The bedroom door whooshed open and Westley stepped out, hair still wet, dressed in a beige and white linen outfit, cool sandals on his feet, looking like a total beachcomber, drop-dead gorgeous, high-end model.

"Are you ready?" Her voice came out all agitated, even though she appreciated every moment of his evocative physical presence, his core-clenching appearance.

He smiled and raised an eyebrow. "Are you?"

"Have been for a while."

"Then let's do this and compare notes later."

Not exactly her thoughts...but yes. They had to fulfill their job requirements, the agency expectations.

He thrust his hand onto his hip, and encouraged her to wrap her arm through his. She did, without question, because the pretense helped reinforce their story and, even if she only admitted it to herself, she liked it. Liked him taking charge. Liked that she had an excuse to keep close to him.

Blood rushed to every erogenous zone, making her all tingly. Diverting her attention from rational thinking. She couldn't have that. Afterward, yes, but not now. Not on their way to a discreet interrogative dinner.

She took a long, slow breath, rejuvenating her lungs with fresh oxygen. It jump-started her brain to come up with a question. "Did you find out anything on your *surveillance*?"

He tucked her hand in tighter, stepped through the door and ensured it clicked closed behind them. The warmth of his body seeped into hers. "Only that there's a small, under-resourced police station with a single cell, on the other side of the island, and that Marcus has paid island security to monitor the comings and goings from the main house.

"The best thing we can do is make the most of opportunities to get close to Marcus and the others, and see what they have to say. The more we argue with anyone, the more likely he'll have us evicted, putting ourselves and others at increased risk, in increased danger."

She had to agree. Made absolute sense. "Anything else?"

"Nothing of significance." It should have been a simple response, but the way his hot breath caressed her ear had her wanting to forget dinner and revisit him in all his delicious bare-skinned glory.

Later. Maybe. If he'd meant what he'd said, what he'd proposed. But she wouldn't hold him to it. People changed their minds. And that had to be respected, on each side.

She could easily amend her choices too, but after his wonderful, unexpectedly earth-shattering attentive expertise, she'd be an idiot not to indulge in some more pleasurable hands-on fun. Up until him, no one had come close to providing her with that level of orgasmic satisfaction.

So while they were away and had the means and opportunity, she may as well make the most of it, whether what they shared evolved into anything more or not. However, going by what he'd stated, she'd have to give him the indisputable green light.

And she would because, assuming he didn't drive her insane with his incessant Mr. Politeness talking, why wouldn't she subscribe to more bliss? The man knew his way around a woman's body, knew how to use his tongue and fingers and cock to best advantage. And given the stress of the assignment, she needed some regular relief. She imagined he did too. So why not incorporate it into their schedule?

Partway along the path, he shifted her hand from his arm and held it, intertwining their fingers, his heat infusing her skin with silent promise, and they continued their stroll to the main building, which glowed with golden light in the setting sun.

"I'll let you do most of the talking." She said it softly but loud enough for his ears, and he stopped and held both her hands.

Westley pressed the gentlest kiss to her forehead and nuzzled her neck. "Whatever you're comfortable with. But if you have a question, ask. The more information we glean the better."

He pulled away, flashed her that devastatingly gorgeous smile of his, kept hold of one of her hands and led her inside. Everything about his manners screamed gentleman. But in the bedroom, he had a devilish Dominant dirty side. Exactly what she realized she really, really liked.

Initially she'd thought his pleasant, courteous demeanor was an act, but he showed legitimate, consistent etiquette. Behavior that couldn't be faked. Not for long, anyway.

Politeness as well as protector qualities were part of his personality. Even when he took charge with, well, anything. Other than someone's work performance and consistent friendship qualities, sex was a great way to ascertain a person's true self and, so far, he'd shown a confident, generous, considerate character.

He hadn't just poured on the charm, using it as some scammer device to win over women. In fact, he didn't at all come across as a womanizer type. Though, his lover expertise suggested he'd had heaps of experience. Could be with a handful of women or many, and either way, she wouldn't complain. Not while he solely focused on her.

Could he keep it up? Sustain what they'd started? Or had their chemistry combusted, created the perfect sexual storm, in that one moment. The idea of having another go, for scientific, let's-prove-a-hypothesis reason, had her body tingling with anticipation.

But for the next few hours she'd have to put her libido on ice, be on her absolute best, loving, newly married behavior. Basically engage in a sort of edging foreplay.

Thank goodness some touchy-feely, hands-on interactions were required and no one would think anything of it, including Westley. She'd be playing her role and thoroughly enjoying every second of it. To everyone else, it'd look normal, expected.

However, she also needed to remain alert and focused on anything and everything Marcus said and did, right alongside her hopefully equally physically expressive partner.

Westley let the maître d' know they'd arrived, and the immaculate, well-dressed guy ushered them into the super quiet dining area. The large table remained the central focus, beneath the sparkling chandelier, but this time with only four place settings.

So Marcus had invited another guest. If she had to guess, she'd say it'd have to be his business colleague, Rei. He and Marcus looked pretty tight, and she imagined they were strongly invested in the outcome.

The magnificent windows drew her curious gaze, as they had the night before, offering an unobstructed view of the choppy sea, windswept sand and sinking sun. Would they sink or swim during dinner tonight? Would they unearth the information they sought?

A ray of sunlight shot a rainbow-colored beam off one of the drops of crystal hanging from the chandelier, and straight to the flawless fireplace. The hearth remained as spotless as Dexter's kill room.

Did they ever light the thing? She loved an open fire but she couldn't imagine a tropical island had much use for one. Most likely fake, promising a lot but giving little, much like her assessment of Marcus. So far.

As per the previous evening, Westley pulled out her chair — but this time she didn't protest — then sat beside her, opposite the unoccupied seats directly across from them.

Why hadn't his chivalry pissed her off on this occasion? She ran through the revised list of thoughts in her head. Maybe because she knew him better, or possibly his body-shuddering orgasm skills had something to do with her calmer state.

The cedar, citrus and clove fragrance of Westley's cologne had her craving a mulled wine, had her craving him. Again. She tried to distract herself from overdosing on his delectable scent, from succumbing to his arousing presence.

With a shaky hand, May poured herself a glass of sparkling water and studied the seating arrangements. Given Marcus' narcissistic, megalomaniac personality, would he move one of the chairs to the head of the table? Everything about him radiated an air of arrogance and superiority.

"You all right?" Westley's hot breath stroked her ear.

"Yes, you?"

"For the moment." He pressed the lightest, sweet-yet-seductive kiss on her earlobe, and gestured to the red and white wine bottles in the center of the table. "Which would you prefer?" Like he understood she needed something more to smooth out the pre-meeting jitters. And more. They'd had quite the personal and professional day of discovery.

"Red, please."

"A lady after my own heart."

Was she? Or did she fit into the opportunistic circumstances? She hated having a cynical attitude, but better safe than forever sorry. Trust required time to build, from their fetus-relationship stage upward. Assuming they both wanted to take that gamble.

He unscrewed the lid of the shiraz and poured them each an underwhelming amount of wine. Smart, but somewhat frustrating. She needed at least double that to take the edge off. But, thankfully, the bottle remained in reach so she could always top up, if needed. Within reason.

She and Westley didn't have to drive, but they still needed to be on point. Attentive, observant, vigilant. So she had to watch how much she had. How much they both had, or it could significantly impact on their receptivity to subtle, yet key discussions. To possible case-breaking information.

The longer they waited, her nerves wound tighter and tighter, like a coiled spring ready to release. She needed to expel some pent-up energy or she'd explode. She clenched her fingers around Westley's thigh and continued sipping her wine.

If she knew they had enough time and wouldn't be disrupted, she'd suggest a short break in the universally accessible toilet, drop to her knees and suck him off. She fucking loved having a man fully give himself over to her. And she couldn't wait to taste him. Wished she'd had a chance earlier.

Westley looked her in the eye and gripped her hand before it slid up his leg and palmed his cock. "We'll get to that later." His raspy voice and firm gaze said, *I promise*, with a subtext of *fuck, it's hard to stop you, I want this too, but please don't argue. Listen and obey.*

And although that demanding sort of response normally annoyed her to the fuck, in this instance, she got it. Abided by the restrictive situation. Saw the benefit. Understood the significance of showing discipline.

As well as setting up the right atmosphere to extract useful intel, he wanted to ensure their safety. And she appreciated that. Appreciated him for assisting her on her first official assignment. Appreciated him reinforcing the rules, the guidelines, helping her learn the convoluted ropes.

And he was right—assuming they both remained onboard with the idea, they could indulge, and enjoy each other thoroughly, when they returned to the cabin. Exactly like the newlywed couple they aimed to embody.

The main door whooshed open and Marcus and Rei entered with large welcoming smiles. Most likely cultivated to look legit after years of practice. However, to be fair, she didn't know the two men well enough to determine whether they had perfected faux interested, cheerful facial expressions, or whether they purposedly tried to manipulate the truth.

Everything about them, from their brand-name business attire to the way they walked, carried an air of wealth and entitlement, and a strong desire to make the best impression.

She couldn't wait to see whether they lived up to the promoted hype, or if their monetary greed compromised and conflicted with their original agenda, with their regular sales pitch, and made them even more pushy.

Would their results to date have them spiraling into an unsalvageable tailspin? And if they did, would she and Westley be considered a liability?

Highly likely. So they had to play along. Ask questions without being too inquisitive. If Marcus or

Rei picked up on the slightest thing out of place, she and Westley would jump right to the top of their kill list.

Although scary as hell, it influenced their choices. Part of their role entailed reducing the risk to innocent people while keeping themselves safe. And the rest of their time they'd spend on how to foil Marcus' deadly Ponzi scheme.

"Good evening. Thanks for joining us. How was the rest of your day?" Marcus kept that same practiced smile plastered to his face and, surprisingly, took a seat opposite Westley. Rei sat across from her, mirroring his friend's mannerisms. These two had worked their presentation right down to the smallest congruent detail.

"Lovely, thank you. It's almost impossible not to enjoy socializing with such a great group of people, as well as making the most of this stunning setting." Westley squeezed her hand beneath the table.

She smiled up at her 'husband'. "And the facilities are fantastic. I've got a spa day booked in for tomorrow, and I can't wait."

Westley glanced at her. "I might join you, sweetie."

Sweetie? Oh, he was annoyed she'd sprung that on him. Had arranged it without consulting him first. Without his protector presence. But, like her *husband*, she aimed to roll with the proverbial punches.

He needed to recognize that each of their decisions impacted both of them, but they had to trust one another and reach deep down into their backed-up stores of flexibility. Analysis paralysis didn't get results. Sometimes choices needed to be made on the spot. Sometimes they didn't have the luxury to talk things over.

"I highly recommend it." Rei's voice cut into her silent staring war with Westley. She tore her gaze from her *husband* and met the man's dark, calculating, all-assessing eyes. "The massages are superior to anything you'll get on the mainland. And the day spa has a great couples' package."

Excellent. Spending hours being pampered was the opposite of hardship. A sacrifice she would willingly make. Outside of great sex, she couldn't think of a better way to spend her time. Other than successfully completing their mission and acquiring Alex's praise.

Hang on. She darted her gaze between the two guys and kept a forced, hopefully believable-looking elated smile on her face. What was she thinking? They wouldn't do or suggest anything to benefit others, only themselves.

Having her and Westley pleasantly unavailable, caught up in the benefits of what the island package included, most likely formed part of a well-constructed ploy to keep them out of action for a while. Most likely was a ploy to ensure the investors rarely had free time. Rarely had the ability to interact outside of the organized events. Had her partner already cottoned on?

Afterward, she and Westley needed to discuss all the ins and outs of the conversation, including the words and body language, to ensure they followed up on any promises. And others did too. Ensure they all remained true to their characters.

May kept drumming into her head that she and her *husband* had to have an aligned approach to divert any suspicion from their story. They needed to participate—within reason—appear neutral, in love. It only took the slightest slip up to clue in guys as paranoid as these two fuckers.

"That's brilliant." Westley pressed a kiss to her temple. "Once we're done at the day spa, we'll check out the rest of the perks on offer." Westley leaned in, glanced around, then refocused on the guys. "We'd actually planned to do that today but ah…let's just say we got caught up with each other." His low, sexy voice had her squeezing her thighs together.

Westley ran the pad of his thumb lightly over the back of her hand and *oh*. Every thought fled from her brain. Never would she have believed something so simple, so high-school chaste, could be so erotic. Though, his insinuation plus his voice, and the small, seemingly simple gesture did evoke some pretty explicit memories.

Soft, hard. He'd shown the perfect balance of skills during their lovemaking.

No.

Not lovemaking.

Sex.

Fucking.

Release of a primal pressure valve. Pure unadulterated, no-strings-attached pleasure. She had to acknowledge the reality of what they'd shared. Or risk harrowing heartbreak.

With her thighs squeezed extra tight together, she turned to meet Westley's roguish gaze. What he'd said hadn't been too far from the we-can't-keep-our-hands-off-each-other truth.

A new partnership with out-of-this-world chemistry. Yes.

Newly married. No.

But definitely capitalizing on physical marital privileges. To their mutual advantage.

"Well, let's eat and chat. We won't keep you too long. Sounds as though you have some more pressing activities planned for tonight." Marcus smirked, hopefully reinforcing he bought their implied, now somewhat real, we-can't-stop-fucking-every-spare-moment story.

Chapter Twelve

"Dinner, and this proposed investment opportunity, look too amazing to miss, don't they, honey?" She swung her gaze to Westley, and gave him her best ditzy damsel expression. Wide-eyed smile, with an accompanying look that said, *I trust you to make the main business decisions.*

"They do indeed." Her *husband* stared into her eyes, and placed his palm on her upper thigh, his thumb rubbing way too close to her clit.

She jumped at the unexpected extra intimate contact, and did everything in her power not to buck into his questing, teasing hand. Although she'd love to, she could not come at the table, couldn't do it discreetly with eagle-eye suspects watching their every move.

Yes, it would reinforce her lustful connection to Westley, but...so not appropriate. She didn't have one single exhibitionist bone in her body. And on top of that, she struggled to keep quiet when she came.

With a barely perceptible smirk on his face, Westley shifted his focus away from her and back onto Marcus and Rei, but kept his hand on her thigh, gently stroking. "I'm sure we can spare a few hours. We do love good food, and can't say *no* to participating in valuable, enticing projects that benefit people."

A couple of waiters returned with amazing antipasto platters filled with rolled cold meats, pickled vegetables, and a range of cheeses, as well as a serving of high-end caviar on crackers. Westley's favorite, from what she'd witnessed.

And she got the appeal. If the selection of roe was as appetizing as the other night, she might just break her self-imposed rule and climax in company at their shared table.

Her mouth watered. She hadn't eaten much during the day—they'd been a bit too busy feasting on each other. Not particularly filling but sexually satisfying and hormonally rejuvenating and nutritious.

Marcus stabbed his fork into a rolled piece of prosciutto. "Excellent. Then let's talk mutually satisfying business options."

Although his proposal intrigued her, she could hardly wait to indulge in Westley for dessert. He'd well and truly proven his tastiness. Hopefully they wouldn't have to hold out too long before they could, once again, have some intimate time to themselves.

It'd all depend on Marcus and Rei and their agenda and schedule. What amount of time they'd allocated to keep them cornered at dinner. At their mercy.

It all came down to how much the two suspected con artists pushed to get their own needs lucratively met. Going by May's struggle to sit still, this would be the biggest edging challenge of her life. A welcome positive, yet an equally painful, torturous-yet-tempting negative.

So what did a new wife do in this instance? Focus on providing her husband with her undivided attention, while indulging in a range of fabulous food. And appreciating every single moment.

After engaging in superficial chitchat over a delicious degustation-style menu that fully satisfied her tastebuds, she had two areas left to please. Intellectually, she remained ravenous for further details on this 'recommended' investment, and physically, she craved more of Westley's fingers, cock, and magic mouth. And she didn't mean talking…except for his alluring accent.

Marcus dabbed his lips with his pristine white napkin and tucked it under the outer edge of his practically licked-clean plate. "What did you think?"

"Oh, everything was wonderful, thank you," May blurted, her response fully honest. It had been one of the best meals she'd eaten in ages.

Westley propped his forearms on the table and leaned in, his gaze colliding with the host's. "I'm assuming your proposition matches up to the elite quality of the food."

Marcus jolted back ever so slightly, but still perceptible, keeping his mask of control in place. Obviously, he hadn't anticipated pre-emptive pressure from potential new investors. At least not until they'd heard the details.

"Of course. It's a rare, once-in-a-lifetime opportunity. I scoured many applications and narrowed down interested parties to a small group that I thought would connect with the idea."

And be able to afford the exorbitant buy in, essentially fund it without too many questions.

"Thank you. We appreciate you including us on the exclusive list." Westley's straight-white-teeth smile had a tinge of don't-fuck-us-around. "So let's get down to specifics. How much money will make the project viable, and does it have a positive expectancy? Because I'm sure, like me, the other investors want to know the likelihood of making a decent profit."

Westley's charming, grin grew. "So, going by your estimation, how long might it take?"

Rei glanced at Marcus, and they carried out some sort of silent conversation. Marcus kept up an unworried façade while Rei looked a little rattled, creases bunching across his usually smooth, Botoxed-looking brow.

"Show them, Rei." Marcus' voice oozed absolute confidence.

Rei hesitated and retrieved the latest smartphone from his pocket. Using facial recognition, he logged into the home screen and started flicking.

She couldn't wait to see what data he produced. Would it back up Marcus' confident claims, or would it set her and Westley up to be the next too-curious victims?

Marcus' eyes lit up, his gaze switching between her and Westley. "It's an app. One that will revolutionize trading. The research we've done and the algorithms we've put in place are superior to anything on the market. Rei's just pulling up the preliminary test results."

Was that something they could doctor to suit their agenda? How could she and Westley check? How could they know for sure? In the meantime, she needed to show how impressed and interested she found the 'ground-breaking' idea. She propped her forearms on the table, matching her husband's posture.

"Here you go." Rei glanced up and handed his phone to Westley. "You can scroll through the app and find the initial results and likelihood of positive expectancy, as well as future gains, in the last tab."

Westley concentrated on the information, shifting from one tab to the next, then twisted his head and looked May in the eye. "Sweetheart, want to have a look? You're better at this app and mathematical stuff than me."

Did he realize how hot that was, making her sound smarter? As though he had a weak spot for his wife, as though to suggest not to judge a book by its scatterbrained cover.

Kind of shoving it up Marcus and Rei's boys' club assumptions and misogynistic, narrow-minded mentality. Such a turn-on, on so many levels. She'd show him her full appreciation the moment they returned to their cabin.

"Thanks, honey." She took hold of the phone and had a thorough study. Maybe she'd pick up something Westley hadn't. That was most likely his thought too. Always better to have more than one set of eyes scrutinizing the content and feeding back on material.

"Impressive." She smiled and glanced at Rei, then Marcus. "Is it possible to give me access to the prototype so Westley and I can review it further before we commit any funds?"

Rei darted his gaze to Marcus, as though seeking his direction. Was it her imagination or did he look a little uneasy, stressed, threatened? She imagined neither of them had anticipated grilling, ultimatum-style queries from their select group of guests.

They'd probably assumed if they played the 'you're-so-lucky-to-be-considered' card then everyone would show their gratitude by signing up, no interrogative questions asked.

Cool as a cliched cucumber, Marcus addressed them both and smiled, his elbows on the table, his hands clasped together. "We'll see what we can do. I'll need to look into the legalities and get back to you."

He topped up each of their glasses with still, ice water, then placed the decanter down and nestled his drink in his hands. Did he intend to have a swig or did he need the refreshing cold to permeate his skin and temper down his inwardly heated response?

Marcus met her gaze, his feverish eyes boring into hers with overconfidence and conceit. "For me to provide the information to you, I need your express confirmation in writing that you won't share the app or idea with anyone. Once you've signed the contract, if I find out you've breached the agreement with the aim to sell the app as your own, you'll be litigated."

"Understood," Westley answered before she could even respond. "Now, assuming we agree the protype has potential, what are we looking at in terms of buy in?"

Lines of irritation formed around Marcus' eyes, while his practiced smile remained in place. "Well, that's dependent on who else signs up to the terms of the prospectus. The fewer people who commit, the more each remaining investor needs to contribute. So encouraging others to participate is to your advantage. To the advantage of all of us."

And his bank account, no doubt.

"So what figures are we talking?" Westley persisted in his polite, pleasant, English way.

Marcus stared Westley straight in the eye, as though one-hundred percent sure of what he had to sell. "A minimum of one million US dollars."

She barely managed to stifle a gasp. *What the fuck?*

"That sounds reasonable." Westley squeezed her hand below the table, beyond the view of Rei and Marcus, as though to say, what a fucking scam. They'd already suspected it, but this practically confirmed the con.

She worked hard to school her features into an unperturbed, encouraging expression.

Marcus sipped some water, the ice now partially melted, placed his drink on the table and rubbed his hands. "Oh, it is. You early investors will get the privilege of a discounted deal. But, as I said, the pledge amount will increase if we don't get the bulk of funding we require."

So in other words, he wanted suckers to promote the idea to supposedly benefit themselves as well as ensure a healthy number of dollars in his accessible funds.

"We understand." Westley's conspiratorial smile looked almost believable. To them, it probably was. They didn't know him well enough to see the chinks in his ex-sniper armor.

May didn't fully see them either, but in the past few days, living in such close proximity, she'd developed a much better awareness.

She clutched onto Westley's hand beneath the table. "Let us know if you can send through the app prototype, and when we're likely to receive it. If possible, it'd be great if we could review it while we're here on the island. That way, we can confirm if we're willing to support the project before we leave."

Westley gave her an unexpected that-was-awesome side smile. Subtle enough for only her to notice. Hopefully.

"I'll check in with the app developer and get back to you as soon as I have an answer." Marcus might be able to fool some people with his insincere smile, but not her.

Yes, she'd only spoken to him for a short time, but she'd socialized with enough others to know the barely visible yet telling signs. "Thank you." She slid her gaze to Westley, and hoped neither Marcus nor Rei recognized her triumphant grin. "We both appreciate it."

"We do." Her *husband* lifted her palm to his lips, gave it a seductive kiss, then lowered her hand into his lap. He twisted his head to refocus on the guys across the table. "Thanks for dinner. Send us through any additional info and we'll analyze it thoroughly and get back to you as quickly as possible."

Westley let go of her hand and stood. She followed suit and he quickly intertwined their fingers as though he couldn't stand being separated, couldn't stand not touching her for too long. And she welcomed the contact.

"But we haven't had dessert." Marcus' voice came out part desperation, part disappointment. Had he planned to use the extra time to spellbind them with his overall smooth-talking strategy? Use a cult-leader approach to try to make them forget their demands? To trust and fully cooperate with him?

Turning to stare at her, his *wife*, Westley said, "You gents go ahead and eat ours. We already have a sweet feast lined up back at our cabin."

Oh. Excellent. Her heart raced to triple time. She couldn't wait. Their dinner with the guys had acted as extended foreplay and she was more than ready to come. They'd set things in motion, executed their roles to perfection, and the achievement got her extra aroused.

May snuggled in closer to her *husband*. "We do." She stared up at Westley with dreamy, desire-filled eyes — yes, she was playing the required part but she wasn't entirely acting — then reluctantly gazed at their hosts. "Let's meet up again once we have a chance to evaluate all the parameters."

Marcus and Rei rose and shook hands with them, then Westley led her out of the dining room, into the front foyer and onto the well-lit path leading back to their accommodation. They kept hold of each other's hands but didn't talk until Westley waved his card over the reader and whipped her inside.

The door slammed shut behind them and he pushed her hard up against it. "You were incredible tonight."

She stared into his shiny, espresso-colored eyes. "So were y—"

Westley smashed his mouth to hers, drugging her senses. As though he'd coated his tongue and lips with some sort of aphrodisiac. A chemical combination she couldn't ignore, a powerful interaction she couldn't deny.

He pressed into her with an urgency she'd never experienced. Hot, sexy, mind-melting. Like they needed no clothes, ASAP. Like she wanted to remain naked with him, forever.

But that could totally be her horniness talking. Up until him, it had been quite a while since she'd done the dirty with a man. Sure, she'd gone at it with Westley not long ago, but her insatiable self needed him again.

May couldn't remember a time she'd been this hot for a guy. And, yes, it could entirely be a physical, superficial thing, related to the circumstances, the intensity of their roles, their close proximity, his spectacular outer shell. The overall excitement. His refined English accent. Presumably a combination. And she aimed to utilize that to her personal and professional benefit.

They pulled apart for a few short seconds to strip down, then crashed back together against the door, writhing, moaning, the friction of their skin making her go out of her mind with unmet desire.

Suddenly he stopped.

No! She wanted to cry with frustration.

"By the window."

She sucked in a disbelieving breath. "But people might see us."

"With the lights off, it's unlikely. A silhouette maybe. But even if they somehow do make us out, it works in our favor. It reinforces we're a newly married couple who can't get enough of each other. That we just can't wait to fuck."

Fear mixed with excitement raced through her veins. She'd always believed sexual intimacy was a private thing between consenting partners. She'd never even entertained the idea of anyone watching without express permission. Had seen it as too confronting, embarrassing, and yet...

Was it that big of a deal? The windows looked tinted, so if they did it in the dark, as Westley said, those wandering by might see shadows but not much else. Though, enough to provide proof of their relationship story. Not at all a bad thing. Helped reinforce their premise. In fact, the idea was surprisingly hot.

He grabbed her hand and led her to the sliding door overlooking the calm ocean, the tide rolling into the shore. "Press yourself up against the glass and be loud. Leave everyone with no doubt about how much you're enjoying yourself, enjoying me."

Was that to stroke his ego or to strengthen the credibility of their newlywed undercover operation? Didn't matter. She wanted both.

"Don't hold back." He kissed a path down her spine and kneeled behind her. "Thrust your bottom out, and push your pussy against my face."

Just the thought had her juices flowing, practically to the point of dripping. She placed her palms firmly, securely on the glass, and arched her back, as requested, to give him complete access.

He groaned and licked from her clit to her ass. Fuck, he had the best, most adept tongue. So pleasure-giving...except when he chatted incessantly. Which he had no ability to do with his face buried between her legs. The best, most enjoyable way to keep him quiet. And focused.

A slow, soft swipe of her clit had her moaning so loud, the sensation so intense, her knees buckled, and she worried she might collapse to the floor. But his capable hands held her hips steady, and kept her upright, so he could lap at her pussy, creating a sublime climb to climax.

"So sexy. You are such a sexy woman." His rumbly, whispered words pushed her over the orgasmic edge, and she screamed his name, so overtaken with pleasure she'd almost forgotten they may be seen, heard. Ecstasy had a way of blocking out anything but bliss.

May slumped against the cold window and jolted back, her nipples super sensitive. She spun around and clasped his face, encouraging him into standing so she could kiss his wet lips just as he'd ravished hers.

He penetrated her mouth, delving his tongue deep, and she wrapped her arms around his neck, pulling him impossibly closer, their bodies plastered to one another, rubbing, gyrating, needing more.

Westley palmed her ass and grinded his hips against hers, seeking more friction. And it felt glorious. But if they kept this up, he'd come against her stomach, rather than inside her, which she sensed neither of them wanted right now.

So she dropped to her knees, grabbed his gorgeous erection, pre-cum already leaking from the slit, and stroked. His eyes practically rolled back in his head, and he growled.

With her fingers still encircling his hard-as-fuck dick, she sat back on her haunches and glanced up until their gazes met. The passion pinging between them had her pumping harder, faster, and he thrust into her hand.

"I need your mouth on me." His voice had never sounded so husky, breathy, so damn sensual.

"And I need you in my mouth." She gave him the dirtiest smile and slid his swollen cock between her lips, retaining full eye contact.

May stroked him in combination with sucking and licking, and he stumbled. He threaded his fingers through her hair and angled her head, encouraging her ministrations exactly where he needed them.

Fuck, she loved seeing a man let go, give over control to her, trust her with his pleasure. She upped the pace and depth and rhythm, and just as she deep-throated his dick, he came. His stuttered breath, followed by a booming roar, had her going harder, wringing out every last bit of his release.

He slammed a hand against the glass to keep himself from falling over, and she took that as a massive sign of success. She relinquished his cock from her mouth with a pop and licked her lips, savoring the remnants of his fresh masculine flavor.

From what she'd witnessed, he ate well, didn't drink much alcohol, and had high standards of hygiene, which obviously added to his extra delicious taste. She couldn't wait to suck him off again. And knowing they still had at least a couple more days to make the most of this incredibly pleasant diversion, filled her with inexplicable joy.

He released his death grip on her head, unfortunately—she'd always enjoyed having her hair pulled—and held her face between his hands. "I desperately want to do you here, up against the glass, take you from the front, then from behind, but my legs won't hold up."

"Bed it is. Maybe we can give this spot a go tomorrow." She couldn't help the satisfied smirk from sliding onto her lips.

"First thing, because if you suck my dick like that beforehand, it's not going to happen. I'll be thoroughly spent. It's all about physics, and recovery."

She laughed, pleased she'd affected him as much as he'd affected her. "Thanks for letting me know. I promise I'll be mindful, and aim to adhere to your request."

"I appreciate it." He grasped her hand and assisted her to stand, his potent stare remaining fixed on her eyes. And although he'd just had an epic climax, his cock started to rise. "Let's go. I need to be inside you. Now."

Chapter Thirteen

"So what's on the agenda for today, aside from our couples' massage?" May's sleepy voice reinvigorated his cock. But then again, what didn't?

"More sex?" Which would be beyond amazing—May had been insatiable during the night, and as a result, he'd hardly slept, fucking her into ultimate oblivion—but they'd been sent to do a job. He wrenched his thoughts away from detouring down a delicious, self-indulgent path.

She smacked his arm. "I meant workwise." Though, the look in her eyes suggested she'd prefer some adult fun first too.

It took his mind a few extra seconds to get back online. To temper down his arousal and focus on a practical plan. "Try to have a chat with the remaining investors. Try to find a way into Marcus' office to search for more incriminating evidence."

May rolled onto her side, propping up on one elbow. "Do you really think he'll have damning information lying around?"

"If he's as arrogant as he seems, he probably believes he's several steps above everyone else. So he won't be worried, if anything he'll be complacent. And that will be his undoing."

She stared into his eyes, her forehead crinkling with adorable concern. "I hope so. We can't do much without a warrant."

"Unless we catch him doing or saying something dodgy." Which he intended to do through thorough, expert preparation. May might be new to security work, but she had mechanical and military smarts, and he aimed to tap into every bit of her expertise.

"Such as? Attempting to kill someone? I doubt it. He's arrogant, but clever enough not to be too blasé."

"So what do you suggest?"

She stroked wayward strands of hair off his face, the pads of her fingers soft and warm. He wanted to close his eyes and lean into her hand like a shameless, bunting cat.

"Get to know the other investors, as you've recommended the whole time. Check out any holes in their stories, their thinking. Determine if there are any lingering disputes with Marcus, any lawsuits, or if anyone has negatively promoted his business, particularly to the public.

"Note whether they mention any of the missing investors from previous recruiting parties, particularly the last time they saw or heard from them. Answers to these questions might help get Marcus arrested or identify who might be next on his hit list."

"So you're assuming he's guilty." He wanted to hear her reasons, her rationale, without biasing her reply with his answer. A way to see if her conclusions matched his...or added to them. A way to reduce skewed, group-minded thinking and focus on facts.

"Going by his wife's statement of concerns, and my gut, *yes*." She shivered. Apparently, everything about Marcus put them both on edge, had their nerves on high alert.

Her enchanting eyes stared into his with confidence and conviction. "He's up to something. My fight and flight instinct activated the moment I met Marcus and his smarmy mate, sending immediate red flags to my brain. That tells me whatever they're doing is not quite right. Now we need some sort of proof, ASAP, before someone else goes missing."

He combed his fingers through her lustrous long locks, enjoying the silky slide of the strands, desperate to roll her beneath him, twist her hair around his hand and tug hard.

Because although he spoke courteously, she'd awakened his baser urges, his Dom tendencies raising his craving for carnal pleasure way above what constituted proper. And he sensed she enjoyed the contrast between his well-mannered words and down and dirty sexual interplay.

"You speak too much sense." Westley breathed out long and slow, trying to redirect some of the blood in his throbbing cock back to his brain.

"I'd intended to talk through everything we've discussed so far, problem solve and fill in any gaps, but I'm too distracted to think." He stared into her eyes with clear intent but verbalized it for extra emphasis.

"The facts are, I want you. Again. And then some more."

Her eyes went wide and dark with distinctive longing. "Maybe up against the sliding door before breakfast?" As they'd discussed last night. *Hmmm…tempting. So damn tempting.*

He ran his hand along her back. "But we'd only be able to fit in a quickie and I want us to take our time."

"Oh, yes." She trailed her hand over his chest, his abs…

He grabbed her wrist before she could reach his overeager dick. "Unfortunately, we desperately need to discover what's going on below the surface. To make the most of the small window of opportunity…then we can celebrate later." His believable-sounding words impressed him. His heart, his libido, not so much.

Her forehead crumpled with disappointment. "I guess I can't argue with that." Though her body language didn't match her words. Her subtle gestures said 'let's further explore each other, even if we only have time for an express bout of sex'. And fuck, did he want to.

Discipline. It all came down to willpower, self-control, mental strength. Succumbing to emotional needs and ignoring pressing practical tasks could end in disaster. He'd seen it happen. Many times. Had been close to letting it decimate his career, his life.

So although he wanted nothing more than to fuck his partner into next week, he needed to prioritize. They needed to stay alive first, obtain the intel, then partake in an intimate party for two. Or so he hoped.

Once they returned to their normal existence, would she choose to continue what they'd started? He definitely would. He'd had enough experience to know what worked for him, what he desired. She had spunk. And although he generally didn't like gobby, combative women, he enjoyed her intellect, her well-thought-out arguments, her passion.

Enjoyed the fact he could be one-hundred percent honest about who he really was, that she knew the real Westley and still chose him as a fuck buddy, and maybe more. Maybe even considered him long-term romantic-partner material.

Westley gave her ass a large, forceful grope. "Let's get ready."

She moan-groaned, and after a brief, reluctant pause, rolled out from his embrace and instead of heading straight for the shower, she detoured past her bag. May bent over and fished through her suitcase, giving him a fabulous view of her beautiful butt and pretty pussy, selecting clothes and making his dick wish he had less sense, and instead, went with his primeval instincts.

He squeezed his eyes closed and waited for the en suite door to shut.

Safe.

Sort of.

For the moment.

Not seeing her seductive body gave him the breathing space to silence his cock-driven dirty thoughts, and get his mind back into gear. To factor in fundamental tasks like making breakfast. Shift into a clear trajectory of activities that prepared them for their day physically, mentally, emotionally.

Although tremendously tempting, they couldn't afford to remain fuck-struck. It wasn't a real honeymooner's holiday. They needed to redirect their focus from the do-me-now, overwhelming sexual-drive moment, to weighing up the investor party information, connecting causal relationships, and discovering the required evidence.

Simple to say but not easy to enact. For anyone. Westley considered himself extremely disciplined and he still found delaying his desires challenging. Especially with her. It had become almost impossible to ignore her magnetism.

May had an equally strict, regimented work background that had seen her thrive. So he had no doubt she harbored the same set of systematic skills. An ability to separate out, reconfigure, compartmentalize. Or so he hoped.

If she caved to their potent, hypnotic attraction, he doubted he'd have the required strength to say *no*, to resist her advances.

He swung his legs onto the floorboards, threw on some cotton boxers and got started on his go-to breakfast. Many a man fancied himself a BBQ specialist, but he knew where he excelled. And yes, he could manage a grill, a hot plate, but he outshone most other men when it came to delivering a fantastic, fry up.

"Mmm…that smells yummy." May's voice bordered on orgasmic.

He twisted his head to find her heading for the fridge…in a towel that just covered her best bits. No. Not totally true. She had a stunning face and sexy-as-fuck legs, and petite, sweet feet. All of her got him going.

She opened the door, pulled out a bottle of apple and blackcurrant juice and poured them each a glass. She handed him one, her hair still damp, her gaze infused with I'm hungry sentiments. And not just for food. Pretty much mirroring his mood.

But if they succumbed, it'd eat into their limited, remaining investigatory time. He needed to uphold an exemplary attitude. He needed to lead from the front. Be firm. Be focused. Ensure he showed appreciation and love, yet lean on his experience in the field to emphasize the required behavior that aligned with their agenda.

A hard ask, for him, for her, but vital.

He accepted the drink and gulped it down. "Thank you." As sweet and delicious as her.

She swept her gaze to the fry pan, the short-cut bacon sizzling. "Thank *you*." May hesitated beside the bench, her juice almost finished. "Need any help?"

"No, thank you. I've got everything under control." *Mostly.* "Take a seat. Breakfast is almost ready. You can wash up." A cheeky smile slid onto his lips.

"Happy to. Thanks for doing this."

"Thanks for being open, flexible, accommodating."

"It's a pleasure." Her sensual smile made him want to screw breakfast, toss the table aside, and eat her pussy instead. Again. However, the quicker they resolved the case, came to some enforceable conclusion, the sooner everyone could positively move forward. The sooner they could get back to each other. Safely. Enjoyably. Pleasurably. With low to no concerns. With all the desired time in the world.

They devoured their bacon and eggs with mushroom, tomato and avocado sides, cleaned up, got dressed in leisurewear, and in less than thirty minutes they met at the front door, and headed off to their couples' day spa session.

Afterward, still buzzing with bliss, Westley led her outside. He held her face between his hands, struggling to stop staring at how tuggable her beaded nipples looked in her stretchy tight tank top. "Now back to reality. Ready?"

"I hope so. You?"

"With you by my side, yes." He stared into her eyes with absolute conviction. "We can do this." He believed in her, he believed in them...as individuals, as experienced career professionals. As romantic partners, the results remained to be seen.

"Aww...not only polite but sweet too. Now let's go." She gave him her cheekiest, smart-ass smile, and broke away. Right at that moment, a warm, gusty breeze, blew up her short, activewear skirt, swishing it around her sexy thighs like Marilyn Monroe in *The Seven Year Itch*.

Westley subtly adjusted himself and followed her, like a one-track-mind, on-heat puppy. He sidled up to May and clasped her hand. "Don't forget, at every opportunity, we need to show a combined, aligned front. Convince everyone we have an unbreakable, cohesive bond."

And that meant frequently touching, snuggling and speaking in a loving way to each other so those they came across believed what they portrayed without question.

As he did. But did she? Was he the only one who wasn't pretending?

"I know. And I agree it's essential. I promise I'll be on my absolute best adoring-wife behavior." She held his face between her small, soft hands and planted a deep, X-rated kiss on his lips. Hard for anyone to dispute. Hard for anyone to question her attraction. Hard for him not to believe the façade, for him not to get hard.

Eventually, they broke apart, her eyes a little dazed, his arms tightening around her swaying body. Once she'd gotten her balance, had somewhat stabilized, he kept an arm in place about her waist and guided her along the path heading away from the main building toward the sea.

To the right, Benjamin and Phoenix ran along the beach, looking like a couple of models on a photoshoot, chatting and laughing and barely breaking a sweat.

They couldn't waste this opportune moment to speak to them alone. "You intercept Phoenix and I'll take Benjamin," Westley whispered. "Text me when you're done."

He planted a quick kiss on May's lips, before she could reply, then broke away and sprinted to catch up with Benjamin. The guy separated from Phoenix, and while slowing to a jog, shoved ear pods into his ears and fiddled with his phone, oblivious to his surroundings.

Westley gained on the guy and Benjamin turned, a curious expression on his face. He yanked out the earphones and stopped, the water crashing onto the shore right near his heels. "Can I help you?"

"I'm not sure. Perhaps." The salty air stung his nostrils. "How do you know Marcus?"

"Through an online investor group. What about you?"

Defensive? Did he have something to hide? Or was he naturally guarded? "Through word of mouth. I'm just trying to work out whether what he's proposing is a lucrative deal."

Benjamin bent forward and propped his palms on his thighs, sucking in oxygen. "Who knows. There are no guarantees, like with any stock."

Westley mirrored the man's posture in an attempt to develop a bond through body language. "I understand that, but I'm trying to make sure that whatever I invest in has some sort of promise."

Benjamin bowed his head and raked his fingers through his thick, ruffled hair. "Me too. Any tips on what to look for?"

Ah…so apparently, he was also a new recruit to the scheme. Or a smart ass. Or trying to suss out other investors' attitudes for himself or to feedback to the head honcho.

Aside from the private investor group Benjamin had joined, Westley didn't doubt that the guy had tapped into anecdotal info from those in the financial field and run some further internet searches. Westley hadn't yet pursued the investment route in his personal life but he'd read a lot on it and all the greats said the same thing—the only good stock is one that goes up in price.

Having thoroughly checked out Marcus' history online, Westley hadn't found anything of significance. Anything much at all. Already concerning. Had Benjamin discovered more info? Had Phoenix? Did they have the skills to search for, and hone in on, telltale specifics? "Data. Past results. Have you seen statistics along those lines?"

Benjamin shook his head, his expression totally believable, entirely sincere. "No. Not yet. My high-end, successful acquaintances that established the forum, recommended him and I had no reason to doubt their endorsements. But following our chat, I won't put in a cent until I do some additional research."

Birds of a feather remained glued together. Worrying, but not particularly surprising. Support guaranteed support. "And how about Phoenix?"

"What about her?"

Ooh, protective. Westley hadn't expected such a snippy response. He'd apparently tapped into a weak, significantly sore point. Either Benjamin was related to her or wanted to be...by marriage.

"Has she had similar recommendations?"

Benjamin stood tall, his hands squeezing into fists by his side, his jaw clamping down hard. "Why are you asking me?" Did he feel insulted, affronted? Like Westley believed the guy had somehow coerced her, or would take her word over Benjamin's?

Westley summoned his best, most subtle, soothing smile. And hoped he'd done enough to prevent the younger man from throwing a retaliatory punch. "Because I've seen you together and figured you're friends. And before I sign to anything, like you, I want to know what I'm getting into. So I'm interested in obtaining as much information as possible from as many of you as possible."

"Well, then go and ask her yourself. I can't speak on her behalf."

Hopefully May had successfully extracted some intel from Phoenix during their discussion.

Keeping his voice low, calm and measured, Westley continued. "I'll be sure to get everyone's opinion before I invest any money. I've worked too hard to throw it away. I believe it's worth taking the extra time to collect details and not be impulsive."

Benjamin stayed silent, almost reflective, as though weighing up Westley's words.

Gesturing gently with his hands, Westley said, "Look, we both want the same thing—a successful investment."

The tension started dissipating from Benjamin's body, his hands relaxing at his sides, his facial expression turning from surly to receptive. Thank fuck he'd successfully talked him down from the frustrated, reckless ledge.

Westley glanced around. Outside of May and Phoenix, no one else stood on the beach within view. The breeze blew strands of May's silky blonde hair off her beautiful face, while the water nipped at both their ankles. The permanent-fixture, scavenger seagulls, ducked and weaved and shuffled around them, angling for food.

"You're right. I'm the same."

Bingo. Westley had gotten the guy onboard, switched his wariness to rapport.

Benjamin looked around, then refocused his blue-green eyes on Westley. "Phoenix is a trust-fund baby so she's new to all this. Too trusting. I want to try and protect her as much as I can.

Nice. Considerate. Kind.

Once again, Benjamin scrutinized the surroundings. "I've taken over my dad's dwindling estate and made it something, so I refuse to lose any of it. I want to see growth, expansion, positive outcomes."

"As we all do."

"Before I commit to providing any capital, I'm going to review every dollar of business earnings to date, as well as the projected income for this project. Not just trust the recommendations. Like you suggested, the more data the better.

"Although there's always a level of uncertainty with investing, I won't risk the majority of my money on an unfounded, untested idea. And even if I choose to trial a small amount, I'll ensure I have a stop-loss."

Westley's thoughts exactly. Which could be a huge red flag for someone like Marcus. Going by his approach so far, he'd wanted his wealthy party of people to blindly accept his proposition, his terms, and willingly outlay their funds.

And if not, he'd have a few short days to come up with a way to convince each investor his scheme would provide lucrative results. The guy was so compromised, who could even trust the figures he put forward? Unless they were impaired themselves. Hence why sensible investors sought answers on their own, rather than relying on his skewed view and data-mined details.

But he had to give it to Marcus—the man could talk. He'd shown natural, articulate, salesman-like traits. He consistently used pretty, evocative language and demonstrated knowledge and intelligence. Exactly what most people wanted to hear to ensure success. Particularly if they had a history of low self-confidence, if they carried lifelong emotional damage and lack of self-belief.

Benjamin's switched-on reasoning made him both smart and a massive target. Westley mentally added Benjamin and Phoenix to his and May's safety list for monitoring.

Westley forced a friendly, disarming smile. "A stop-loss is essential, I agree. Like you, I'm eager to seek out the most effective, least risky opportunities."

Benjamin stroked his stubble, scanned the area around them again, and re-established eye contact. "Good to know I have an ally." He kept his voice quiet, just above the level of the squawking seagulls and crashing waves.

Only a few seconds later, he darted his eyes behind and around Westley. "I'm not familiar with the others, but from what I've seen, each person is here for their own individual benefit. Don't get me wrong, I understand that, I want to set myself up well too. And make sure Phoenix isn't taken advantage of. I'm happy to consider something that has promise but I refuse to be a part of any criminal activity."

As in, he had started to suspect Marcus' deals might have a dodgy aspect. And based on Penelope's confidential testimony, and Westley's meetings with Marcus so far, he did too.

Hence why he and May were investigating. Hence why he needed to determine any link between Marcus' business dealings and people's disappearances.

Benjamin started jogging on the spot, a silent but clear message he needed an out, needed to escape. Dissipate some pent-up, stressful energy. Hopefully impulsivity, the need to alleviate anxiety, wouldn't drive him into deadly hands.

"I want clean investments as well. If you hear anything, let me know. Thanks for your time." Westley glanced at the tide, now sneaking up over the sand and tickling their ankles. "If you want to talk about anything, come and see me, or my wife, May." He loved saying that way too much.

Chapter Fourteen

"Phoenix?" May hated jogging, but she pushed through her displeasure to catch up with the woman.

The slender young lady stopped, and using a black elastic tie off her wrist, wound her long golden hair into a low bun. She dug her toes into the soggy sand but didn't turn around. She stared at her feet, squelching into the shore, avoiding eye contact.

Shy? Perhaps. Avoiding something? Possibly. May needed to determine which was true.

She stopped in front of the woman, preventing her easy escape. The waves crashed on her left, the overflow of water racing up to their feet. "Are you enjoying your stay?"

Phoenix glanced up, her baby-blue gaze short of meeting May's eyes. "Who wouldn't love an island getaway?"

Nice deflection, but it didn't quite answer the question. May was far from born yesterday. She knew all the avoidance tactics. And planned to utilize whatever she could to get accurate answers.

May needed to find a way to develop rapport or she'd get nowhere. "Just between us, I prefer a winter holiday. Hot weather and sand-coated feet aren't my thing. Being a schnitzel doesn't fit into my idea of a dream vacation. Far from it. I don't mind rugged coastlines with rockpools and cliff-faces, but Westley isn't so picky. Coming from England, he loves any sort of tropical beach, any sort of sultry weather, and I love him, so here we are."

Phoenix bit her lip and laughed. "I'm with you. I'm an Autumn-Winter girl."

Yes! She'd reeled her right in with her first attempt. Westley would be proud.

"It helps having great air con in our, I mean, my accommodation. I can watch the water through the window."

Ah…so she and Benjamin had had some intimate time together. Not surprising. But obviously neither of them felt comfortable admitting it…yet. So May wouldn't call her out…at the moment.

They both laughed.

Phoenix's gaze remained below eye level. "Honestly, if it wasn't for the business opportunity, I wouldn't be here." The business opportunity and Benjamin, more like it.

"Me either." May slid the most conspiratorial smile onto her lips. The weather could be as sticky hot and humid as ever, yet she wouldn't regret her sexual experiences with Westley. He was beyond sex-god status. Consistently sparked every pleasurable sensation, even in areas she'd never considered erotic. He had indisputable, mega skills as a lover.

"Everyone I speak to, including financial advisors, keep telling me I need to invest wisely but I have no idea." She ran her hands over her tied, rich flaxen hair. "And then I heard about this and…"

"You saw the potential benefits."

"I did. I needed to tune into someone who had knowledge, who could lead my investments in the right direction. And when I spoke to Marcus, he ticked all those boxes."

As any great salesperson did. They had an amazing ability to say the right things at the exact right time, to take advantage of the ignorant, to play into what people wanted to hear. "Do you have anyone else independently looking into other share options?"

"No. Except Benjamin. He's been great, but he can't answer all my questions either. Other than him, I'm not sure where to start. I'm new to this. It's hard to know what's the right advice. My parents weren't supposed to die just yet."

"Oh, I'm sorry. I didn't realize…" She reached out and ran her hand over the woman's goose-bumped biceps.

Phoenix shivered. "I didn't either." She crossed her arms over her chest. "But I plan to get the best outcome from a difficult situation." The corners of her lips quivered.

"I'm sure you will. You seem sensible, driven, determined."

Phoenix glanced up, her gaze meeting May's eyes for the first time. "I am. I just hope I do them proud. I hope I can grow their wealth in a healthy, positive way that benefits me, and my family, and others."

May smiled. No way was this woman behind any wrongdoing. Too sweet, too innocent, too lacking in confidence. She couldn't wait to hear Westley's feedback on Benjamin. Was he as easy to strike off the persons-of-interest list? And even if he was, did he meet the criteria for the missing-person, death list? "That's my dream as well."

Phoenix reached out and clasped May's hands. "I hope we both achieve what we set out to do."

"Me too." May squeezed the other woman's fingers. "But just be open. If this doesn't work out, something else will. Whatever happens, don't give up."

Phoenix clutched May's hands harder. "Thank you. Ben's been encouraging me to review information with more perspective before committing to anything." She smiled. "It's always good to get an external person's opinion."

May swallowed her repressed reply, which burned like corrosive acid in her throat. Yes, she wanted the best for the woman, for any innocents stuck in Marcus' web of deceit. But she couldn't give away her cover. Doing that would put every single one of them at heightened risk.

All she could do was subtly steer people in a better, less deadly direction. "It is, I agree. Particularly when enjoying the perks of such a pretty place." She let go of Phoenix's hands. "Anyway, I should let you get back to appreciating all the stunning views. And there are plenty. You don't want to miss them."

May snatched her smartphone from her handbag and checked the time. "And I'm due to meet up with my hubby any minute."

"See you at dinner tonight?" the shy woman asked with a hopeful smile.

"I'm not sure yet. I need to check in with Westley. But if all goes to plan, yes. Otherwise, I'm sure we'll see each other sometime tomorrow."

"Cool." Phoenix smiled, then turned and power-walked toward the spectacular cliff face and rock pools.

May went to send Westley a text, when she caught a glimpse of him in her peripheral vision, striding toward her. Women went on about the allure of gray sweatpants, but him in his form-fitting white tracksuit bottoms, setting off his increasingly tanned, olive skin totally trumped that fallacy.

His dirty-as-fuck smile thoroughly fell in line with their newlywed guise. And had her lady bits begging for more attention, had her virtually disintegrating into the sand. But did his response reflect his truth?

Was he as enamored with her as she'd become with him? Would her first case be her last? She couldn't fall for each partner she worked with! Didn't intend to. Assumed her feelings for Westley were an aberration. Getting involved with a colleague frequently ended in career suicide. A total occupational hazard.

Could he be an outlier, or had her solace-seeking led her straight into the arms of a smart, skilled man, willing and eager to show her some attention? How could she ever be sure of his motivations?

He wrapped her in a whole-body hug, affection flooding her every cell, deluging her heart. He felt so right. Like he connected with her not just subconsciously but also physically, psychologically, spiritually. Emotionally. Maybe even consciously, but beyond what her inner self recognized. Beyond what she'd ever known, what she'd ever believed possible.

Westley? A love interest? More like *lust* interest. She'd only known the guy for five seconds, in the scheme of things, however, she trusted his professional opinion. Could she also trust him at a personal level?

Just because he excelled at security work, didn't mean he successfully transferred the same high-level expertise into his relationships. She'd come across many police and military men over the years who did extremely well at their jobs, won all sorts of medals, all sorts of accolades, but struggled to hold a conversation, let alone a long-term love affair.

"How did you go?" he whispered in her ear, his hot breath tickling her skin, not-so-subtly asking for so much more.

"She's an innocent. Vulnerable. Drawn here by the promise of building her wealth, and increasing her connection with Benjamin. What are your thoughts about him?"

"Not so innocent. More strategic. But he doesn't seem deceitful. I believe he legitimately cares for Phoenix, and he thought Marcus might provide a positive financial outcome. He still may. But at what expense?"

She shifted away enough to look into his eyes. "That's what worries me. Will he dispose of anyone who questions his plans?"

"Has he already?"

"It's looking that way."

"It is. But we can't condemn him until we have more concrete proof."

True. They both wanted a quick and easy solution, one that would put away culpable people. But in order to do that, they needed evidence that would stand up in a court case. "There's the group dinner tonight. During the meal, one of us needs to find a way to get into Marcus' office. Use some sort of ruse. See if he's left anything of significance lying around. Unlikely but possible."

"Me. I'll do it." He'd nominated himself before she had a chance.

Shit.

Shit shit shit.

Maybe she shouldn't worry. Westley knew what he was doing, right? He had stealthy sniper skills. Skills she didn't have. Worrying was probably one of the biggest, most common mistakes of her life, except she couldn't ignore how she felt. Couldn't ignore the players and the ultimate game. Who would win?

In the end, she didn't want anyone to get hurt. If she could help it. She wanted to work with Westley, who'd also shown protective, life-saving traits, to ensure no one got injured, or even worse, killed.

"And if you can't find anything, we'll work on where else he might store the information. Without secure storage, physical or electronic, he can't provide the required data backing his proposal. And people will want to see results, especially now that we've started prodding them, reinforced the idea. They'll want to see a well-thought-out, evidence-based prospectus."

Without transparency, if Marcus was culpable, they'd expose his grandiose mission. Based on May's gut and the information to date, she'd bet her life on the guy's guilt.

They needed to safely access as much of Marcus' office and the main homestead — get invited into the spaces where possible — in order to search for a legit hint of proof to support their request for a warrant.

She reviewed Westley's guarded words and her strategically trained thinking. Reviewed all the possibilities within her current frame of reference. "My guess is he has a safe or something similar. Could be physical or electronic. Something that gives him temporary security, some time to shift any valuable documents to another protected area."

Could Westley add to the possible considerations? He'd had a heap more experience in this area.

He stroked his thumb over her cheekbone. "If we don't find anything in his office, his home, there's a small bank on the island. We'd then need to check if they have secure envelopes, safety deposit boxes. Or equivalent."

"And if they don't? Or don't give us authority to access them?"

"Let's start with ruling out the main options first. Then we'll devise a strategy from there."

"So we need a way to get into Marcus' office unnoticed. Any ideas?"

Westley kissed the concerned crease above her nose, and held her tighter. "Give them an excuse for my absence. Tell them I've got to make some business calls. Keep them distracted, and I'll slip into his office and home."

"But what about securing court-approved evidence? We can't admit anything that isn't found within a legit search."

"At this stage, we only require enough of an indicator for a search warrant. Once we have that, the areas can be thoroughly explored, and anything of significance will be admissible in court."

Hopefully the authorities didn't give Marcus enough notice to relocate any potentially damning evidence. She stood on her tip toes and pressed a long, languorous kiss on Westley's lips, eliciting an undeniable, enthusiastic groan…from both of them.

"So we need to find and chat to Franc and Odette as well as Edgar and Billie before we act?" she said, all breathy.

"If possible." His voice cut out like a faulty microphone.

"No pressure."

He held her face in his hands. "None at all. If we can do it, great. If not, we work through things, step by slow, careful step."

"But we have limited time."

"We do. Though safety comes first. Risk management. I don't want to compromise us or our results. We can only do what we can do without drawing unnecessary attention to ourselves."

She wrapped her arms around his neck and pulled him close. "I one hundred percent agree."

He slid his palms along her back and stopped on her butt, gripping, massaging, kneading. And she loved it. Loved his hands on her. Loved his hard cock nudging her stomach. His full undivided attention. "We must find that balance. We have to ensure no one suspects anything, that everyone believes we're here for the financial benefits. Nothing else…other than a honeymoon-style holiday escape."

His dick dug harder into her abdomen, clearly stating he wanted what she did. Wanted to clearly back his irrefutable words. Another fuck. In fact, based on his previous skills, and recovery, she craved more than one.

And yet, they couldn't ignore their Solve Security work. Responsibilities and obligations before pleasure. The clock ticked, reducing the time to discover enough tangible facts to prove their presumptions and prevent more deaths.

And if circumstances permitted, they'd also slot a few fucking moments in between. To reinforce their story, and for their own enjoyment. He glanced at his smart watch. "We've still got a few hours to extract more details from Edgar and Billie, and Franc and Odette. Let's find them and try to determine their hopes and aspirations and any issues or concerns they may have with Marcus or Rei prior to the group catch-up later. It might also help us work out an effective escape strategy."

She pressed her lips to his and thrust her tongue in his mouth, the rippling waves crashing against their ankles, the salty breeze buffeting their bodies. Yet neither of them moved, didn't even flinch. As though totally caught up in the magic of what they shared.

Rousing from a passion-induced daze, she stepped back and shook her head, her legs still wobbly, her shoes sinking into the wet-concrete-style sand. "I suppose we should focus on our mission."

"We should." His eyes said he had the same debaucherous mission in mind. The one that focused purely on them and exploring their new, explosive connection, rather than the job at hand. The one that took them away from what they needed to do workwise to discover the required intel.

Loud voices broke their intimate moment, and they swung their gazes to a cabin a few hundred meters from theirs. Edgar stood in the doorway, all sheepish, while Billie yelled at the top of her very shrill lungs.

"When are you going to pay it back?" Billie shook her head and stomped down the path, leading away from the front door. After a couple of meters she stopped and turned to face Edgar, throwing her arms up. "How about the mortgage? Did you even think about that? About me?"

"I...I...come back inside, let me explain." He kept his voice low, the tone bordering on begging. Smart move.

A strategy to let her simmer down, to neutralize her temper and keep quiet before others started asking awkward questions.

Either the guy was a spend thrift or a gambler. Maybe both. Explained his interest in options to feed his habit, to potentially gain quick money. But could Marcus provide that? And even if he could, would the gains flow through Edgar's fingers like a flood, preventing him from holding onto any earned cash?

How many debts did he need to service, how many did he need to pay off before he could see a profit? Did Billie even know the extent of his situation? Did he? How much money could repair the rift he'd created?

Billie stormed off. Had she known about his spending issues earlier and avoided the ramifications? Or had she been in denial and just made the stressful discovery? Had he promised he'd get on top of the monetary muck up and shown he hadn't? Had he possibly driven the debt deeper? Had he insisted that this trip would fix everything?

Westley nibbled down May's neck and whispered, "Follow her."

Chapter Fifteen

May gave him a quick peck on the lips and power-walked after the woman. She assumed her 'hubby' would check on Edgar. Then they'd regroup later and provide updates.

Hopefully the couple provided some crucial info to help them decide how best to proceed. Hopefully whatever they shared would help determine who might be at the highest risk of 'disappearing', who was in Marcus' deathly sights.

May needed Billie to slow down if she had any chance of catching her in her heightened, uninhibited state. "Billie?"

The woman stopped, her straight ash blonde hair whipping about her head, her front foot shoving into the sand, her hands clenching and unclenching at her sides. And froze. With Billie standing as still as a marble statue, May had to step into her line of sight in order to seek out some eye contact.

"Are you okay?" May ducked down and attempted to search the woman's averted stare.

"Depends what you mean by *okay*."

May angled her head, eager to lock into her gaze. Eyes often told a whole different story to what a person said. They truly were the windows to a person's soul...reflected their mindset, anyway.

"I don't want to pry but I overheard your argument with Edgar and wanted to offer a friendly ear. Another woman's perspective. If you need it." May fucking hoped she did.

The more details she and Westley could obtain the better their chances of breaking this case wide open, and stopping the culprits. Stopping further needless deaths.

Billie dug the toes of her sneakers into the crumbling sand. "Edgar is full of promises, but he's a gambler. Keeps chasing that money-winning high. He's pissed his funds up the wall, right alongside all of my hard-earned cash. Or in his case, deposited it into slot machines, across poker tables, and into get-rich-quick schemes. I can't keep supporting his addiction."

Like the Ponzi schemes Marcus had a history of perpetrating. Why wasn't that a surprise? But by Billie's response to her the other night and now, the woman had no idea about the depth of Marcus' scams. Did Edgar?

Obviously, he'd fallen for the hype before, going by what she'd said. Fingers crossed Westley used his strategic skills to insidiously slide beneath the guy's skin, below his radar, and extract a useful response.

Billie briefly met her gaze, anger and frustration, like dark pools of venom, swirling in her big brown eyes, then stared at her wringing hands. "I've tried and tried, but I'm sick of it." She shook her head, a muscle in her jaw ticking. "I don't know what to do."

Neither did May. What could she say to appease a woman who had been emotionally and financially pushed to the brink? Awkward and unpleasant, she had to give her space, time, focus on active listening, facilitate her to continue to speak freely.

After what felt like ten minutes but was probably no more than thirty seconds, Billie glanced up, refocusing on May's eyes, a deep crease etched into her brow. "I still love him. Does that make me a pushover, a masochist?"

"No. Staying with Edgar and trying to work it out shows strength. Masochists enjoy pain, but it sounds like you're getting no pleasure from what he's offering."

"So what would you do?"

"Speak to him, once you've calmed down. Reinforce your needs and expectations of a romantic relationship. Make it specific. Let him know any deal breakers. Let him know what will make you walk away. Permanently."

If only May had the guts to do the same... "Give him a chance to rectify what he's doing. But put a time limit on it or else the behavior could drag on. And you don't want that. It already sounds like you're past your tolerance point. Work out a performance contract if you need to."

"Something to make sure we're meeting what we each want?" Billie's eyes latched onto hers with undeniable optimism.

May smiled. "That's exactly it. A strategy with doable steps toward a shared goal."

"Thank you!" Billie threw herself at May without warning and squished her in an appreciative hug. "That's such a huge help. I feel so much clearer. Like I have something to work with."

May gently patted the woman's back. "I'm glad."

"Me too. This conversation has been life changing." Billie broke away, her eyes moist yet alight with eagerness.

A positive change from the emotional pain she'd already endured.

Billie could barely stand still, brimming with renewed, uncontainable nervous energy. "I don't mean to be rude, but I need to find Edgar and talk about all this while it's fresh in my mind. See if we're destined to head in the same direction."

The slim woman's contagious enthusiasm had May brimming with vicarious excitement. "Go. And good luck."

Billie virtually flew across the beach and disappeared over a sand dune.

Time to rejoin Westley. Hopefully her discussion with Billie had given him enough time to draw out additional useful snippets from Edgar. She could hardly slow herself down, keen for them to share and discuss their news.

The refreshing sting of salty sea air created a stark contrast to the polluted machinations Marcus had masterminded. He'd gotten away with these lethal tax-write-off junkets for way too long. She and Westley had to find a way to catch him in his web of lies and deceit, without succumbing to the guy's growing death toll.

Fighting her desire to prematurely spill all she'd learned to her partner, May strolled, mindful of soaking up her surroundings, controlling every single step along the coastline. Every single step that brought her closer to joining him.

Although desperate to share with Westley all she'd discovered, she needed to tamp down her impulsivity and give Billie time to reunite with Edgar. See what panned out there. If Edgar withdrew his pledge, it'd increase his risk of being added to Marcus' kill list. Billie too.

She scaled the sand dune and her man came into view.

Her man.

Yeah right.

Neither of them had spoken about relationship longevity, but it didn't mean they couldn't enjoy each other for as long as possible. So why did the idea of keeping their fling as a short-term thing fill her with emptiness?

What started as annoyance at Westley's polite, prim and proper, aristocratic, super-chatty, overprotective manner had quickly turned to appreciation when he showed his depth of character, when he demonstrated that in the bedroom, and out of it, he was thoughtful and intelligent and filthy as fuck. That dichotomy totally got her going.

A sly, knowing smile slid onto her face. And she couldn't wait to feel his hands all over her again. And again. And again. His multifaceted personality and broad skillset fascinated, intrigued and excited her. And their 'marriage' allowed them to make the most of touching and treasuring each other. Publicly, privately.

Yet it also caused some concern. Could he be acting the whole way through? With the guests, with her? Playing the mandated part in order to get the required results. Stopping a murderer had to supersede their love life.

Sex life.

Westley clocked her approaching and gave her the dirtiest, most sinful smile. Totally in keeping with what they'd physically shared, and their cover. She exhaled. Such a gorgeous guy. On so many levels.

However, stopping a madman, a charlatan, a killer had to be the primary goal. Except she didn't want to be used and discarded, especially when she'd started forming an attachment to her colleague. A huge occupational hazard.

How would it affect them when they returned home? Would it impact on whether they could partner up for future jobs? Assuming they made it out of this mission unscathed.

She'd sworn she wouldn't get involved with Mr. Politeness, with a man who underestimated her, with a guy from work, and yet, how could she not fall for someone so irresistible? Someone who'd proven he wasn't as superficial, and 1950s beliefs driven, as she'd assumed. Westley embodied a depth she hadn't anticipated, a man who had an annoyingly charming *Lucifer*-like essence.

And boy, had she had a crush on that smoking-hot man. She imagined Tom Ellis in that highly memorable part, one that had set many a straight woman's heart on fire with pure, unadulterated lust.

Westley refocused on Edgar, with Billie snuggled into her guy's side. Going by the visual vibe—smiles, laughter, and generally open body language—she assumed Westley had wound down the conversation pretty quickly upon Billie's arrival, if he hadn't already.

From what she'd learned from him, he'd had a long, covert, successful military history so he presumably possessed the skills to flex and bend and adapt, within seconds, depending on the circumstances. He could turn on the smallest of coins.

"Hi," she said as she approached. "Wes, honey," she added, unable to resist. She hadn't ever referred to him in the shortened form of his name, didn't know if he hated it, but the circumstances called for familiarity. And yeah, okay, she wanted to test him. She wanted to see how far she could push.

With a roguish, unmistakable twinkle in his eyes, he gave her the widest, most wicked smile ever. Totally non-defensive, totally tuned into her hint of fun, while acknowledging the need to subtly regroup. And sexy as all fuck. All expressed through his stimulating, hypnotic coffee-colored eyes. Just her sort of man...

"Hey, sweetie, done with your walk? I got talking to Edgar so didn't sort out lunch. Sorry." He shrugged and gave her an apologetic look. Believable. No actor could have done better.

Although appeasing the situation, it made her question every single word he said. If he could lie convincingly here, had he bullshitted to her, too? Did he mean the endearments he'd expressed, or were they part of the broader plan? Get her onside in order to increase the effectiveness of the outcome. Do what it took to successfully solve the case.

Having known him only a few days, it made it hard to discern the full truth. For the short time they'd worked together, she trusted him, rated Westley as a sharp, confident, reliable partner, but beyond that... They didn't have enough history.

She plastered the prettiest, no-worries-babe smile on her face. "I'm sure we've got supplies at the cabin. But let's go check. Otherwise, restaurant it is."

He stepped away from Edgar and Billie, wrapped an arm around her and pressed a loving kiss to the top of her head, sending tingles right to the tips of her toes.

She nuzzled into him, appreciating the affection, but wondering about its legitimacy. Even if she confronted him about it, would he tell her the truth? Or would he wait, ensuring they kept up a believable in-love, newly married couple façade until the end of their job? Especially given her initial skittish response to his advances.

From a practical point of view, it made sense not to prematurely fuck things up. Emotions had a way of screwing with a person's thinking. Big time. And that would be extremely detrimental to what they aimed to achieve.

The more they played their role to perfection, the less likely they'd be found out, and the less likely it'd compromise their mission. Unless they got caught in some sort of crossfire in the meantime.

More involvement, more sharing of themselves created more risk, but also a greater likelihood of achieving the required result. It all came down to rational understanding and balance.

"We'll let you go." Edgar's green eyes sparkled, and he winked as though he'd understood *lunch* as code for *sex*, then glanced at Billie. "We have some things to talk about."

They sure did, and so did she and Westley. The more they spoke to everyone, the more the puzzle pieces came together. Exactly what they'd hoped for, exactly what they needed. The only way they could solve the situation…preferably with no more casualties. Except they still needed clear-cut, admissible evidence.

"See you later." Westley squeezed her tighter and turned them onto the path toward their accommodation. "Do we actually have lunch supplies?"

She laughed. "Big breakfast not enough to fuel our sex-fest?"

"Far from it. It's been years since I've physically worked so hard."

She stopped and feigned a glare. "Are you saying I'm hard work?"

He ran his warm, capable hands along her arms, and stared into her eyes. "Not at all. I'm saying I need to increase my fitness and calorie intake to keep up with you."

May laughed. Best, most unexpected response ever. And that accent…extra sexy. She could never get sick of it, would love hearing his voice direct her across town through her GPS. As well as regaling her with dirty talk in the bedroom.

The guy had charm down to a fine art. Quick-witted, funny, self-deprecating. Elite timing. Not a surprise, given his successful sniper background.

His super-sinful smile reached right up to his enticing cocoa eyes and he slid his hand around hers. "Come on…before I fade away."

May couldn't stop grinning even if she tried. He did that. She'd never felt so happy, so carefree. And yet, she couldn't shake that uncertain niggle at the back of her mind. She couldn't stop worrying about falling for a man who might be a chameleon. A man who could break her heart.

Westley whipped the swipe card out of his pocket and broke away from her as they approached the front entrance. She started talking and he shoved a finger to her lips. She froze, a surprised frown on her face, and he silently gestured with his head toward the door.

Ajar.

Shit.

They had definitely closed it when they'd departed. Someone had been in their cabin. And had left in a hurry.

Not housekeeping staff. They always locked up afterward. Their job was on the line otherwise, particularly if any items went missing.

Or was the intruder still inside? Had they ransacked the place trying to find incriminating information on them, planted a bug, a bomb? Tried to set them up?

She sucked in a breath and attempted to remain calm. Difficult to do with her mind racing and her heart hammering.

May wound her arms around Westley's neck and kissed her way up to his ear. "What do we do?"

He swung her around and pressed her against the outside wall, nudging his knee between her legs, his breath hot against her skin. "I'm going to kiss you hard, X-rated, a show for anyone watching. And because I bloody love your mouth."

Westley did what he'd promised, making her dizzy with lust. She thrust against his thigh in a fast, furious rhythm, chasing an orgasm. Not only did she want to play into his plan, but also he'd driven her right to the brink.

He groaned. "The second you come, I'm going to make sure you're grounded before I move inside." Oh, how she loved it when he moved inside...but he hadn't meant it *that* way. *Unfortunately.*

He kissed her temple, grabbing her hips and grinding her clit against his leg. "Then you're going to wait out here while I do a quick internal sweep of the cabin."

"But—"

"Think of an excuse. Drop an earring. Start searching for it. Something. Got it?"

"Yes!" She cried out, her climax hitting right in line with her answer. The perfect timing. Like meeting him. Like being paired together. Out of her control but in the best way.

Whether they could pursue something meaningful, whether he wanted to sustain a relationship outside of this contrived situation, she tried to have no expectations. But if they did or didn't, she couldn't deny they made a great team.

Her eyes flickered open to find his staring into hers with pure desire. Maybe not so pure, given the I-want-to-sink-into-you glaze in his potent gaze.

Westley kissed her forehead, the tip of her nose, then the delicious spot behind her earlobe. "You are so bloody hot." He breathed out a warm, heavy breath. "I'm going to go in now. Check everything. Give me ten minutes."

"Yes. Be careful," she whisper-breathed both in agreement and in response to his delightful nibbles along her sensitive skin.

He broke away, his focus intent, determined, almost possessive. Then he swallowed, focused on the unlatched door and pushed it open.

May tried to catch her breath, ground herself in some sort of new healthy reality. Because, even if Westley was pretending, she couldn't go back to how she'd lived. He'd changed her, right down to her DNA.

Made her realize that past boyfriends had lacked any future significance. Explained why she'd never had any interest in getting serious with anyone.

She had put up with so much, given guys so many chances, thinking that's what it took, when really, she'd grappled with low self-confidence. Let them disrespect her, and her actions had disrespected herself.

Never again.

All these changes, this love affair with Westley, working so closely with him had highlighted her awareness. Highlighted that, going forward, she needed to have a fresh new approach, to do things differently. To feel appreciation and affection, possibly even love.

As discussed, she reached up and subtly caressed her earlobe, covertly removing the earring. Safely palmed in her hand, she forced a frown, and dropped her gaze to the ground.

She swept her stare across the path and meticulously manicured grass—as smooth and even as a golfing green—as though searching. Step by slow step she moved forward, scanning from left to right, and right to left, retracing the trail they'd taken.

Counting almost every second of retracing the track and close surroundings, she started to struggle with the charade when Westley's refined voice rang out, "May? Sweetie?"

She shot up and turned. The gorgeous man filled the doorway, his arms braced on either side, his dark hair disheveled, his eyes penetrating.

"Found it?"

"Not yet." And then it clicked. What a great tactic. If he didn't play chess, he should. His strategic mind and planning were more than ten steps ahead of her.

"Keep looking. And I'll do the same inside. Between us, I'm sure we will." Code for *give me some more time. My preliminary search yielded no alarming breaches but that doesn't mean no bugs were planted.*

She gave him a half-smile and nodded. Pretending for a little longer to guarantee their safety. A no-brainer. She'd do her bit. Part of her hoped he'd find something that would reinforce they'd gotten close to the truth, and part of her wished he wouldn't.

A violation of their private space meant they had to be on guard every single second. And the other guests, too. Most likely all their villas had been wiretapped. But unlike her and Westley, they didn't have the same level of knowledge, the same level of worry.

The intensity of the investigation already ate away at every ounce of energy. Hypervigilance would only further deplete their well-worn stores. Except she had to push through. *They* had to. The slightest lapse in judgment could mean their undoing, could mean the loss of someone else's life.

Although sex helped with boosting endorphins, it provided a temporary reprieve. Although positive, it devoured their restricted physical resources.

Instead of getting frustrated, irritated, anxious, she focused on her one simple task, until Westley's voice, once again, broke into her mindfulness.

"Sweetie, any luck?"

"No, you?"

"I'm not surprised."

"What?"

"I found it inside."

"Really? Oh. Great!" Except it wasn't. Not if he'd discovered what she thought he had. However, she had to play the relieved-wife card.

Squishing the earring into her palm, she stepped into the front foyer and shut the door. May threw herself into his arms, gave him a passionate kiss and pulled back, revealing the earring.

"Nice work," he whispered.

"I thought so." She kept her voice super soft. "And what did you find?"

He nibbled along her neck. "Evidence of tampering. I disabled three bugs. We need to be extra careful."

Oh God. Was Marcus onto them? "We do. Maybe one of us needs to stay here at all times?"

"That's what I'd recommend, but it may raise suspicion. We need to behave *normally.* As normally as we can...for a highly sexed newlywed couple." He squished her against his lean, hard body. "We should be fine as long as we know what to look for, are careful about our conversation, and disable any obvious threats."

"Any threats, obvious or not."

"Indeed."

The more they got pulled into the intricacies of the case, the simmering, underlying current of drama, the more she needed a detailed list to keep on top of all the ever-changing moving parts. "So if the person who planted the bug doesn't get any info?"

"They could assess the transmission or device as faulty."

"Not that they'll ask us directly but, if they start fishing around, I'm assuming we play dumb?"

"You assume correctly. If they don't receive any intel, what can they say? They have to suck it up or else give themselves away. They've made their bed, and have to lay in the consequences."

"And what about the other guests? I'm assuming it would look too suspect if none of the bugs worked."

He huffed out a frustrated breath. "I would prefer to disable each and every one of them, but you're right. It might look questionable if all of the bugs are ineffective."

Instinct had her winding her arms around him in an attempt to absorb his strength. It didn't work as well as she'd hoped. She still couldn't help but worry about the outcome.

If she or Westley didn't get the required info soon, what would Marcus do? Progress his plan out of ignorance? Out of desperation? Or had he cottoned on to their covert attempts at interception and devised an alternative strategy? If he'd spotted their deception, how long could she and Westley remain safe? How long could anyone else?

"Are you all right?" Westley whispered, his hot breath scorching a path from her ear to her neck.

"No. Not even close. But I trust you. I trust our skills to reduce the risk of harm to us and others. I trust and believe in what we're doing."

"I do too."

She waited for Westley to say something else, add an intimate endearment reinforcing she meant more to him than just a workmate. But he didn't. Her emotions begged her to wallow in disappointment, but instead her brain took over and she reverted to what they needed to do to define and strengthen their strategy. What would assist in keeping them, and the others, alive. "So now what?"

"We discuss the finer points of our plan in great depth and enjoy each other thoroughly." His espresso eyes and self-assured manner, energized her dwindling reserves.

"We need to work our way around to each and every proposed investor. Focus on the ones we have the least amount of information on first. Determine their motives for attending, tap into their deeper, underlying agendas, assess if they're at risk of disappearing."

"I agree. Have you fed back to Alex?"

Chapter Sixteen

"Not yet."

Oh. May had assumed he'd be right on that. She'd had full belief in him, but should she? Had she overestimated his abilities? Their short time together meant she hadn't experienced enough of him to determine whether he consistently backed up his words with actions.

"Have you?" He didn't say it with concern or judgment. His easy tone suggested he trusted her to converse with their boss, with or without his consent.

"No." How could she expect something of him that she hadn't done herself?

He didn't look phased in the least. Her shoulders dropped—she hadn't even realized they'd been so raised.

When it came down to it, most people worked in self-preservation mode. She'd only experienced how Westley behaved in her presence. A very small indicator of his true character.

Outside of that, she had no idea. As far as she knew, he could have perfected his Mr. Charming routine to the point that he could camouflage any lies, making them almost impossible to detect.

And he might think the same about her.

What influenced his decision-making? Did he need people to like and approve of him? Believe in whatever story he spun, believe in his hype? Did he feel driven to prove himself, his skills and masculinity? Did he get pussy-struck? Require regular female attention? Require a regular fuck? Did any or several or all of those inform his choices?

She fucking hoped not. May had already invested too much interest in him and his apparent abilities. And she knew hers. If he fell short now... She couldn't go there, couldn't go down that line of thinking or she'd fail to retain the required focus. Which could have devastating consequences.

May needed a man who shared her vision of positive growth and not stagnation. She needed a man who wasn't full of shit, she needed the opposite of a stereotypical, self-serving charmer. A guy who wouldn't fence-sit out of fear. Although she understood the temptation.

"Let's pull a summary together right now. Before we do anything else...no matter how much I want to." The sly smile on his face reignited her desire to jump the man.

But somehow, someway, reality kicked in and she held off. She admired her sudden strict adherence to discipline. Something she usually didn't consider her forte...in her personal life.

She went to move and he grasped her hand, his stare penetrating her eyes. "Just so you know, I don't like to bother Alex until I've vetted the info I've obtained. Checked and double-checked it, making sure it has worth. Value. Between us, we can do that. Then once we've reported back, he can secure the required resources and send us some additional supports. Because I'd say we're going to need them."

Oh. It was as though he'd read her apprehension. She'd assumed only Marcus, and possibly Rei, were involved. But after Westley's assessment, who really knew? Marcus could have recruited a number of people to his cause.

She had to keep an open mind, however, from what she'd witnessed, she doubted any of those on the island were caught up in Marcus' scheme. Other than considering what he put forward as an investment opportunity.

None of the others had any connections to existing criminal organizations, and not one guest had shown any links to questionable internet searches. However, elite operatives excelled at keeping themselves and their movements hidden.

Without knowing exactly who was involved, they had no idea what they'd do. And depending on the leverage Marcus had over them, they had no way of knowing what lengths anyone would go to. What they were sure of was that someone had broken into their cabin...but to do what exactly?

Spy on them, definitely. Make sure they were who they said they were. Marcus came across as a totally paranoid fucker, so probably doubted their cover story. Or had he planted bugs in each cabin to hear his guests' honest opinions on whether they'd commit to investing in his proposal? And what, if anything, held them back?

Marcus could afford to pay for people's patronage, but he couldn't afford negative press, a conviction, jail time.

How much was he willing to protect his lifestyle, his funds? Had he offered select recruits a fee, a lifetime guarantee? And if they didn't uphold the terms, then what? Did he seek retribution?

So much to think about, so many complexities to consider. This whole case had them diving down a rabbit hole from the start. And the twists and turns kept coming, and coming, and coming. But it was important not to become paranoid.

Marcus showed clear signs of schmoozing to deflect from his staunch self-preservation, self-enhancement mode. Rei...he remained an unknown. She and Westley had yet to discover much about the guy other than what messages he and others had posted on social media, and that Marcus considered him a business associate, and lifelong friend. Far from an endorsement.

"Right." But did Alex have enough justification to send over back-up? Not yet. Maybe soon, depending on what they discovered.

Did he have enough staff to provide the required support? And even if he could spare some agents, would they arrive in time? Nothing either of them knew for sure. Alex probably didn't either. "How about you grab the laptop and do a deeper dive into everything Rei and Marcus, while I make us some lunch?"

"A bacon and egg roll would go down a treat." His impish smile had tingles converging in the epicenter of her core. Bacon and eggs and bread—so British. Well, the abridged version of a traditional cooked breakfast or, in their case, brunch.

"I'll get started on it." But she didn't move.

"While you're cooking, I'll do another cursory glance, but I'm pretty sure we've exhausted all available online avenues. No obvious red flags there. Marcus has well and truly concealed his electronic tracks.

"From what I can see, his website looks clean, upfront, and professional. He's more than covered his bases." He held her face between his big warm hands. "I'm certain there are more subversive dark-web decisions being made but under what names?"

Good point. Neither of them had any possible leads. It appeared that Marcus had gotten away with a hell of a lot of deceitful shit for a long time, proving he not only knew but also had mastered the drill.

"The plan hasn't changed. We need to speak to everyone and keep our ears pricked for anything odd, listen for anything out of place, anything suspect. Anything that could lead us to where we need to go."

Because currently they had no fucking clue. They suspected Marcus and possibly his mate, but instinct didn't equal arrest, didn't equal conviction. Only admissible evidence would pave the way for the perpetrators to be found guilty. Not hope. Not a gut feeling. Not speculation or assumption.

She wholeheartedly agreed with Westley's take. His thinking, his strategy, made perfect sense. People didn't realize how easily they gave themselves or their intentions away with something as simple as word choice and body language.

It was so much harder to hide true intentions when in person. The slightest tone change, or body movement, could give insight into someone else's real agenda. "I'll keep my eyes and ears and Spidey senses on full alert."

"Good girl."

His smooth, sexy English accent never got old. Arresting, velvety, core-clenching. It repeated over and over in her mind. And although she considered herself a feminist, when it came to sex, she got off on her partner taking charge. It allowed her to relinquish control, which bizarrely gave her a sense of peace and emotional freedom.

A sequence of sublime shivers rolled over her body. She'd never been called *good girl* before and she liked it. A lot. Coming from him, it didn't sound patronizing, arrogant, condescending. Not in this instance. *Good girl* sounded like high praise.

He'd managed to infuse each syllable with potent, masculine energy so that those two simple words slipped seamlessly into her stimulated senses.

Their eyes locked, subliminal hot-as-fuck chemistry flowing between them. Who needed verbal communication when body language said so damn much? So much more. Every little conscious and subconscious message on display.

"I'd better get started on brunch," she said — before she jumped him, and they spent the rest of the afternoon devouring each other. Delicious idea, but super short-lived. Avoiding the challenges of reality and indulging in pleasure, wouldn't help them successfully complete the case.

Unable to erase images of Westley taking her to climax, multiple times, she savored the memories, while trying not to burn the bacon or the bread. And attempted to ensure the egg yolks remained runny, to their liking, yet the whites solid. The day before, she'd successfully cooked pancakes with lemon and sugar, but could she meet his fry-up requirements?

Westley pressed his front to her back, the heat of his body permeating her clothes, her skin. "Mmm…yum. The bacon and eggs too." His sexy-as-fuck voice penetrated her ear.

Fuck eating. Fuck Westley instead. But if she fell victim to that mentality often enough, she'd die of starvation. The man was addictive. Irresistible. Scrambled every last speck of her senses. So she needed to be aware, mindful, resolute.

Giving in to his allure each and every time would be to her detriment, to their detriment. First and absolutely foremost, they needed to stay energized, hydrated, and not surrender to momentary baser needs.

Or else they'd be caught way off guard. Might not even make it back to mainland Australia. Might disappear, along with several others caught up in Marcus' tangled web of deception. The guy's M.O., his suspected specialty.

But they still had to prove it.

So far, it had all come down to hearsay. Circumstantial evidence. No one had any facts. They had nothing to directly link Marcus to the disappearances outside of his wife's concerns. And his connection with those who had never returned home, had virtually vanished.

May reluctantly slapped Westley's groping hand aside. "We need to eat. We need sustenance."

"We certainly do." Westley's voice oozed with sensuality, every syllable striking the perfect note in her core.

She wanted to sink into his embrace, melt into his strong, secure arms... The temptation beyond real. Overwhelming.

No.

As amazing as a quick fuck on the kitchen bench would be, they could devour each other later. Take their time. Enjoy every single sensual moment. Once they'd sought out more substantiated information and fed it back to Solve Security, once they were safer. Alone without interruption. She whirled to face him, with a stern, we-have-no-time-to-play-right-now stare.

Westley put his hands up in capitulation, but couldn't hide his I-know-what-we-both-really-want smile. And that added to her arousal. Kind of like a long-game edging session, which meant their orgasms later on would be epic.

He nudged her toward the table, carried over their plates, and joined her. "Thanks for this."

Did he mean the food, her work, or the sex? Maybe all three. Hopefully her personality factored in there somewhere as well. "It's a pleasure. I enjoy cooking."

Westley swallowed a large mouthful of his roll. "And I enjoy eating," he said, and licked the remnants of dripping egg yolk off his lower lip.

She squirmed in her seat, cognizant she'd have to hold out for a while before they could taste each other again.

Focus. She snapped her gaze to her meal and dug in, savoring the multilayered flavors. They needed nutrition, energy, in order to think as clearly as possible. They needed it to help them crack the case wide open.

They needed to stop the maniac, and his checkered history of dodgy dealings, and save lives. Including their own.

"When we're done, let's head over to the main house for a drink in the cocktail lounge, and see if you can cause a distraction so I can sneak into Marcus' office unnoticed. And then, if I can, I'll also check out his cabin."

"What sort of distraction? You need a decent amount of time to factor in both."

"I do. So we need to think of something Marcus and Rei can't resist…"

They both went quiet, their focuses shifting internally.

An awesome idea sprouted in her brain. "I know." She swung her gaze to meet his inquisitive eyes. "I can speak to them about adding more personal funds into the investment, but reinforce I'm keeping it from you as a surprise."

"A surprise?"

She shifted her plate aside and propped her forearms on the table, leaning in closer to him. "As in, I anticipate it doing so well that you'll be rapt once I tell you what I've done, once I give you the good news that we've made even more money."

A wicked smile spread onto Westley's lips. "I like it. However, they may want to discuss that sort of business proposition in Marcus' office."

"They may or may not. Depending on my attitude. If I'm cool with it, maybe they'll be happy to discuss it openly. It's worth a try. From Marcus' point of view, it might encourage others to invest more too."

He tapped the pads of his long, pleasure-giving fingers against his lips. "So what's your strategy if they suggest continuing the conversation in private?"

"I'll give them reasons why that's not possible. I'll say I can't go to our cabin in case you return during our chat, and if they're adamant about meeting in Marcus' office, I'll schedule another time. If I have to, I'll feign some previous engagement. A facial or some shit. Then while I discuss more details with him, you can search and bug his office and possibly his villa…if you haven't already."

"You've got everything covered."

She glanced down at her clothes. "Unfortunately."

His husky chuckle had her struggling to sit still.

She fixed her gaze on his intense eyes. "I have tried to think of every possible angle so I can confidently cut them off if they try to railroad me."

His grin grew. "I wouldn't expect any less."

"Any less than what?"

"Your best. At anything and everything you do."

Oh. A massive positive. A massive compliment. But it didn't mean long-term affection, it didn't mean a long-term romance, a sustainable personal, or even work-related, relationship. They might make it back in one piece physically, psychologically, spiritually, but not necessarily emotionally.

"Thank you. You do all right too."

He threw his head back and laughed. "Touché. I knew I liked you from the very first second we spoke."

Smart man, focusing on their discussion rather than her appearance. Though, she valued his appreciation of that too.

They finished brunch, washed up—with a shit-ton of kiss and cuddle breaks—and managed to pull themselves away long enough to get ready without a much-desired fuck stop. Then, hand in hand, they headed to the main, communal house.

On a beeline for the bar, she and Westley scanned the area for any premature interception.

Nothing.

No Marcus, no Rei. Not even a sighting of the other investors.

They parked themselves on a couple of bar stools in the sumptuous lush-red cocktail lounge, and Westley ordered a pitcher of margaritas. A fantastic choice. Almost as though he knew her better than she knew herself. Hot days lent themselves to jugs of cool cocktails.

When the lemon-lime concoction arrived, she sat back and waited for Westley to pour her a glass. She trusted him to mete out the drinks or she might get tipsy without realizing, and be unable to effectively enact their discussed plan.

A no-go scenario. May refused to let him down, let Solve Security down, let herself down.

He raised his full glass to hers, his eyes speaking words he couldn't say. Not in public, anyway. *Any concerns? How are you feeling? Are you ready?* "Cheers."

May clinked her crystal goblet to his with a bit too much gusto. A ripple of margarita rolled over the side, splashing away some of the salt around the rim, and ran down the stem. Tracing the errant overflow with her tongue, she glanced up and met his fiery gaze.

Flames practically danced in the man's eyes. He looked wild, almost primitive, like he wanted to snatch her out of her seat, thrust her against the bar, and fuck her right there. And didn't that create inextinguishable sparks that smoldered in her core.

Ridiculously tempting, but no. No on so many levels. Levels that superseded emotional compulsion.

With supreme steadiness, she raised her glass to her lips, the tang of salt slamming into her tastebuds. And she loved it, loved a challenge. Placing her unfinished cocktail on the bar, she stared Westley in the eye with the utmost assurance, as if to say, *don't-worry, all-good, I've-got-it-under-control.*

And she did, mostly.

Her partner polished off the rest of his drink in three, well-spaced gulps. "Sweetie, I need to get a few things done this afternoon. You all right to entertain yourself for a while?"

All sorts of sordid images flooded her head. May had already touched herself for him once but, in this instance, he didn't mean masturbation. Sadly. They'd both gotten off on her self-pleasure, big time.

Right now, he wanted to give her one last out. Westley wanted to ensure she gave him clear endorsement to do what they'd discussed, workwise. For him to slip into Marcus' private domain, plant bugs, and — time permitting — search for proof of his guilt. And anyone else who may be connected to the whole murderous, self-indulgent scam.

"Of course, honey," she said, with her sexiest smile. May leaned in and pressed a deep, passionate, make-sure-you-come-back-to-me kiss on his irresistible lips.

When they finally broke away, he breathed hard, his stare penetrating, his pupils turning his coffee-colored eyes as black as a freshly poured espresso. Hot, dark, enticing. "I should go." But he didn't move. He gave her another are-you-sure glance.

She wound her arms around his neck and nuzzled in right near his ear. "I'm good. If I have any issues or concerns, I'll text you or find whatever way I can to get you the hell out of there."

May kissed his temple, then his lips, and relinquished her hold. She lifted her glass in a sort of well-wishing toast. "Look forward to seeing you later."

Westley sent her the sweetest, sexiest smile, his eyes crinkling at the corners with true affection, making her almost break down into tears. Tears of pure joy, pure love and indescribable, heart-tugging emotion.

Even if things didn't work out between them on the romantic front, she couldn't bare if he got hurt, wounded, killed. She swallowed a large gulp of her drink to stave off any premature, uncalled-for crying. No need to worry…yet.

Separation put them at increased risk but it didn't warrant an overly anxious response. If she were able to do her part and keep Marcus and Rei occupied, there shouldn't be a problem.

Once Westley assessed what was needed to access the guy's office, he could slip in and out without notice. Fingers crossed. Luckily, he showed more consistent longevity when it came to sex. In fact, he'd kept going and going until she shattered. His adaptability to each environment made him highly skillful, highly respected, highly appreciated and in demand.

So how could she hold onto him? Definitely not by force. He'd retaliate against that, against relinquishing his freedom. He needed to want her exclusively. Recognize she fit into his life picture. That being with her wouldn't compromise his career…or hers. That being without her would impact negatively across the board.

Westley spoke to the bartender, within hearing range, to essentially let her know he'd set up a tab, and left. She could order more drinks for their party, or any others who stopped to chat, without stressing about payment.

Any costs, she imagined, would be rung up as job expenses. Within reason. Not that either of them had taken advantage. They'd been incredibly careful and considerate of what they spent, of the limited agency budget, of not taking the piss.

However, they still needed to get the job done and that incorporated some latitude, some adaptability. Solve Security had sent them to the island posing as a wealthy married couple, so they had to spend accordingly. If they skimped, it'd draw unnecessary attention and scrutiny.

May gestured for the young, handsome bartender to come over. "Could you please give Marcus and Rei a call? I need to discuss something with them."

The guy had the customer-service smile down to a finer-than-fine art, his bright white teeth almost blinding. The overall effect encompassed a combination of interest, happy-to-help, and nothing's-a-problem. A three-pronged attempt to increase his chances of a lucrative tip, no doubt.

He picked up the pitcher and refilled her cocktail glass, then returned behind the bar, grabbed a mobile phone from beneath the counter and called.

"Marcus? It's Brad from the bar staff. May, an investment group member, asked me to contact you. Are you and Rei free to come and speak to her now?"

He squeezed the phone between his ear and shoulder and stacked dirty glasses and dishes in the dishwasher. "Uh-huh. Okay. I'll let her know." He finished loading the shelves, added a dishwashing tablet, and closed the door, then pressed a few buttons, and the machine whooshed to life.

Brad put the phone away, grabbed a sponge and wiped across the countertop. On the way over to her, he made eye contact and smiled. "They'll be here in a few minutes." In total barman mode, he kept going, clearing glasses, making chitchat with her, chatting to coworkers out the back, wiping up any spills. The ultimate hospitality professional.

Nerves twisted into a tight bundle in her stomach and unraveled when the two male suspects came into view. They'd taken the white marble stairs, instead of the lift, and headed into the bar, speaking softly. Probably solidifying their game plan.

Marcus zeroed in on her in seconds, his gaze latching onto her eyes and freezing her in place. Not that she planned to move until they'd spoken, but still… His presence, especially beside his best bud, essentially two against one, sent icicles of fear dripping down her spine.

However, she sat in a communal safe space, and Westley knew her whereabouts. They'd confirmed their game plan. So as long as she stayed put, no matter how frightened, she just had to focus on delaying the two suspects. Capture their attention for as long as absolutely possible. Give Westley the most uninterrupted time she could manage.

This supremely small window of opportunity might be their only chance to poke around. This might be the one and only occasion they had to find what they needed.

In less than a couple of days, they'd lose their access to a potential wealth of information. The current, hopefully attainable resources might not reveal all they required but they provided a start.

At the very least, they'd follow a probable line of inquiry that could help them devise a clearer plan of action. Like with anything, remaining stagnant prevented success. It kept people cocooned in their overconfident or fear-fueled bubble, their comfort zone.

Remaining static often ended in disaster. They required the complete opposite. Didn't matter how scary and unsettled the circumstances. They needed to stay open-minded, to adjust to the environment accordingly.

Not allow any navel-gazing, any inward focus on their limited beliefs. They had to go with where the leads led. And hope they didn't get fucked — in a bad way — in the interim.

Chapter Seventeen

"Thanks for coming so quickly." She forced a sweet smile.

"If only," Rei murmured to his mate.

Ick. Had he meant for her to hear his smart-ass remark? Had he carefully chosen his words and tone and volume in a broader strategic move to unnerve her?

Didn't matter. They could say whatever they liked. All she had to do was stick to the plan, keep them busy for as long as possible. Not let their lad-like behavior affect her mission. "I have something important to discuss with you."

They glanced at each other, their brows furrowed with obvious intrigue.

Marcus' eyes reconnected with her steadfast gaze. "And what would that be?"

She gestured to the stools lined up beside her like attentive soldiers ready for battle. "Let's discuss it over a drink or two."

Thankfully, they each took a seat without argument, without further delay, and requested their beverage of choice from the barman.

May sucked a large mouthful of margarita through the cocktail straw. A burst of liquid courage without impairing her judgment. She had to stop short of a buzz, no matter how tempting, or else risk over-loosening her tongue and not remembering specifics to relay to Westley later. A clear-headed approach was the name of this killer game.

Swiveling to face the maniacal male duo, she crossed her legs and leaned in, propping her forearm on the dark shiny bar top. She glanced around them, to make sure no one else had arrived, that no others were within earshot, including staff, and refocused on the men. "I want to surprise my husband."

They looked at her, their brows creased with confusion, but within a split-second Marcus' mouth morphed into a knowing leer, while Rei outright ogled her, as if to say we-can-suggest-a-few-X-rated-ways. Westley had checked for bugs in their cabin, but how about cameras? Maybe the two horrid men had watched them go at it?

Heat rushed up her face and she sucked down a little more of her refreshing margarita.

Marcus quickly schooled his facial expression to pompous rich businessman mode. "And what does that have to do with us?"

Meanwhile, Rei stayed silent, unable to stop undressing her with his eyes. Shit, maybe they *had* gotten their voyeuristic jollies viewing her and Westley fucking on every available surface in their villa.

With supreme difficulty, she stopped the avalanche of erotic images crashing into her brain. Her and

Westley on the couch, the kitchen bench, the stovetop, over the dining table, against the glass sliding door, on the bed, in the shower.

Oh God.

If all went to plan, she'd be screaming that later.

Several times.

Pretending she didn't notice Rei's sleazy gaze, she tried to send a subtle but clear vibe that said, I'm loyal and one-hundred percent dedicated to my husband.

"Well, he has a big birthday coming up next year and I couldn't decide what to get him. Then it came to me. A gift that keeps on giving." She forced her lips into a huge, innocent-yet-excited smile and paused for effect. "I have my own personal trust fund and couldn't think of what to buy a man who has everything. But now I know."

She pushed her unfinished margarita away and turned back to them. "I want to spend it on you." She shook her head and laughed. "I mean, your proposed project. If I add my separate funds on top of our combined pledge, then I can show Westley all the extra earnings I've made."

Marcus lifted his martini and stared into it, as though contemplating her suggestion. He picked out the skewered green olives, tugged them into his mouth with his teeth, chewed, then had a sip from his glass and swallowed.

"It's a great idea, and I encourage it, but we need to warn you that there are no guarantees that we'll make a significant profit that quickly. Sometimes it can take several years to receive the best benefits."

Rei raised his red wineglass right up to his nose, sniffed and had a swill of the blood red liquid. "There may be some initial, occasionally large, short-term gains, though this kind of venture is usually more of a slow-burn scenario, a long-term investment, something that grows over time."

She clapped her hands together with spirited self-congratulations, acting as ignorant and naïve and trusting as possible. Almost ditzy when it came to anything outside of her limited sphere of knowledge. Going by the few interactions she'd had with them so far, playing scatterbrained seemed the best strategy.

Her supposed lack of understanding could draw out their discussion. She'd have more questions they'd need to explain, giving Westley more opportunity to search and hopefully find incriminating notes and documents.

"See, the gift that keeps on giving. Just like I'd hoped." She plastered on the biggest, most enthusiastic smile she could muster. "Thanks for the disclaimer, but I understand the market has ups and downs and cycles, but like people say, you need to be in it, and have some patience, to win it."

Marcus glanced at Rei and they exchanged a smug, superior look, taking her I'm-a-bimbo bate, hook, line and super self-absorbed sinker. "Indeed. Almost our exact motto."

Rei tapped his glass to Marcus' martini.

No words required. If she hadn't been sure before, their behavior this afternoon practically reinforced their collusion. But it remained third-party information, a hunch, circumstantial. Either she or Westley or both of them needed to discover tangible evidence. Something that would stick in a court of law.

Currently, if Westley found something questionable, they couldn't use it without a warrant. So they needed to produce the required paperwork without Marcus' and Rei's knowledge. They needed to surprise them or else their key suspects could dispose of anything dubious.

However, if he made it into Marcus' inner sanctum, and found anything of use, he could take photos, possibly even collect data on a USB stick, for them to discuss in detail. Later. Hopefully he captured enough incriminating information to implicate them. Hopefully she'd given him enough time to find something.

The guys finished their drinks and shifted in their seats, suggesting their meeting had almost come to an end.

"So can I count on you to accept my additional cash and keep quiet?" She twisted her head to look around them, as though to ensure no one stood nearby and heard her proposition. Except the two predatory partners in crime.

May darted her eyes between them.

They remained silent. What did they have to think about? She'd offered them more money. Five seconds passed, six, seven, eight, nine...

"You can. But don't you still want to review the app first? And even if it meets your needs, we'll require your monetary confirmation in writing." Marcus pinned her with a no-margin-for-movement stare.

Oh shit. Yeah, she had to look determined to stick with her original proviso. "Let's call it a preliminary deal, then, until I review the app." She stuck out her hand.

Marcus shook it, his palm warm and sweaty and disgusting, followed by Rei, his cold, clammy grasp making her want to immediately hand sanitize.

Gross. She tried not to snatch her hand out of his slimy grip. "So when should I expect to receive a working version of the app?"

"I'll get it to you this evening."

"Great. So assuming I think it's viable, where should we meet to make my pledge official?" May smiled and, while they glanced at each other deciding on a suitable time and place, wiped her hand on her skirt. She couldn't wait to change.

Marcus met her eyes with a don't-fuck-with-me, discerning stare. "When can you get away from your husband without his notice?"

"Tomorrow. After breakfast. I'll stay behind at the table finishing my coffee, while he goes for his usual run."

"Great. Let's lock it in."

May forced her best so-grateful-and-excited smile, pretended to tap the meeting into her calendar but instead sent a quick *get out now* text to Westley, and left. Had her ninety-minute meeting given Westley enough time to do his thing? She'd soon find out.

She tried harder than hard to walk at a steady, relaxed pace back to the accommodation, when all she wanted to do was run and discuss where things were at with Westley.

Not just update him. She also wanted to hear what he'd been able to achieve.

After what felt like ages, she made it inside the cabin, slammed the door shut behind her and leaned against it. Out of breath, even though she had strolled the whole way.

Westley strode out from behind the kitchen bench and caressed her cheek. "What happened? They didn't touch you?" The they-better-not-have warning look in his eyes made her smile, feel more at ease. Westley had her back in so many ways.

She had to admit she enjoyed his extra protective side...when it came to relationships. "They were smarmy, but fine. They took the bait and promised to send me a preliminary version of the app to review tonight. Then I've agreed to meet them after breakfast tomorrow to discuss everything in more detail."

May scrutinized his unsettled stare. "What did you find?"

"A camera in the hallway leading to Marcus' man cave. I'm going to need to somehow disarm it, obscure it so I can get into his office unseen."

"How?"

"I don't know if it's wired, or wireless. So the quickest way to disrupt the thing without immediate notice is to cover the camera."

Of course it couldn't be as straightforward as she'd hoped. Of course the guy had to have cameras placed strategically around the place. "How are you going to do that?"

"I bought some black spray paint, a spray can extender, and a backpack."

Her heart rate shot up to fainting level. "What if you're caught?"

"I won't be. I'll thoroughly check the surroundings beforehand, cover my face and use the blind spots as best I can, before I act. Then if I can't get in, or don't find anything there, I'll try his villa...if I have enough time."

Westley turned his head and stared out of the large window, the clouds gathering, dark and looming over the rough, angry sea. A sign that it might rain on their upcoming parade. She hoped not. May hoped for a swift, effective resolution so that no one got hurt.

He clenched his jaw and twisted back, studying her eyes. "I don't like you having to schmooze with them again. I wish there was an easier way...but there isn't. I need time to get into his office at least."

"You do. I agree." She pressed a quick kiss to his lips. "They're meeting me in the public dining space so not much can happen there. And while I go through every possible specific, hopefully you can sneak in, crack Marcus' computer login and access something useful." Although not ideal, they had to make the most of the restricted options.

The burgeoning smile on his face suggested her response somewhat appeased him. Thank goodness. They couldn't do their job effectively otherwise. Worry and fear affected clear, rational thinking and impacted on attention and concentration. And they couldn't afford to miss a single sign, a single beat.

The afternoon cleared and they spent the rest of the day sunbathing and swimming in the ocean, dissolving some pent-up stress and enjoying each other's company. And not just for show. The more time in Westley's world, the more she admired and appreciated the man, and wanted him to remain a permanent fixture in her life.

Did he want the same? Or would this turn into a weird sort of work-holiday fling? Bets were off until they made it back to the mainland, back to reality. Something that worked in extreme circumstances couldn't always succeed in routine normality.

She'd been there, more than done that. Without the right fuel, lust had a way of petering out. And love? Well, that took a consistent source of energy. Or so she believed. Up until now she hadn't had the experience to confirm or deny.

However, without tender love and care, without patience and perseverance, she couldn't have kept cars and military vehicles operating, couldn't have retained a career as a successful, sought-after mechanic. She figured the idea had a translatable cross-over effect.

Bordering on sunburn, they traipsed back to the cabin, showered together, and decided to ditch dinner at the main house and focus on fine-tuning their plan for tomorrow. So they ate in their cabin, discussing specifics for their upcoming time-restricted mission, then indulged some more in each other.

As promised, Marcus sent a digi-sign non-disclosure agreement to prevent her stealing the idea and promoting it as hers, and once May had signed it, he gave her access to the app prototype later that evening. She and Westley studied it in bed, and she forwarded a copy to Solve Security to review, along with Marcus' strict terms and conditions. Hopefully their tech expert, Chris, would find something incriminating.

May and Westley made love twice, before slipping into an exhausted sleep. Expending some nervous energy helped heaps, or else they'd have been up all night. They needed a fresh, alert, clear-headed mindset, one ready for anything.

In the morning, Westley held her extra tight, staring into her eyes with indisputable passion, kissing her with reverence, driving slow and deep inside her until they climaxed together.

Still panting, he practically cling-wrapped her to him. "Be careful. Promise me."

She kissed the sweaty spot where his neck joined his shoulder. "I promise." And she did. To do her job well, and to not wind up injured or dead. To wind up with Westley. Permanently.

But she didn't want to freak him out. Neither of them had uttered the 'L' word — it was way too soon for that — so up until then, she didn't want to presume. The guy was a natural protector, so of course he wanted to look after her, and enjoy the benefits. Whether he wished for more, she couldn't be sure. Yet.

They showered and got ready, then as agreed, selected a range of food from the buffet of the main-house dining room.

As soon as Westley finished his apple and blackcurrant juice and plate stacked with bacon, sausages, poached eggs, mushrooms, avocado, spinach and tomatoes, he patted his mouth with his napkin, shoved it beneath the cutlery, and leaned into her ear. "Whatever you do, don't agree to move anywhere else without me present. Okay?"

She stared into his eyes. "I won't. I'll warn you the minute we tie up the meeting so be ready to run."

He brought her mouth to his, delving his tongue between her lips with a claiming kiss. She had no doubt his primal-caveman show rammed home the we're-hot-for-each-other message to anyone watching.

When they broke apart, her head swam with dizziness. In the best possible way. The man sucked out every ounce of oxygen, penetrated every one of her cells with his pleasurable, overwhelming presence.

He stroked his thumb over her cheekbone. "Meet you back at the cabin in a couple of hours?"

"Sounds good." Clever of him to signify the limit out loud for any eavesdropping ears. Plus it set up for her to commandeer the guys for at least sixty minutes, hopefully longer, to give Westley ample time to enter

Marcus' office undetected, hack into his computer and access any incriminating information.

He grabbed an apple from the fruit bowl and bit into it as he exited the room. She sipped her black coffee and played with her phone, ready to send Westley a message to let him know the moment Marcus and Rei appeared at the entryway.

"Hope you enjoyed your breakfast." Marcus' soft-yet-menacing voice scraped her eardrum.

May hit send and glanced up, both men towering over her table. With a forced smile, she gestured to Westley's vacated seat and Rei pulled over another chair. "I certainly did."

She looked around, as though checking no one was close enough to overhear. Fully playing the part. "The app looks extremely promising, so shall we get down to business?" she said, keeping her voice quiet, but loud enough for them to register.

* * * *

The moment the coast was well and truly clear, Westley shoved the hood of his black jacket over his head to obscure his face, then slipped back inside the main house and slunk along the hallway until he reached the corridor leading to Marcus' office. Glancing around him, he noticed no one. Not another worker, not a guard, not another investor party member.

Sliding a black mask into place to further reduce identification, he then extracted a telescopic extension pole and spray can from his backpack, and covered the camera with black paint. After waiting several seconds, without guards, or the man himself, intercepting, he shoved the mask, extension pole, and spray can back in his bag, and hid it beneath the closest staircase.

With thin black gloves on, using a quick-and-easy lock-picking method — a couple of Allen keys effectively placed — he jimmied open the door with no visible damage, and shut it behind him with the softest of clicks.

He snatched his phone out of the back pocket of his sweatpants and called Alex. "I'm in. If I can get Marcus' computer online, can you get Chris to crack the code?"

"How long have you got?"

"About forty-five minutes before I need to leave. Could be less."

"I'll get Chris hooked up remotely now."

"Thank you." Westley pressed the power button, and the computer screen came to life, a multitude of colors almost blinding him, like staring at a camera flash.

A deterrent? A security feature? Or just an extension of the guy's garish taste? He glanced at the time. Fifteen minutes had already passed since May sent him the all-clear message, which meant he had an even tighter deadline. "The computer is on. Is Chris in?"

"Not yet. She's almost there."

"Good, because time is bloody ticking." Westley paced, darting his eyes between his watch and the door. Anyone could walk in at any minute. If not Marcus or Rei, it could be the cleaner, or reception needing to give him a message. And he needed to have his plausible answer ready as to why he stood in the guy's office unaccompanied. He needed to sound convincing.

Bloody hell.

Normally he excelled at waiting...but it helped when he was hidden, on a rooftop or inside an apartment across the road. With a gun aimed to take a shot. Not when he wandered around a one-way in, one-way out office like a cornered sitting duck on speed. Not when *he* became the potential target.

"Any updates?" Westley thrummed his gloved fingers against the fancy desktop. The whole outfitted office, probably cost more than his entire home. Everything, from Marcus' furniture to his IT equipment to stationery, appeared high-end, elite, designer.

"Chris has connected and started a scan."

"For what?" He raked his hands through his hair and tried to stay calm. "I need her searching the files ASAP." Bloody hell. He had to exit the private space quickly and efficiently, before Marcus drew any concerning conclusions. Before Westley and May lost the guy's belief and confidence in their 'marriage'. Once that happened, they were fucked.

"I know." Alex spoke in a low, steady, trust-me tone. "But first she has to check for and disable any alarm devices, any triggers that could set off all kinds of notifications, and create devastating destruction."

Oh. Yeah. He should have realized that. Like he'd realized the importance of wearing gloves to prevent him leaving any fingerprints. Stress had a way of making a person narrow-minded, desperate to hurry, to cut corners to get the fastest result and ease their anxiety. However, like with CPR, the working area required thorough safety checks for danger before proceeding.

Westley tried to focus on calming breaths, the ones that had taught him patience, prevented him from too much PTSD. Except, he couldn't translate the skill to this very different environment.

Not yet. He needed more experience in this face-to-face field before he developed the required toughened nerves, the nerves to match his sniper career.

Come on. He scrubbed his clammy hands over his face. "Anything?"

"Not yet." Alex sounded way too patient, way too calm.

Westley wanted to keep talking, go hard at his boss, distract himself from the urgency and pressure of the situation, but he needed to remain as silent as possible. He needed to have his hearing on alert for any noise nearby. Worst case scenario, he had to implement the reasonable-sounding excuse he'd thought up earlier.

"Did Chris find anything suspect with the app?"

"No, unfortunately." Alex's disappointed voice rumbled down the line. "Going by her in-depth assessment, it looks sound. She didn't identify any scammer, hacker type software. Not anything she's aware of, anyway. But as we all know, new technology is coming out all the time."

Fuck. He'd really hoped she might see something that could implicate the prick of a man.

Westley glanced at his phone. Still no warning text from May. A good thing. Hopefully she could draw out her conversation with the suspected partners in crime past an hour, without it sounding contrived. And fingers fucking crossed, no network delay impacted on him receiving her text in a timely manner.

In the meantime, with his heart pounding against his sternum, he scribbled out a note, fitting with his preplanned excuse, asking Marcus to meet up to discuss solidifying their investment pledge. And planted a couple of listening devices — one inside the smoke alarm and one in his phone charger.

The whole operation had *precarious* written all over it. But, working in the security field, it formed part of the everyday deal. It came with the risky territory.

"Got it. Type in SUCRAMInvest." Chris' cool, calm, collected voice broke into his anxious thoughts.

"His first name spelled backwards?" Couldn't be right. Way too simple, way too easy to crack.

"Yeah. Obviously not the sharpest tool in the showy shed." Alex never failed to come up with some cracking comments.

"Far from it. Arrogance has a way of dumbing people down, of shredding their safety net." The words spewed out before he could stop them, concern and stress the catalyst behind his bouts of severe verbal diarrhea.

"Are you in?" Alex asked, jolting Westley back to the urgent task.

"Wait," Chris' crisp, clear voice shot down the line, stopping Westley right in time. "He has multi-factor authentication. Have you got an authenticator app on your phone?"

Phew. "I do."

Alex and Chris blew out a collective relieved breath.

"Open it, and when I tell you, type in the numbers on your screen."

"Okay."

Five seconds.

Ten.

Fuck me.

Twenty.

How much longer? Westley's leg started shaking.

"Now."

He entered the sequence of digits and…success.

Yes! "I'm in."

Within seconds the screen loaded up, and he searched through emails and folders, precious time racing away.

Nothing suspicious in Marcus' email app. Nothing stuck out in his File Explorer page or on the cloud. Maybe he'd saved info onto a transportable hard drive or USB stick. *Fuck.*

Westley shoved his hands through his hair. Still, anyone with such a lazy password had to have slipped up somewhere.

"Anything?" Alex asked. "Can you share the screen?"

"Not sure how."

"There's a way to do it, but given the short timeframe, it's not worth it. Focus on what you can find." Chris reinforced his need to use his speed-reading skills.

Westley's eyes practically blurred from scanning page-upon page of data. "Nothing."

"Have you checked his deleted file history?" Chris' suggestion had him immediately clicking into the folder. Why hadn't he thought of that? That's why she was the quick-thinking tech expert and him the field agent.

Westley navigated to it and...*whoa!* He struck evidentiary gold. Chris was a bloody legend. Documents included guest lists and confirmed that the missing people had all attended the various 'investor parties', disappearing soon afterward.

He sifted through the notes, skimming as quickly as possible, and determined that anyone trying to blackmail or compete with Marcus, or tried to steal his ideas, soon vanished. And even more disturbing, correspondence between Marcus and Rei demonstrated they'd turned it into a sick game.

Snatching a clean USB device from his pocket, Westley inserted it into the relevant computer port and started saving the incriminating files.

Within moments, his phone buzzed.

He glanced at the screen—a message from May letting him know he needed to get out. Now.

Shit.

One more minute and he'd have downloaded all he needed.

He kept an eye on the door, and one on the download time.

Five

Four

Three

Two

One.

Westley ejected the USB, shoved it back in his pants pocket and closed down Marcus' computer. He stood, shoved his gloves in the front pouch of his hoodie, and hurried to exit the office. Before he could even grab the handle, the door swung open.

Chapter Eighteen

"Westley? What are you doing here?" Marcus raised a scrutinizing, suspicious eyebrow.

Rei stood close behind with an equally accusatory stare.

"I finished my run and came to see you about the investment. I knocked, no one answered, but the door was unlocked so I left a note. It's beside your computer."

Marcus scowled and strode over to his desk, most likely to double-check Westley hadn't spun him a shitload of crap. He picked up the Post-it note and all the tension in his face dissolved.

Westley stood in the doorway and fixed a demure smile on his face. "I'll be in touch."

Rei muscled past, and shut the door in Westley's retreating back.

* * * *

The moment Westley entered the cabin, May rushed over to him, wrapping her man in a tight, relieved hug. "You okay?"

"For now." He pressed his palm against her lower back and stroked her hair with his other hand.

She pulled away and searched his eyes. "What do you mean?"

Westley leaned in until his mouth practically caressed her ear. "I don't know what security measures Marcus has in place. He may have hidden devices I couldn't detect. He could have installed cameras that click into action any time he leaves the office and someone enters unannounced. Or anyone else tries to access his computer."

Really? She was so out of the loop. Was this how things had progressed? She felt her forehead crinkle with disbelief. "So he could have set up some state-of-the-art, fandangled, supposedly infallible system within the last twenty-four hours?"

"Or maybe beforehand. Who knows if he saw me hovering, checking things out yesterday and is just biding his time? Either way, with the right contacts, and the required amount of money, he could make almost anything happen."

Oh. Shit. That made it very real, and terrifying.

He stroked the soothing, warm pads of his thumbs over her cheeks. "Don't stress. At this stage, we're one, maybe two steps ahead of him. So we need to use that to our advantage. For as long as it lasts. Milk it for all it's worth because, like with anything, circumstances can change at any time."

Westley's phone buzzed as if on cue. "Hang on."

May hated it when people prioritized their phone above people, but in this instance, it might mean something significant…

He retrieved his mobile out of his pocket and swiped. "Marcus. Let's see what he has to say. And to who."

Westley turned up the volume. "We're all set up." Marcus sounded clear and confident through the phone bug software.

"You sure no one knows?" Rei's distinctive voice trembled down the line.

"How could they?"

"I don't know. Just a gut feeling."

Stressed silence ticked by…

"That Westley guy puts me on edge. There's something…off about him." Rei said it with the utmost certainty, conviction. Fear.

"He's British. Formal. Hoity-toity. Of course he's going to sound different, out of place, like he recognizes more than he does. But he knows shit, he's an amateur sleuth at best. Westley is no secret agent, he's no James Bond."

They both laughed.

May's hackles rose, offended on Westley's behalf, prepared to set the two dicks straight. How dare they think him incapable. She went to speak, act, uphold her man's honor, but he put a finger to her lips in a *shhh* motion.

She clamped her teeth together and nodded.

"So we're still on for tonight?" Rei asked.

"We are. First to the marina is the winner."

Winner? These two were psychopaths to the max. Who played a game with people's lives?

"Done deal."

As in, they had already selected a victim or two, and had determined a designated finish line.

The conversation went dead.

Fuck. With only her and Westley in place, hands-on working the job, how could they keep the remaining guests safe? They couldn't watch all of them. They needed Solve Security back up, but if they waited for other agents to arrive it'd most likely be too late.

May swore a string of obscenities beneath her breath. "We still don't know who's the target."

"So far almost everyone we've spoken to is on the list of possibles." Westley plugged his phone in to the closest power point to charge. "Let's talk to Franc and Odette and see if we can rule them out. With only two of us, the fewer people we need to monitor the better."

"Makes total sense."

"We need to divvy this up as safely and sensibly as possible. How about you try and speak to them, and I'll attempt to keep an eye on the others. From a distance."

"Okay. I'll see what I can find out."

She pressed an all-too-brief kiss to his lips and took off to the couple's cabin close by.

May knocked on the door.

Nothing.

She tried again, and waited.

No response.

They could have gone for a walk or jumped on the island circuit bus.

A moan penetrated the door.

Shit. Had Marcus or Rei broken in and attacked them?

She raced around to the back entrance and... *Oh!* A woman's palms pressed up against the back window, the glass door shaking. Apparently, Franc and Odette were going at it good and hard. And by the sounds and looks of it, they both loved every second. As she had with Westley.

May averted her eyes and retreated. Not the best time to try to gain their cooperation. She'd give them a good thirty minutes and come back. See if they were up for a little chat.

In the meantime, she wandered by the rest of the cabins lining the street, Edgar and Billie's door wide open. With slow, cautious steps, she snuck up to the entryway and peered inside.

Empty.

Water gushed, and a vacuum cleaner roared to life.

Cleaners?

She knocked, and waited. "Excuse me?"

No answer.

No sign of Edgar and Billie. Had they left of their own volition or... Had the housekeeping staff been instructed to clean the room ready for the next occupant? And what sort of mess had the workers found?

May entered and scanned the space. No stand-out stains or damage. Not in the main living area, anyway. "Hello?"

The vacuum cleaner stopped, and two women came running out of the bedroom. They both studied her without speaking.

"Hi, I'm trying to find my friends. Have they left?"

The younger lady made eye contact. "*Si.* Ah...yes."

Left to go where exactly? The bottom of the ocean? A lime-filled barrel? The hairs on the back of her neck rose to attention. Why hadn't they said anything? Had they made it safely home, escaped once they realized they wouldn't follow through with the investment, or had May jumped to unfounded conclusions? "When?"

The older woman met May's gaze. "*Non lo so*. I, *come si dice*...I don't know."

Damn. She needed to leave and report to Alex. Have him and the team investigate whether the two of them had in fact safely left the island and made it back home.

"Thanks for your time." May exited the cabin, thoughts fighting for attention in her head. Had they gone voluntarily? Did Marcus and Rei know? Or had they intercepted them before the couple could escape? Maybe she and Westley had been too late?

While pondering all the possible outcomes, she grabbed a take-away mocha from the main house bar, then walked to Franc and Odette's place, hoping to find them ready to talk.

She discarded her empty paper cup in the bin along the main road, and continued onto their front path. Once again, she knocked on their door and waited.

In seconds, footfalls, some heavy, some light, padded on the floor. A good, positive sign, a great sign.

The door swung open, and Franc stood in an upmarket black tracksuit, his cognac eyes staring as though trying to work out her agenda. And what that might mean to him and his partner. "How can I help you?" His clipped, heavily accented words and back-off tone shouted *do-not-disturb*.

Under any other circumstances she'd have abided by the vibe and left them alone, but she couldn't, knowing they might be the next targets. She had to do her due diligence.

May beamed her most brilliant, rapport-building smile. "Do you have a moment? I haven't had a chance to properly introduce myself or get to know either of you, and the weekend is almost at an end."

He stayed silent so she continued. "My husband reinforced that this event is a great networking opportunity, somewhere to make relevant, valuable connections, so I didn't want to pass it up."

Franc studied her eyes. "Your husband is a wise man." He waved her inside and gestured to a lounge chair. "Sit."

Attempting to remain relaxed, she did as requested, running through how best to interrogate them in the most subtle way possible.

"Coffee, tea, water?"

"A coffee would be lovely, thank you." Thank goodness for the excellent facilities—a pod coffee maker in each room—because she couldn't do instant.

He placed a pod in the machine and glanced at her with a quirked eyebrow. "Sugar, milk?"

"Neither. Black is fine, thank you."

While he returned to making their coffees, she surveyed the surroundings. Nothing out of place...from what she could see. Pretty much a mirrored version of the cabin she shared with Westley.

But where was his wife?

As if reading her mind, Franc called out, "Odette, *mon chéri*?"

Seconds later the woman in question emerged in a summer dress, her long titian hair wet. "Hello. May, isn't it?"

"It is."

The woman sat beside her, her hair cascading over her shoulders. She looked youthful but close-up, the fine lines around her honey-brown eyes suggested she had entered her forties. "Lovely to meet you. Finally." Her pronunciation had a less conspicuous French lilt.

"Same. How are you finding the island?"

"It's beautiful." She sighed, somehow sounding more French. "We've attended a few of the investor retreats and they've all been wonderful."

Although she'd love to explore Franc and Odette's history in more depth, she had to hurry. She needed to drill down to extract key information as quickly as possible. "This is our first investment party invitation, so I'm keen to hear your feedback. By what you've said, I'm assuming you've invested with Marcus before?"

"*Oui*. Yes. Though, as he says, it takes time to get results. We are patient and see the potential benefits. But we are also sensible. We don't invest our whole portfolio in one area. This is just a play money venture for us."

Franc brought over their coffees on a tray. "And what is your plan, madame?"

Was he asking out of interest, or did he have a silent partnership with Marcus, one where he sussed out prospective investors and fed back who sounded serious, and who he believed wouldn't commit?

May grabbed her cup and smiled. "Me and my husband discussed a similar strategy. Good to know that it's working for you."

Franc stared at Odette and rattled off some words in French that May couldn't understand. And Odette replied, gesturing with her hands, her voice raised.

Neither offered a translation.

"Sorry?" May swung her gaze between the husband and wife.

Odette faced her with the fakest of fake smiles. "Nothing. My husband's English isn't as good as mine.

He just asked for clarification about our discussion. And I explained."

"Oh." *Yeah, right.* More like he'd contradicted what his wife had said, and Odette told him to keep his mouth shut. She blew on her coffee and had a sip of the delicious brew, the rich color and mouth-watering scent reminding her of Westley. "So, no concerns? You're happy with the investment options Marcus has promoted?"

"We are. He's ahead of the standard curve. He has a progressive insight. We believe his ideas will allow us to continue to move in a positive direction." Sounded like he'd well and truly brainwashed them with his salesman talk.

However, from what they'd related, they didn't seem a threat to the guy. Quite the opposite. They helped recruit by promoting his idealism. Rather naively, but still. They may even be giving him a heads up on serious versus questionable candidates.

But their actions didn't appear to have malicious intent. So she didn't think they were involved in any criminal activity. Either way, it significantly reduced their risk of harm.

Going by her behind-the-scenes investigation on the couple, they had money to burn. So losing a million dollars here or there would be like losing one hundred dollars to most people.

Doable. Wouldn't break their bank account or make a dent in their lush lifestyle. Not a great attitude, but obviously they'd considered it acceptable when the possibility of earning more remained on the table.

May finished her drink, went to stand and stopped. "Have you kept in touch with any investors from past pitch parties?"

"Some, yes. Others we have tried to contact but had no luck. Why do you ask?"

"Westley and I are interested in speaking to all those who have been involved with Marcus and why they've chosen to invest or not. We'd just like to get as broad of an understanding as possible."

"Ah…this makes sense." Except Odette's facial expression turned sour. Did it play into her concerns about continuing to provide funds to the man or highlight her involvement in possible criminal activity? A lead she and Westley would also need to pursue.

"Anyway, I'll leave you to it. Thank you for your time, and for the coffee. You've given me lots to think about."

Franc gave her a kiss on both cheeks, his dark scruff scuffing her skin, then collected the empty cups, and returned into the kitchen.

Odette grasped May's hand and pulled her in for a double-cheek kiss. "Will we see you at the official launch tomorrow?"

"We're intending to be there, yes." Unable to totally rule them out, she'd update Westley and Alex. Ask the team to do a deeper dive. And she also needed to ask her boss to make inquiries about Edgar and Billie to ensure they had safely boarded the plane and successfully exited the island.

Afterward, she and Westley could divide their time between Sterling and Felicity, and Benjamin and Phoenix. Separately monitor each couple and hope they mostly stayed together. Still not ideal, but it helped. However, if the partners split up, she and Westley had no way of keeping an eye on all of them at once.

Chapter Nineteen

May power-walked back to her villa and slipped inside. "Hello?"

Silence.

Was Westley asleep?

In the shower?

Not returned from his surveillance of Marcus and Rei and the other guests?

She checked the bedroom and en suite, and no sign of him.

Nothing looked out of place, no evidence existed of a struggle, so fingers crossed he'd chased a lead, checked on the others and hopefully followed their two suspects, to the best of his solo ability. All of the possibilities had their challenges.

A weird cocktail of apprehension and excitement coursed through her veins, her heart thudding loud and fast and frantic. The caffeine had not helped, creating an additional anxious, persisting spike in her system.

How could she and Westley effectively keep an eye on four people plus Marcus and Rei? And do it in an inconspicuous way, while preventing further deaths? She desperately needed to discuss options with her 'husband' and see if they could problem solve the most workable solution.

A natural adrenaline junkie, she'd faced her fair share of fear and thrived. But this, this took her to another level of functioning in dangerous conditions.

After she changed into some dark, stretchy surveillance gear, she poured herself a Scotch on ice, and paced, and paced and paced, reviewing all the data to date.

A couple of hours later, the front door swung open. Westley.

Thank fuck.

She raced to the foyer and wrapped him in a grateful hug. "You're okay."

His strong arms clamped around her and he kissed her crown. "I am. You need to have more trust in me."

She nestled into his neck. "I do. I don't trust others."

"Great answer." He kissed her forehead, then looked her in the eye.

"I thought so." With her palm, she rubbed his sternum. Westley was so hard and fierce. Her man epitomized warrior.

"I wish we had more time to…"

Fuck. She agreed.

He sighed. "What did you find out?"

"Franc and Odette seem safe. They are totally in support of Marcus' bullshit proposal. Not sure if they're involved with the homicide side of things, but I don't think so. I've let Alex know, just in case."

"And Edgar and Billie?"

"Gone. When I checked in with Alex, he confirmed that they left the island and returned home, according to the flight records. Billie must have confronted Edgar, as she swore she'd do, and he chose her over more gambling. A massive positive for their relationship, and their lives."

She searched his eyes. "What about you?" *Are you really okay? Would you tell me if you weren't?* "Any updates?"

"Phoenix splashed in the sea while Benjamin stared at her from afar, and Sterling smoked through a pack of small cigars, lounging on a deck chair overlooking the ocean, while Felicity went shopping at the designer stores. Nothing of significance. No red-flag alarm bells. So any of these four could be the possible next targets."

"Bloody hell." May had hoped they could have further reduced the possible victim pool. But no such luck. She swiped her hand over her face. "So, how do you recommend we do this? What if they all go off on their own? There are only two of us and four of them. And then we have Marcus and Rei to watch on top of that."

He held her face between his hands and pressed a gentle, loving, lingering kiss to her lips. "I think we follow Marcus and Rei. They'll lead us to their targets. And we'll intercept.

"I know it's not ideal. I'd prefer we concentrate on protecting the others, but with only two of us, we can't. We have to mitigate the risk as best we can."

He locked his dark-chocolate gaze on her eyes. "You focus on Rei, and I'll keep a close eye on Marcus. Like with our situation, they can't split themselves in half, they can't spread themselves too thinly. So they need to have a plan to address this, and any plan is fallible."

Including theirs. May sucked in a strained breath. Things had suddenly gotten scarily real. She might lose Westley. She might lose her own life. And all for a job. All for the broader safety of others.

And yes, her past career had placed her in precarious positions but this meant more. Westley meant more. So instead of making her retreat, it bolstered her resolve, reinforced why she and Westley were there in the first place.

A more intimate, worthy cause, but just as important. For everyone's best interests. Except now that she'd finally found a man she loved, the thought of possibly not having him in her future shattered her heart. Surely the universe couldn't be so cruel.

Circumstances meant she had to do her job, and hope for the best. Come what may. They both had to. No matter how much they cared about one another. He hadn't said he saw her in a serious light, hadn't spoken about pursuing anything long-term once they returned, hadn't said he loved her, but she hadn't confessed her feelings either.

And right now, it didn't matter.

What mattered was them both making it back, and she had everything crossed that they would, unharmed, then they could discuss where to go from there. Talk in a neutral, more stable, hopefully sustainable, environment.

May kissed her man, deep and intense, yet way too brief. What if she never saw him again? A tear rolled down her cheek and he swiped it away.

"We'll be fine." He ran his hands up and down her arms. "Call me if you have any concerns. Anything that makes you feel ill at ease, unsettled, scared, okay?"

She nodded. "You do the same."

"I will."

They stood there, staring at each other, neither of them moving. But they had to, before the deviant duo attacked their next victims.

"I should go. See what Rei's up to." Her voice radiated both reluctance and resignation.

He stroked her cheek with the pad of his thumb. "Be careful."

"You too." Why did it feel like the end? And right when they'd formed a strong attachment. Right when she'd first felt true love.

She kissed Westley again and shot out of the accommodation to locate Rei, before she changed her mind. Before her overwhelming emotions wouldn't let her go, anchoring her to the spot.

Where could she find the creep?

May started with the main house and bingo!

Rei shook hands with Marcus and left, a smug smile on his fake-tanned face.

With absolute subtlety, she stalked the guy, following from afar, to his villa, checking for any weirdness. Checking for anything untoward. Anything that pinged her instinct radar.

From her discussion with Westley, had he assessed Marcus in the same light, with the same criteria? Had he chosen a similar, stand-back, careful strategy? Observe and only intervene where required? Had he chosen to play it safe or take more risks? They hadn't had enough time to fine tune their tactics.

They had no idea whether Marcus or Rei would make the first move. Neither her nor Westley could presume. Maybe in this case Rei would lead. Maybe not. Maybe they'd planned to strike in tandem. It depended what they'd decided on between them, in a private place like the beach, somewhere without a bug. Plus what opportunities presented.

Like her and Westley. They might have certain ideas, but they had to go with what played out. Be adaptable to the environment. Anything less and they'd fall far behind the eight ball. It'd set them back as well as put others' lives in danger.

In less than twenty-four hours, people had to commit or not, then leave the island. And she and Westley had to ensure they were all protected. Physically, financially, psychologically.

Hidden in the bushes, she spied on Rei, ensconced in his cabin. Waiting for him to be distracted enough for her to make her move. Because going by his conversation with Marcus, they planned to act tonight.

With her phone on silent, she waited and waited. Finally, his mobile rang and he got caught up in an animated discussion. She scoured the surroundings and with no one close by, she snuck up to his car in the driveway.

Using an electronically operated switch, she tapped into Rei's key fob signal, broke into his vehicle, popped the hood, and removed the starter relay, disabling the engine. Just in case he tried to use it to kidnap or transport someone or assist Marcus. Just in case he tried to flee.

Right as he finished his phone call, she disappeared back into the bushes.

Her mobile buzzed in her pocket.

A message from Westley.

I've just sent this to Alex. Listen…

She clicked on the audio file.

"You ready?" Marcus' hushed voice.

"Yeah." Rei sounded sleepy.

"Good. We need to act now. Get rid of them before tomorrow."

So the commitment breakfast ran without concern, without anyone causing conflict? *Shit.* What had they planned to say if a couple went missing? That they'd decided against the proposition and returned home? Like Edgar and Billie. Probably. Who'd even check? Most of them knew very little about each other, and she imagined Marcus had made it that way.

"I'm leaving now."

"Meet you at the marina in an hour or less. No fuck ups."

"Don't worry, I'll get the job done."

"You sure? It's not going to be like last time. I can't keep covering your ass. I can't keep picking up the slack for your incompetence."

"I promise I'll uphold my end of the agreement. No one will see them again. They'll disappear without any obvious trace."

The recorded call ended.

Damn. Neither had mentioned any specific names. But it was enough to notify the island police, which she did, also sending them a copy of the audio file.

A few minutes later, Rei stepped outside, setting off the sensor lights, and locked the front door.

She shoved her phone in her pocket and clung closer to the sandy ground, her heart thundering in her chest, blaring in her ears. Forcing her eyes open, she took in as many details as possible. All decked out in camouflage gear, Rei skulked forward with what she assumed was a killer kit in tow — a pack slung over his shoulders and strapped to his back.

Using his keyless entry fob, he pressed the 'open' button, and the lights flashed. Had he not noticed that the car was already unlocked after her tampering?

Obviously not, given he dumped the backpack in the boot, then jumped in the driver's side. Maybe his mind remained too caught up with his mission to notice small anomalies. Maybe he knew jack shit about cars.

Rei went to start the motor, but nothing. No clicking, no chugging, no hint of any movement.

Dead.

Exactly what he'd promised Marcus. To kill those in their way. Except she'd beaten them to it and, as a result, hopefully saved lives. She'd killed his car, preventing human deaths. Pre-empting his plan meant he'd have to go on foot, ensured he couldn't go anywhere too far away, couldn't fulfill his end of the murderous bargain. *Fingers crossed.*

While he tried to revive his car, hood open, fiddling with the engine, the police arrived and a couple of officers took Rei in for questioning.

As soon as she got a chance, after giving the authorities a statement, May returned to her cabin, jumped in an island buggy and traveled to the marina. She raced up the road clinging to the coast and… *Oh.*

Oh fuck.

Chapter Twenty

Marcus waved a gun at Westley who sat back on his knees, hands behind his head, positioned alongside Sterling, Felicity, Benjamin and Phoenix. No one had glanced May's way yet.

Hopefully the sound of the wind and the water crashing against the dock drowned out her arrival. Thank fuck the buggy was significantly quieter than a car.

Heart thumping in her chest, May rolled into a sheltered spot camouflaged by boats bobbing in the water, and switched off the engine. Adrenaline coursing through her system, she jumped out of the buggy and slinked closer, service pistol drawn. Trying to keep her hands from trembling.

Creeping as quietly as possible, focused on slow, silent steps, she attempted to avoid squeaky timber boards and closed in. Seagulls squawked and a couple swooped too close to her head. She slammed her hand to her mouth, barely stifling a scream.

Thankfully, Marcus remained focused on Westley and the others, apparently not alerted to her presence. She breathed out and shook her shoulders, trying to recalibrate. Trying to tamp down her racing heart.

What was the guy planning to do? If he killed them all it'd look incredibly suspicious. Unless he intended to dispose of them in different ways, or by making their demise appear as natural as possible.

A sailing expedition gone wrong, perhaps? Maybe he could force them onto a boat, sedate them, and make sure the vessel sank. Or ensure the engine had a 'fault' so that it exploded, instantly killing the entire party, except himself. Basically, some sort of believable boating accident.

Raising her gun, within a close enough position to take an accurate shot, she held her arms as steady as possible and shouted, "Drop your weapon."

Marcus startled, his head jolting up searching for her position, giving Westley a few precious moments to tackle him to the ground.

"Go!" Westley yelled, and the others ran, shooting past her.

Yes! Guest deaths averted. She blew out a relieved breath, still aiming at Marcus.

The two men struggled, and *bang*.

Bang!

She gasped and jolted backward.

Marcus' gun had gone off.

Twice.

No!

With some effort, Marcus rolled on top of Westley, jumped up and hobbled away.

May jolted into action, calling an ambulance as she ran toward her motionless man.

Blood.

So much blood.

Soaking into the weathered wood.

She dropped to her knees beside him, discarded her gun, and put pressure on the small, bleeding hole in his chest. "Westley, stay with me. You need to live, okay? Promise me."

A gurgle, a clear sign of fluid building in his lungs, no speech.

No.

No!

He couldn't die on her.

They'd both endured way too much for it all to end in despair.

Blood continued to ooze onto the sun-bleached boards, creating a large, slowly spreading maroon stain. His life ebbing away. Without urgent medical intervention, how much longer could he survive?

But he had to.

He fucking had to.

She squeezed his shoulder, her other hand saturated with his blood. "Stay with me. Please."

He couldn't leave her now, not when she'd just found him.

She sucked in a stilted breath. And another. And another. Vision blotchy, breathing strained, hyperventilation threatened, but she couldn't let it take over or she'd faint. Pass out.

And she couldn't risk leaving Westley unattended. She pushed harder on the steadily seeping wound. He needed all the life-giving care he could get…she had to try to stem the bleeding until the paramedics arrived.

They needed to stabilize him, airlift him to the closest, biggest hospital in the vicinity, stat.

May checked Westley's vital signs and *shit!* He'd stopped breathing.

No.

No dying. Hadn't he heard her?

Kneeling in position, focused on saving her man's life, she commenced CPR, fixated on giving Westley the best chance of survival. She lost total track of time, keeping up the chest compressions and rescue breaths until her arms burned, and she fought for breath, the ambulance officers finally arriving and taking over.

Using a defibrillator, they got his heart rate stabilized, his breathing in a labored but steady rhythm, and transferred him into a helicopter to fly to the closest mainland hospital for emergency medical treatment. His worst nightmare, her worst nightmare, but the only way to receive the attention he required as soon as possible.

She couldn't thank the universe enough. He needed urgent, life-saving attention. The best, most thorough intervention in the world. Because he needed to stay alive.

But now with him in the best of care, and his survival out of her control, she focused on what she could do. Where she could make a difference. Something, anything to distract her from Westley's fate.

Marcus. The guy that had injured many others, including her man. The guy who needed immediate apprehension and interrogation. Where had he disappeared to?

May rubbed her hands over her cold, windblown, sea-spattered face, fiery, unrelenting tears trickling over her cheeks. She had to gather herself. Pressing her bloody palms into a praying position, she lifted her thumbs to her lips. Although the opposite of religious, she wouldn't knock back any additional assistance. She couldn't help but hope for justice.

Flicking on her phone torch, she snatched up her gun. Drops of blood led away to a bunch of warehouses on the wharf. Distraught, but determined to get the guy, she followed the bloody path past the pongy fish mongers, the telltale red trail ending at the entrance to an abandoned warehouse on the water.

With her senses heightened, she eased open the metal door, the salt-encrusted hinges creaking, and stepped inside, careful to make the least amount of noise. She stopped, clicked it shut behind her with the smallest of squeaks, and listened out for any sounds. She swallowed the lump of stress clogging her throat.

Dark.

Quiet.

Unsettling.

Like walking into her own, private horror movie.

Salty sea air stung her nostrils and her eyes watered while she waited for her sight to adjust, her heavy breaths to slow, to silently reregulate. Hopefully Marcus couldn't see her and attack before she had a chance to retaliate.

The crack of a gunshot, and a bullet whizzed past her head, piercing a hole through the door she'd just entered.

Fuck. She dropped to the ground, air rushing in and out of her lungs. Desperately, she tried to calm her shattered nerves. A difficult task when all she wanted to do was run. Escape. Not confront this psychopath who had already injured her partner and was the prime suspect in several other murders.

But she couldn't trust Marcus' paid island security team, or wait for the skeleton police staff to catch up. They had a lot going on. Attending to survivors, taking their statements. If she sat back until they were ready, Marcus might get away. She needed to find the man before he caused more trouble. Fuck, for all she knew, he'd ended Westley's life.

No. She breathed out a pent up, paranoid breath. She couldn't let her mind wander down that detrimental path. Negativity created negativity, and she needed hope, positivity, success.

You can do this.

May kept hold of her Glock and gradually stood. She inched forward, the darkness dissipating, like a lifted curtain, and a range of metal machine parts and storage containers filled the cluttered space. Marcus could be hiding anywhere. He had the absolute advantage.

Slowly, cautiously, May scanned the aisles, sticking close to the shelves. Where was the prick? Aware of every movement, the slightest sound, she crept deeper into the massive shed. On high alert.

Another two bullets whizzed past her.

She ducked, her pulse pounding at her temples, at her wrists, in her ears. Deafening. Thankfully only she could hear the persistent beat of her fear. One careful step at a time, she searched the internal space.

Marcus couldn't have gone too much further unless he'd managed to jump one of the island ferries. She'd need to check the whole place before she accepted he'd escaped.

No, she'd never accept that outcome. She'd spend every spare moment devising a capture plan and putting it into action. Because she wouldn't allow Marcus to get away with his crimes, with hurting

Westley. She couldn't allow anyone to get away with murder.

Continuing to creep by the high, thoroughly stacked shelves, she emerged at the end of the aisle into a small clearing with dim, overhead lighting. A sudden clatter had her spinning around, her eyes darting to the origin of the sound, her heart rate shooting through the ceiling.

Could he see her? How many rounds did he have left in his gun? Could he aim and shoot and try to kill her too? Dropping down into a crouch she backed up to the closest wall, behind a barrel, and surveyed the chaotic surroundings.

A sudden barrage of bullets poked holes in the rusty barrel, one just missing her head. She plastered herself low against the wall, hardly able to breath with her heart beating so damn fast.

Quiet.

Unnerving.

Had he used the commotion to unsettle her, to approach her when she least expected?

More silence.

What should she do? She needed a sound strategy. Now.

She needed to know where he was.

May edged to the side and further forward.

A silhouette?

No, Marcus holding a gun in a small alcove in the opposite corner, less than thirty meters away.

She stood, aimed her Glock at the guy, and closed in on him. "Put your weapon down."

"Why should I?"

"Because you're out of ammunition."

"Are you sure about that?" With a groan, he pushed up into standing, favoring one leg, blood trickling from a wound on his thigh, pistol held firmly in front. "Do you really want to test me?" His labored breathing and gritted teeth suggested he struggled to keep on top of the pain.

And she'd use his compromised condition to her advantage. Totally ready to back her bluff. "Do you really want test *me*?" They faced off against each other, her finger on the trigger, ready to shoot…if she had to. Hopefully he wouldn't disable her first.

A police siren grew louder.

"You know you're not getting away. Not from here, not from what you've done."

He darted his gaze around the area, possibly looking for an escape.

"I'm sure you can hear that. The police will be here any minute. Put your gun down, cooperate."

"Or what? Go to jail?"

"Either that or possibly die. It's your choice." She tried to hold her hands steady, her revolver trained on his chest, hoping she'd convinced the guy not to do anything rash, not to injure or possibly kill her too.

"So you're a cop?"

"An agent, but close enough."

"I should have known. You two were too…inquisitive."

A car with flashing lights pulled up in the opening between them and the ocean, a couple of officers exiting and striding straight over. "Drop your weapons."

They both did, and Marcus raised his hands in surrender, still staring at her. "I didn't mean to hurt Westley. You have to believe me."

"Right. Sure you didn't. Just like you didn't mean to hurt the others."

While one of the police handcuffed Marcus and assisted him to the patrol vehicle, May spoke to the other. "I'm an agent with Solve Security. I've been working with my partner, Westley, on a case to investigate Marcus and his dealings. I can give you the agency details and you can check with the owner, Alexander Barrett. You can take my word for it or not, but I believe you'll find you've apprehended a murder suspect."

Chapter Twenty-One

The police officer confirmed May's story with Alex and released her. Jumping back on the buggy, she raced to the cabin, packed up everything and got on the next available flight to the mainland, desperate to see Westley.

Although strapped into her seat, she couldn't stop fidgeting, worry chewing through to the sharp, agonizing center of her nerves. No one had sent her a message or called with any Westley updates. Not Alex, not the hospital.

Was no news really good news? Could no one get access to his medical status, his likelihood of recovery? Or had they held off telling her the gut-wrenching, traumatizing reality — that he hadn't made it?

Her breath caught in her throat, her heart stuttering in her chest just at the thought. In the shortest time, he'd made a significant impact on her psyche, on her beliefs, on her life.

She'd never needed a man, had always successfully managed herself and her choices, and she could again, yet she didn't want to even imagine returning to a single-minded, solo existence.

He had changed her in the most profound, positive way, preventing her from ever reverting to her previous, outgrown ideals. Showing her respect and reinforcing what it took to work in a successful partnership. And she hoped she'd also had a similar impact on him. She hoped, more than anything, that he survived.

Whatever destiny had in store for her, she couldn't unlearn what she'd learned, couldn't be the same May before Westley.

Alone with her thoughts, her internal monologue refused to switch off, oscillating between self-reflection and fixating on Westley's serious chest wound. Would he make it? Wouldn't he? Had the paramedics gotten to him quickly enough?

If he died without her telling him she loved him... How would she cope? How could she handle not having the charming, chatty, quick-witted infuriatingly gorgeous man as a permanent fixture in her life?

Burgeoning tears burned the backs of her eyes but she refused to let them fall.

Positivity.

She had to remain positive. As soon as she landed, she'd check in with Alex and the hospital to try to get the most up-to-date info. Review and respond once she had the facts. But rationality and feelings mixed like olive oil and spring water.

May forced in some airline food, further feeding her rising nausea. But she needed some nutrition to fuel her strength. At least physically. And the energy would also nourish her brain, reducing her risk of falling into the hangry, irrational, negativity trap.

Once she checked into the closest accommodation to the hospital, and dumped their bags, she'd make her way to his bedside, camp out beside him, and hold an in-person vigil.

The flight took forever, as though her life had switched into slow motion. Ten minutes virtually equaling an hour. She needed to hear how he was doing, an update on his condition. May needed to get to him.

The moment the plane touched down, she called Alex. "I'm sure you've heard that Marcus and Rei have been arrested. How is Westley?"

"I don't know." His voice sounded tired, frustrated, wrecked.

"What?" Unbidden tears welled behind her eyes, and she fought the sob threatening to burst from her constricted throat.

"They won't tell me anything. Not a relative and all that."

Shit. "Of course. I didn't think…" If she had to play up her relationship with Westley to get answers, she would. And if he couldn't deal with that white lie, so be it. His reaction, if she was lucky enough to hear it, if he hadn't sustained any long-term major trauma, would say a lot about their relationship moving forward.

"As soon as you learn anything else, you let me know." He said it like he knew she'd find out somehow.

May stood, ready to bolt out of the aircraft, collect their luggage and see her man. "I will."

Within an hour, she'd taxied to a hotel, checked in, freshened up and power walked the five minutes to the hospital. She arrived sweaty and puffed out, not caring how she appeared. It didn't matter, as long as Westley was all right.

The main reception directed her to the ICU, and she rode the elevator up, determined to lie and tell the nursing staff she was his fiancée. At this point, she'd do whatever it took to be with her man. Do whatever she could to help and support him through this.

The lift doors opened, the super-sterile disinfectant smell smacking her hard in the face, and she scanned the clinical white passageway searching for signs to the ICU. Up the corridor and to the right. She hurried along the hallway, trying not to knock slow walkers aside.

Finally, *finally* she reached the secured doors and rang the buzzer. Each moment she waited felt like an eternity. Seconds stretching into minutes. She lost count of how many times she hand sanitized before the doors whooshed open.

"I'm Westley Richards' fiancée, May. Please, can I see him?" she blurted.

The nurse nodded, handed her a face mask, ran over a string of visitor instructions, then gestured to Westley's bed in the far corner of the room, near a window. A peaceful view over a picturesque park. Not that he could see much of it from his bed…if he'd even regained consciousness.

The dim, sanitary space smelled of astringent antiseptic and struggle, filled with beeps and gasps from life-saving machinery. Westley lay still, eyes closed, plugged into his own host of monitoring equipment, including oxygen prongs in his nose.

His face and body looked deceivingly relaxed, peaceful. Hopefully the doctors had dosed him up on pain meds so he wouldn't feel too much discomfort. She slid between his bed and the window and gently stroked his dark hair. She'd never seen him so quiet. So out of character for the man who'd stolen her heart.

May bent down and pressed a light kiss to his forehead. "Please be okay," she whispered. "I can't lose you. I love you so much." She clamped her jaw together to hold back a gut-wrenching sob.

"You're blocking my light." His soft, slurred, raspy voice jolted her upright.

He watched her with glazed, bloodshot eyes, an unmistakable smirk on his face.

"What?" A mix of emotions overwhelmed her. He was alive and responsive, and his usual, gobby, smart-aleck self.

He sucked in a labored breath. "You heard." Croaky, hoarse, but so Westley.

Her Westley. A laugh burst from her lips. "I can't believe you just said that!" She wanted to scold him, but relief overrode any annoyance.

"I can't believe you admitted you love me." He sucked in a stilted, wheezy breath. "If I'd known it'd take this, I'd have injured myself much earlier."

"Stop it!"

He let out a husky chuckle, which turned into a coughing fit.

"Are you okay? Should I get a nurse?" She gripped his shoulder and darted her gaze around the ICU, trying to gain eye contact with one of the staff on duty.

He grabbed her arm, his grasp surprisingly firm. "F-fine."

She searched his eyes. "You sure?"

Westley stared at her with absolute conviction. "As sure as I love you."

He loved her too. Fuck. *Fuck.* Her eyes flooded with happy tears. She cared about this man way beyond words. With total tenderness, she wrapped her arms around him. "Then promise me you'll get better."

"I will, on one condition."

"You have a condition?" She frowned at him with utter disbelief.

"I do." Westley didn't blink, his gaze intense and serious.

"And what's that? That I remain your partner?"

"Across the board, yes."

Oh. Did he mean what she thought he did? "What are you saying?"

"Professionally, personally." Without breaking his courageous, no-holds-barred connection with her eyes, he reached for her hand and held it between his. His palms surprisingly soft, smooth and warm. "Be my wife."

"Your wife?" Was the man still delirious on pain meds?

"Is there an echo in here?"

Apparently, he was more with it than she realized. She wanted to smack his arm but there were too many tubes, and she was too overcome with happiness. "Yes."

"To the echo or my proposal?"

His distinctive, yet somewhat slurred laugh, combined with his smart-ass commentary made everything real, the avalanche of emotion crashing onto her cheeks in a persistent stream of tears. Tears of relief, gratefulness, joy. "Both."

Using the pad of his thumb, he swiped away the flow of descending drops, all the joviality disappearing from his face. "The moment I'm discharged we lock in a day."

Would Westley stand by every word he'd spoken? Being high on medication could skew a person's thinking. "Are you sure you want to commit to anything right now? Maybe you need some time to review everything once you're more medically stable?"

He squeezed her hand so tight, as though to say, *believe me*. "No. I know what I want, who I want. And that's you."

More happy tears spilled out of her eyes, his gorgeous face blurring. Like some sort of surreal-cross-impressionist painting—her favorite type of art. "Even more motivation for you to recover as quickly as possible." She tried to stifle a sob.

He grabbed the bed remote and pressed the raise function until his lips almost met hers. "To claim you as mine, and have you in my bed every day, every night—best incentive ever." And he sealed their verbal vow with a kiss.

Epilogue

Four weeks later, May took Westley home, and stayed. Upon his request she'd shifted out of her house and permanently moved in. He'd lost weight and strength and endurance, but was still as gorgeous as ever, and he could walk and talk. Boy, could he talk. His absolute, indisputable forte. And although she'd initially found it frustrating, everything had changed. She bloody loved it now, loved having him in her life, her future.

After doing some grocery shopping, a week later, she returned to his place, her arms loaded up with bags, to find Westley pottering around in the kitchen, and a delicious meaty scent emanating from the oven.

She dumped the bags on the bench and strode over to him. "What are you doing?"

"Attempting to check on the roast. Oh, and hello to you too."

Fuck, she loved his smart-ass smile, felt so privileged and grateful he was still here, alive, and getting better by the day.

"You should be resting, trying to recuperate." She took the spatula out of his hand and opened the oven door. Her mouth watered. She crouched down, then peeled off the foil on top of the tray. Mmm…pork with crackling and roasted veggies. Hearty comfort food. May hadn't had a decent roast in years.

"I've already done plenty of that today. So I wanted to do something for my wonderful wife-to-be."

Her stomach fluttered with indescribable joy. She could never get sick of her fiancé reinforcing their commitment to each other.

"I've also been busy with some other things."

She stood and placed the spatula on a utensil holder beside the stovetop. "Such as?"

He wound his arms around her waist. "Well, I think it's time we set a date."

"A date?" Was he saying what she thought he was saying?

"To get married. Make this official. I've found the perfect place down in Mornington Peninsula. It's a stunning winery by the sea. They can do a package that factors in everything. Finger food, drinks, a three-course meal, a DJ, and they even recommended local accommodation and a photographer."

Her eyes welled up and she hugged him super tight. Such a sweet, thoughtful man.

"You're not upset, are you? If you want to look at other options—"

"Shut up! Do you know how to shut up?" She laughed, tears trickling down her cheeks. "I love it, I love you. Thank you so much for looking into places and narrowing it down to one that you think we'd both love. I trust you. I believe you understand me well enough to know what I like, so the sooner we can lock in a venue, the better."

His smile practically split his gorgeous face in two. "Yes! I love you so very much."

More tears fell from her eyes and she sniffled, burying her head against his chest.

"After dinner, I'll show you what I've selected and if you agree, we'll make a booking and put down a deposit."

She glanced up at him through glassy eyes. "I can't wait."

"Me either." He brushed his lips against hers. "I also have some other exciting news."

"Really? And what's that?"

"I finally have physical clearance."

"For?" She searched the depths of his rich cocoa eyes.

"Making love." He let go of her and clasped her hand.

"Hang on, what about dinner?" She wanted to be with him more than anything but she didn't want all his good work to go to waste.

"It'll still be at least thirty minutes. I'll set the timer." While he did, she put the groceries away, then he grasped her hand again and tugged.

"Are you sure?"

"Very. Though, you might have to ride my face, then my cock, while I rebuild my endurance."

"Westley!" She smiled and shook her head. Fuck she loved this man, especially his sexy sinful side.

"Come on, you know how much I love it, and you can't deny that you do too."

Westley was right, and she made a pact with herself to never deny him again, allowing her husband-to-be to lead her into their bedroom to fully reconnect and start training for their upcoming wedding night.

* * * *

Drew 'Render' Renderson exited the elevator and stormed to Alex's office, greeting the receptionist with a rash *hi*. It was late, he had an early start, and still needed to head back to the bar and close up.

He raked a frustrated hand through his overgrown hair, catching a glimpse of himself in the large waiting-room mirror. His normally short, dark-blond locks desperately needed a cut, but he had hardly had a second to spare. His faux day job had practically commandeered all his time. More like all-encompassing day-night job.

And a woman. One he couldn't eradicate from his thoughts, against his better judgment. Breaking all the self-imposed rules he'd thought he'd locked up tight.

Without waiting for another word from the receptionist, he pushed Alex's door open, walked right up to his boss's desk and slammed his palms on the perfectly shiny surface. "Nine o'clock. Really? What's so important?"

In all his jobs with Solve Security, he didn't think he'd crossed any boundaries. Screwed with his security role. Alex would have let him know. The guy was a straight-as-straight-can-be shooter, so he'd tell him instantly if he'd breached any protocol. Or so he assumed. Maybe he needed to raise it in his next professional development meeting?

Yeah, sure. The epitome of tongue-in-cheek. Maybe big businesses could tout that shit but not small organizations. They didn't have the time or resources or energy. They needed results, and as efficiently as possible.

No one waited for waste-of-time shit meetings. Any issues got highlighted then and there, in his limited experience. No fucking around. The sooner someone knew their faux pas the sooner they could address it. And the sooner they didn't, the sooner Alex had a reason to move them on.

"Good evening. Thanks for coming in." Alex glanced up from his desk and waved to a seat opposite him, ignoring Render's imposing stance and aggressive tone. And he fucking admired that. Admired the guy's ability to stick to the task and not fall victim to intimidation.

Hence why Alex successfully headed Solve Security. He refused to take shit…and he held all the control. If agents didn't like it, he didn't stop them leaving. "I have a job for you."

Fine, good. He could always do with the extra cash. The bar had only ever been his side hustle. Something to help him pay the bills and live his life between agent jobs.

Render sat but kept fidgeting, his adrenaline spike still dissipating. He propped his forearms on his thighs, one leg unable to stop shaking. "Okay. When. Where? I need to organize staff for the pub."

"I know. And you have some time."

Which in Alex terms pretty much meant five minutes. But he'd argue for some leeway. "Send me the info and I'll review it tonight."

"You'll review it right now."

What? Right now? He'd expected some resistance, but not this level of rigidity. Every other Solve Security job he'd done, he'd had a decent chance to go over the specs. What was it about this circumstance that required immediate attention? Had to be something extremely serious. Which revved up his internal driver, his interest.

Alex glanced down and clicked a button on his tablet screen, highlighting the dark smudges beneath his eyes. Taking on too much? Working too hard? The ex-military guy had a strong desire for fairness. How did his wife cope?

There was a reason Render had stayed single. Fucked for fun. Nothing else. Workaholism didn't foster successful relationships. It didn't allow for any semblance of a relationship whatsoever. Not in his experience. Not until the unexpected hook up with CJ. The first time ever someone had made him question his beliefs.

How did Alex do it? How had he gotten the right balance? Maybe the guy was just a really good fuck? He should ask him. Maybe he could learn something.

Alex's wife, Sage, was a saint of a woman. Render had gotten to know her reasonably well from her stints on Solve Security reception. She showed indisputable love for her husband, sincere interest in the business, and legitimate concern for the staff and their health and wellbeing. But she'd have her needs too. And Alex would have had to find a way to provide her with the required satisfaction.

In terms of Render's love life, in terms of his ability to provide feedback to Alex about his marriage? Too hard basket. What did he know about successful romantic relationships, anyway? He was just a contracted employee. How Sage felt about her hubby's long hours and dedication to his enterprise wasn't Render's problem.

He just needed to focus on his current assignment. And do what was required of him. Pull his agreed-to weight. Not keep wondering why CJ had never made further contact.

A vibrating blip confirmed Render had received Alex's message.

His boss locked his computer tablet and refocused on Render's eyes. "I've sent you all the information. Go over it, no skimming, and let me know if you're in. Then we can devise a plan of action tomorrow."

Between a handful of hours of sleep and a full day manning the bar and sorting out invoices, he'd be lucky to have thirty minutes to himself. "I'll do what I can."

"No." Alex slapped his hands onto his reflective desk. "If you agree to the job, you'll do what's required. You'll find a way to fit in with what's needed. Understand?"

Annoying, but he appreciated the guy's dedication and drive for excellence. For positive results. His drive to save lives and uphold justice.

Alex sucked in a stuttered breath, shoved a hand through his tousled hair, and searched Render's eyes. "I'd usually ask other free agents to assist but only Lexie and May are available, and they have a conflict of interest."

A conflict of interest? Intriguing. Explained the pressured vibe radiating from his boss. Did his fellow agents know a key person in the investigation? They must. His gut instinct flared, like gastric reflux. Hot, burning, the kind that caused unrelenting indigestion.

However, he didn't have the right nor the security clearance to ask more questions. All he needed to do was fulfill his agreed work requirements. As simple and as complicated as that...if he agreed to take this on.

Render snatched his smartphone out of his pocket and reviewed the documents. Even though every single cell in his body suggested he should get more details, be more wary before committing to anything, his defender tendencies took over.

From what he'd read, the widow's case looked pretty typical, pretty straightforward, a pretty standard protection case. She'd probably been her sweet, friendly, innocent self, and the alleged perpetrator had misread the cues and expected more. And Render had to make himself known, prominent, step in, intervene and ensure the guy got the clear message that he had to back the fuck off.

However, there had to be more to it. Why would Alex have called him in so urgently otherwise? So he'd sit and listen and absorb all he could, the intriguing unanswered questions directing him to accept the case. He fucking loved a challenge.

One thing he couldn't stand was a man who refused to listen, who didn't take *no*, or any explanation, for an answer. And Alex had given him a shit-ton of regular work and had proved himself to be upstanding and reliable. As far as Render knew, he'd always upheld his end of the agreement. "I'm in."

"Good." Alex's whole body decompressed with relief, and he pushed a button on his phone that appeared to link him to reception. "Send her in."

Her? As in the client? Alex had been fucking confident he'd accept. And he was right, as usual.

Working for Alex, no matter the role, apparently meant twenty-four-hour availability.

Render turned toward Alex's office door just as a lady stepped over the threshold. An all too familiar, libido-enhancing female. His heart rate shot to stroke territory.

A short, sexy, power-pack of a woman with wavy, long auburn hair entered the room—her assets his biggest weakness. Could it really be *her*, the lady conquest he'd succumbed to six long weeks ago?

The woman he'd had an unforgettable, addictive, one-night stand with — well not in the traditional sense. They'd shared some intense, erotic kissing and oral and naked exploration. They'd shared a rare connection. She'd been sweet, pliant, receptive, enthusiastic, intelligent… Piqued his interest with her honest vulnerability, her engaging conversation, her ability to listen and absorb and respond.

Her gaze locked on his and her eyes went wide with recognition…and was that embarrassment? Stress? Fear? They'd only shared nicknames — no identifying details from their backgrounds, other than her admitting she was a recent-ish widow — a titillating discussion, and a down-and-dirty fun time. They'd agreed to keep their liaison focused predominantly on pleasure. And they had succeeded. Until now.

On that stimulating night, he'd held off on penetrative sex, asking her to call him, thinking it'd guarantee him another date. Because unlike his normal conquests, he saw the hint of potential. Potential for at least a few more nights of no-strings attached enjoyment. Because he'd thoroughly appreciated her company. Except it didn't eventuate.

Render had provided her with his number, presuming she'd phone but she hadn't. Going by previous, consistent feedback, he considered himself a good lover, a good conversationalist, but maybe he hadn't floated her discerning boat. Most women couldn't wait to get in touch.

Or maybe she sensed his deep-seated inability to commit. After losing a husband, maybe she wasn't willing to commit again either. If ever. Maybe she wasn't up to potentially losing another man. Dead or alive.

Without knowing she was the targeted widow, he'd accepted the case. And Alex wouldn't have any idea the two of them had ever interacted. Should he step aside?

In an ideal world it'd be preferrable, but how could he when there were no other available agents? No agents who'd see her in the same light. Be willing to put her safety ahead of theirs in the way he would, in the way he could. Without a family, and living alone, he could fully commit himself.

The woman needed protection, and he'd do everything in his power, work extra time if needed, to ensure she stayed safe. Whether she chose to pursue him romantically or not.

He'd only known her for a few hours but their short time together had made a surprisingly memorable impact. Since their encounter he hadn't even entertained the idea of a random fuck with another woman. How could he put the life of the lady that had dominated his dreams in anyone else's hands?

Sign up for our newsletter and find out about all our romance book releases, eBook sales and promotions, sneak peeks and FREE romance books!

Want to see more from this author? Here's a taster for you to enjoy!

Hearts in Danger: Render Assistance
Sandra Carmel

Excerpt

Charlotte Jaeger, CJ to almost everyone, had given in. Her mates had hounded her to come out for months. Months! Because they cared. She knew that. Didn't make the situation any easier, though. She huffed out a big breath, trying to calm her overwhelming nerves.

Although she didn't feel like it at all, she showered, threw on a comfy, flowy, black dress and a shawl, then drove to *their* bar of choice. On the trendy outskirts of town. They'd offered to come and collect her, but she needed to drive. She needed to know she could escape. Grief had a way of commandeering her emotions, how much she could cope with at any given moment.

Almost as soon as she entered the bustling venue carpark, she pulled into a space. What were the chances? Did it suggest a positive omen? She turned off the engine and stayed in the driver's seat, a wave of guilt-infused anxiety flooding her body.

Breathing in and out, in and out, in and out, she tried to create some self-soothing. She'd agreed to catch up with friends, that's all, right? Nothing to worry about. No pressure.

Didn't matter how much her mates told her it was time. Time to break out of mourning mode and move on. Have some fun. Like they said consistently, and in the kindest way possible, she was young, still alive. She needed to live.

And she did. She got it...rationally. Understood where they were coming from, that they truly were trying to help. Enforcing the idea in her everyday existence, though, meant something entirely different.

To this point, her emotions still hadn't caught up to her thinking. Until someone was in her position, they really didn't understand. She'd never even contemplated the current circumstances until it affected her personally.

Fairy lights wound around the external patio into what she imagined was a beer garden, but the dim, internal environment enticed her inside. So pretty. Enabling her to hide in the shadows. Just what she needed. She hadn't been out of the house to socialize for months. Not since...

Not the time to think about that now. Not the time to think about things beyond her control. She'd promised she'd come and hang out, like they used to. After all the support her besties had given her, she wanted to give back, even in the smallest way. Not be a flaky, whining, excuse-maker. She text messaged her girlfriend group.

Are you here? I just parked.

In seconds she received a response from Lexie.

Me, Sage and May are already inside in a booth, by the fireplace.

Oh. As an introvert, she struggled to walk into a crowded venue at the best of times, but especially when all her friends had already arrived. However, she couldn't sit in the carpark forever. Especially now that they knew she'd actually turned up. Although difficult, challenging, it was better than her having to enter alone and find a spot in the people-filled place.

After checking her make-up and ensuring her wavy red hair hadn't gone into frizz mode, she snatched her handbag from the front passenger seat and stepped into the chilly night air. She wrapped her shawl tight around her, then shut the car door and locked it, her heart racing at record speed. She hadn't experienced that since...

CJ clenched her teeth and tried to hold back the tears from trickling down her cheeks. *You can do this.* It was just a night out with the girls. Nothing more. She could decide the outcome—how comfortable she was, how long she stayed.

Bordering on hyperventilating, she pushed herself forward, joined the heaving queue, and inhaled the soothing scent of smoky eucalyptus. The grounding smell of the forest, of nature, soon had her settling slightly, and she gathered her waist-long hair over her shoulder and studied the ends. The combination of sensory mindfulness techniques had taught her how to avoid panic attacks.

After a few minutes, she finally entered the venue and searched for her friends. Vulnerability, and a fresh surge of adrenaline, shot through her like a hair-trigger handgun.

What was she doing here, in this crazy-crowded, packed place? Yes, she'd promised to come but...

The warm downlights caressed the top of her head, and she caught her reflection in the closest window. Her husband had always loved her free-flowing auburn locks. He'd said time and time again that the strands flickering in the light reminded him of a blazing hot bonfire. Beautiful, striking, unforgettable.

She clamped her eyes closed and breathed out a steadying breath.

When she opened them again, she couldn't miss her girlfriends standing and waving from halfway across the pub, and she bee-lined to their booth, weaving through the throng of patrons milling around the bar.

"Hi." She sat on the unoccupied seat beside May, right on the aisle, ridiculously out of breath. Anxiety had a way of doing that, no matter how much she was supposedly in shape.

Lexie scanned over her with her too-observant, gray-green eyes. "You need a drink."

"I do." CJ couldn't deny it, though, maybe she shouldn't agree to any alcohol. She needed her cool, calm, clear wits about her more than ever.

"Hugo Elderflower Spritz?" Lexie smiled conspiratorially. She knew her a bit too well.

How could she say no to that? Refreshing and not too intoxicating. Enough to take the edge off her frayed nerves.

"Um…yes, please." She'd make sure she sipped it, and focus on discussing the ladies' lives. She was sick of talking about herself and her issues. Sick of the sympathy. She'd spent a year speaking non-stop about how she felt. No more pity party.

Lexie also asked May and Sage for their drinks of choice, then took off to the bar.

CJ manufactured a cheerful smile. "How are you all going? I'm looking forward to hearing your news." And she was, legitimately. She didn't want to become one of those emotionally draining, consistently morose friends. She didn't want to be seen as someone unable to move forward, someone without resilience, someone who'd become a victim.

Sage answered first, speaking about how her psychology practice had met her aspirations, and that Solve Security had continued to grow and excel. With a dreamy smile on her face, she reinforced how much she loved her spouse, and owner of the business, Alexander, and that they'd started trying for a baby.

May then updated them on her husband Westley's recovery and that they were still *very much* enjoying their honeymoon period, in between her continuing to work selected Solve Security cases.

Lexie returned part way through the conversation, and informed them about how her partner, Chase, had resumed his lawyer role, and reinforced their relationship was as amazing as ever. On top of that, she'd committed to a couple of Solve Security jobs, which took up a fair chunk of her non-Chase time. However, overall, she loved her current position, loved her future prospects, loved her life.

CJ offered a safe response, letting them know she'd perfected her violin part for the upcoming Melbourne Symphony Orchestra production. The only thing she couldn't comment on was the man situation, because she didn't have anyone in her life and didn't know if she ever would again.

She'd excelled within the classical music industry, in her role within the strings section, but outside of work, she no longer had a fulfilling personal life, any romantic prospects. Playing the violin remained her only whole-hearted passion. That, and speaking to her close-knit friendship group.

In terms of seeking out a loving relationship with another male, she hadn't even been in the right headspace. Somehow, she kept a smile plastered to her face and hoped it looked believable. "I'm so happy to hear how well you're all doing."

Before her girlfriends could respond, could ask her anything else, which she dreaded, a man said, in the deepest, seductive voice she'd ever heard, "Here are your drinks, ladies."

She stared at the table in an attempt to stop the sudden burst of lust from coursing through her system, to stop *feeling*.

"Render, so nice of you to personally serve us." Lexie had a legendary smart mouth. She made every encounter interesting.

"How could I ignore such a beautiful bunch of women?"

"Always the charmer." May laughed, and the others joined in.

Except her. She wished she could. Wished she could return to being a regularly positive part of her friendship group.

She snuck a peek via her peripheral vision. The guy handed out everyone else's cocktails, leaving hers until last. "Hugo Elderflower Spritz?"

Like he didn't realize every other person had received their drink except her, and yet she couldn't help but glance up, meeting his intense light hazel eyes. My goodness, the man was Adonis personified.

Short dark blond hair — a little overgrown but still sexy as hell — tall, built, buff, ripped, his tight white T-shirt conformed to his torso like clingwrap. Many a hot-blooded woman's dream. Fantasy. Including hers.

No.

She couldn't go there.

Or could she? Her heart hammered, her body tingling with an undeniable, hard-to-ignore, *yes please*! And got into a debate with her mind. Maybe she could give him the benefit of the doubt, give into her desire. Maybe for just a few hours, just for tonight.

Her body made an excellent point, a hard to refute argument. Allowing for a fun, short-term, no expectations, let-off-some-steam experience.

She hadn't had one of those, well, ever. What was the harm? Rationally, she wanted to grow, progress, move in a positive direction. Did he want to as well? And even if he did, even if she did, her mind continued to interfere, throwing all sorts of obstacles in her way, extinguishing her excitement. Her self-talk only reinforced she needed more time.

The current song finished, followed by a pause between tracks. "Yes, that's mine. Thanks." Her voice came out all soft and breathy, betraying her attempt at aloofness.

His lips lifted into the most entrancing smile, which to her absolute pleasure, reached his stunning eyes, practically making her ovaries explode. And his clean, fresh, alluring fragrance, mixed with the smoky scent from the fire, only added to her Render appreciation.

The classic eighties track *Like To Get To Know You Well* started playing, reflecting her dreamy, youth-inspired wishes. And as if in slow motion, without taking his eyes off hers, Render placed her drink right in front of her. "If you need anything else, you let me know."

Why did that sound so sexual, so flirtatious? So enticing. Had he purposely chosen words that sounded insinuating? Words laced with innuendo. Was it a tactic he used to suss out a woman's response, her interest? Or had she jumped to conclusions as a result of her superficial attraction to the man?

Could he tell she desired him, even against her own will? Or had he trained his gaze on her, knowing the other striking women were unavailable. Maybe both. Both options totally drowned her enthusiasm.

With her emotions still so screwed up, and at war with her brain, she didn't even know what she wanted. Concepts sounded good, doable, until reality hit home. And maybe that's where she should have stayed. Why had she agreed to come out? Ignorance, naivety, peer pressure, obligation. FOMO.

She understood her friends had the best, selfless intentions but…tonight had already shown she wasn't ready on so many levels.

The bartender left and returned behind the counter, her eyes following him the whole way. His broad back, how it tapered into his narrow waist, how his blue jeans fit nice and snug around his butt and powerful legs had her squeezing her thighs tighter together.

"You like him." Sage's sweet yet confident voice penetrated the loud chatter, the blaring background music, breaking through her lustful haze.

CJ shot her gaze to Sage. The untameable smile on the woman's face extended to her big amber eyes. "What? No." Except she felt the heat rising from her chest to her cheeks. With her super fair skin, she had to glow a bright, blinding red. Even in the dim light, she couldn't hide her attraction, couldn't successfully enforce her denial.

"You do." Lexie stared at her with a try-and-deny-it smirk, her goth intensity hard to ignore, hard to argue against.

May turned to CJ and touched her upper arm, making sure she had eye contact before she spoke. "He's a player, but he's a good guy." Her spellbinding, sea-green stare reinforced her girlfriend group had a matchmaking agenda.

Shit. She hadn't yet come close to considering even attempting to connect with a new man, any man, even though her mates apparently believed this provided the perfect chance. CJ slipped out of her friend's grasp and glanced at her fidgety hands. "What are you saying?" Because she needed clarification, she didn't want to assume.

Lexie jumped in. "You're attracted to each other. It's obvious. Don't even try to pretend otherwise." Her straight-up, outspoken friend sucked a large sip from her drink and propped her forearms on the shiny timber table.

She waited until CJ met her gaze before she spoke further. "Listen, I've known him a long time and trust me, he's decent. The others can vouch for him too. He's an excellent option for you to dip your toe back into the dating pool, splash around and have some fun. He'll treat you with respect. Rebuild your confidence. He'll work with whatever you want."

What did that mean? How? Her brow puckered. Just the idea of sexually engaging with another guy already pushed her current boundaries, but especially if he did it from a purely 'therapeutic', practical-sexual-intervention perspective. Clinical, detached, passionless.

No. She didn't need someone to hook up with her out of pity, sympathy. A favor. She'd rather fantasize while she touched herself later, without interacting with a do-gooder, perfect stranger.

She swallowed the angst clogging her throat. Although she could do with the physical release, she needed to know that if she interacted with him, he wanted her too, that she didn't doubt whether she was ready and relaxed enough to enjoy another man's touch.

She didn't want to play games with Render, didn't want to lead him on, didn't want him to see her as some sexual charity case either. Or him promise her bullshit he couldn't uphold.

"What we're all essentially saying is you need a good fuck." Lexie rarely minced her far-from-PC words.

A bit of flirting, a bit of making out, sure, but taking it further? CJ shook her head. "I can't." Technically she could — mentally, physically, but not emotionally.

"If you don't think you can, then that's okay, but just remember that change requires stepping out of your comfort zone." Sage reached for her hand across the table and held it, her lustrous cinnamon hair falling forward. "In the end you need to go with whatever feels right for you." She had such a caring, supportive manner. It was hard to go against her reasoning.

May swept her silky blonde hair off her shoulder and pressed her palm to CJ's forearm, the persistent heat penetrating her skin. "Convince us you're not interested, and we'll let it go."

"We wouldn't recommend a guy we didn't trust. A guy who wouldn't work in with what you need. What you both need." Lexie's potent gaze pierced into her soul.

The flickering flames from the fire mixed with the candlelight, creating shadows that danced across the table, drawing her gaze back to the man in question, who stood staring at her from behind the bar.

Goosebumps raised all over her skin. She sucked in a breath and turned back to her friends. "Okay, I admit he's attractive. What woman wouldn't want to do him?"

"We don't care about other women, we want *you* to do him." A sinful smile slid onto Lexie's scarlet lips.

"I don't know." She did know, on a lust level, but if she agreed to go home with him, what would he expect? She didn't want to give him false hope. Or herself.

"Just spend some time speaking to him and see what you think." Sage had this unbelievably compassionate stare, like she could tap right into a person's thoughts, *her* thoughts.

"Fine. I'll talk to him. No promises, though." CJ had to go with how she felt at any given moment, and give consent accordingly. Her husband's sudden death had created a persisting fragility that affected her at a cellular level.

Once she'd finished her cool, refreshing cocktail, she had a soda water, with Render continuing to provide his undivided attention. The alcohol from her first drink had already decreased her inhibitions, enough to break free of her grief-laden shackles, while retaining her alertness and sensibility. It'd provided just enough liquid courage so she could consider a possible new experience without any regrets. And still drive home safely.

While chatting with her friends, CJ had kept a subtle eye on the guy, and he'd shown pleasant, professional but not flirty behavior with any other woman. Only her. Several times, she'd snuck a look and caught him staring back.

So exhilarating...if only she knew how to successfully chat up a man. Unfortunately, she'd never really learnt that skill. And now her unresolved feelings chipped away at her confidence, guilted her into remaining unaware, alone, and unsatisfied.

"CJ, the rest of us need to get going." Lexie's voice jolted her from her unrelenting, self-absorbed thoughts.

Her friend stood and put on her jacket, with May and Sage following suit.

No.

An infusion of panic raced through her veins.

CJ checked the time, and it was close to closing. Where had the night gone? "Not yet. Please."

Sage gave her a goodbye hug. "Render will look after you."

"And if he doesn't, I'll break his balls." Lexie said it with a bit too much pleasure.

"Me too." May wrapped her in a you'll-be-fine embrace. CJ stood to let her out, then planted her butt back down on the leather-covered bench, her mind and body buzzing with all-consuming conflict.

With collusive smiles, her friends waved as they exited the front door. Why didn't she leave with them? What kept her glued to her seat?

Him.

Curiosity.

Nervous anticipation.

What would he do next? What would she do? How would she react?

While she contemplated her missed opportunity to escape, and how to best manage her decision to stay, Render came over and grabbed their empty glasses. "Come and sit at the bar. Keep me company."

Although a little demanding, something about his voice had the tension dissipating from her shoulders and stomach, and made her feel safe. Like he'd sensed her stress, like he cared, like he didn't want her to go. Like she'd made the right choice.

So she followed. Ridiculous, right? But she couldn't ignore the draw to him. A classic example of unexplainable chemistry. She hardly knew the man and yet she couldn't keep away.

Pulling up a stool, she sat silent and watched him. Render had bucket loads of charisma, and could engage with punters while also doing barman duties, like cleaning down the counter-top, collecting glasses and stacking them in the dishwasher. And he knew how to make every drink a patron ordered and did it with poise and flare. Tom Cruise in *Cocktail* had nothing on this guy.

How did Lexie know him? She used to be a cop. Was he an ex-cop too? Or had she met him through the bar? Maybe they'd slept together in the past. Didn't matter. Or at least, that's what her brain said.

Even while he completed the required tasks, he didn't ignore her, frequently making eye contact and smiling, and coming over to check how she was doing, if she wanted anything else. And my goodness, did he have a great smile, framed by that gorgeous golden scruff. It lit up his whole face with undeniable sincerity, winning her over more and more with each second.

But would he take her sticking around as a subtle guarantee for sex? Because although she sensed the mutual attraction between them, she still wasn't sure she could do the one-night-stand thing. Not now, maybe not ever. No matter how much he activated all her arousal buttons.

The final few patrons and bar staff left, and he locked up. The Cure's *Let's Go to Bed* started and he approached her, staring straight into her eyes. "Want to have a nightcap?"

"Is that code for sex?" she blurted out before her brain intervened.

He threw back his head and laughed, a sexy grin settling onto his lips. "If you want it to be."

About the Author

Sandra Carmel is an own-voices bestselling Australian author of racy, flirty and downright-dirty romance novels, novellas, short stories and poetry, who enjoys stimulating herself and others with words. An obsession with Jane Eyre, and her infatuation with Mr Rochester, were key motivators in commencing her romance writing journey. So far, she has taken the scenic route from steamy paranormal to sci-fi to contemporary, creating provocative stories that delve beneath the surface of desire. She reads and writes a lot, frequently disrupted by her ever-attentive, cheeky cats, and sinfully amorous array of book boyfriends.

Sandra loves to hear from readers. You can find her contact information, website details and author profile page at https://www.firstforromance.com

ENTWINED PUBLISHING

www.ingramcontent.com/pod-product-compliance
Lightning Source LLC
Chambersburg PA
CBHW031108030726
47496CB00002BA/440